THE ROAD TO DAMASCUS

CONTENTS

INTRODUCTION

Strindberg's great trilogy *The Road to Damascus* presents many mysteries to the uninitiated. Its peculiar changes of mood, its gallery of half unreal characters, its bizarre episodes combine to make it a bewilderingly rich but rather 'difficult' work. It cannot be recommended to the lover of light drama or the seeker of momentary distraction. *The Road to Damascus* does not deal with the superficial strata of human life, but probes into those depths where the problems of God, and death, and eternity become terrifying realities.

Many authors have, of course, dealt with the profoundest problems of humanity without, on that account, having been able to evoke our interest. There may have been too much philosophy and too little art in the presentation of the subject, too little reality and too much soaring into the heights. That is not so with Strindberg's drama. It is a trenchant settling of accounts between a complex and fascinating individual—the author—and his past, and the realistic scenes have often been transplanted in detail from his own changeful life.

In order fully to understand *The Road to Damascus* it is therefore essential to know at least the most important features of that background of real life, out of which the drama has grown.

Parts I and II of the trilogy were written in 1898, while Part III was added somewhat later, in the years 1900-1901. In 1898 Strindberg had only half emerged from what was by far the severest of the many crises through which in his troubled life he had to pass. He had overcome the worst period of terror, which had brought him dangerously near the borders of sanity, and he felt as if he could again open his eyes and breathe freely. He was not free from that nervous pressure under

9

which he had been working, but the worst of the inner tension had relaxed and he felt the need of taking a survey of what had happened, of summarising and trying to fathom what could have been underlying his apparently unaccountable experiences. The literary outcome of this settling of accounts with the past was *The Road to Damascus*.

The Road to Damascus might be termed a marriage drama, a mystery drama, or a drama of penance and conversion, according as preponderance is given to one or other of its characteristics. The question then arises: what was it in the drama which was of deepest significance to the author himself? The answer is to be found in the title, with its allusion to the narrative in the Acts of the Apostles of the journey of Saul, the persecutor, the scoffer, who, on his way to Damascus, had an awe-inspiring vision, which converted Saul, the hater of Christ, into Paul, the apostle of the Gentiles. Strindberg's drama describes the progress of the author right up to his conversion, shows how stage by stage he relinquishes worldly things, scientific renown, and above all woman, and finally, when nothing more binds him to this world, takes the vows of a monk and enters a monastery where no dogmas or theology, but only broadminded humanity and resignation hold sway. What, however, in an inner sense, distinguishes Strindberg's drama from the Bible narrative is that the conversion itself—although what leads up to it is convincingly described, both logically and psychologically—does not bear the character of a final and irrevocable decision, but on the contrary is depicted with a certain hesitancy and uncertainty. THE STRANGER'S entry into the monastery consequently gives the impression of being a piece of logical construction; the author's heart is not wholly in it. From Strindberg's later works it also becomes evident that his severe crisis had undoubtedly led to a complete reformation in that it definitely caused him to turn from worldly things, of which indeed he had tasted to the full, towards matters divine. But this did not mean that then and there he accepted some specific religion, whether Christian or other. One would undoubtedly come nearest to the author's own interpretation in this respect by characterising *The Road to Damascus* not as a drama of conversion, but as a drama of struggle, the story of a restless, arduous pilgrimage through the chimeras of the world towards the border beyond which eternity stretches in solemn peace, symbolised in the drama by a mountain, the peaks of which reach high above the clouds.

In this final settling of accounts one subject is of dominating importance, recurring again and again throughout the trilogy; it is that of woman. Strindberg him, of course, become famous as a writer about women; he has ruthlessly described the hatreds of love, the hell that marriage can be, he is the creator of *Le Plaidoyer d'un Fou* and *The Dance of Death*, he had three divorces, yet was just as much a worshipper of woman—and at the same time a diabolical hater of her seducing qualities under which he suffered defeat after defeat. Each time he fell in love afresh he would compare himself to Hercules, the Titan, whose strength was vanquished by Queen Omphale, who clothed herself in his lion's skin, while he had to sit at the spinning wheel dressed in women's clothes. It can be readily understood that to a man of Strindberg's self-conceit the problem of his relations with women must become a vital issue on the solution of which the whole Damascus pilgrimage depended.

In 1898, when Parts I and II of the trilogy were written, Strindberg had been married twice; both marriages had ended unhappily. In the year 1901, when the wedding scenes of Part III were written, Strindberg had recently experienced the rapture of a new love which, however, was soon to be clouded. It must not be forgotten that in his entire emotional life Strindberg was an artist and as such a man of impulse, with the spontaneity and naivity and intensity of a child. For him love had nothing to do with respectability and worldly calculations; he liked to think of it as a thunderbolt striking mortals with a destructive force like the lightning hurled by the almighty Zeus. It is easy to understand that a man of such temperament would not be particularly suited for married life, where self-sacrifice and strong-minded patience may be severely tested. In addition his three wives were themselves artists, one an authoress, the other two actresses, all of them pronounced characters, endowed with a degree of will and self-assertion, which, although it could not be matched against Strindberg's, yet would have been capable of producing friction with rather more pliant natures than that of the Swedish dramatist.

In the trilogy Strindberg's first wife, Siri von Essen, his marriage to whom was happiest and lasted longest (1877-1891), and more especially his second wife, the Austrian authoress Frida Uhl (married to him 1893-1897) have supplied the subject matter for his picture of THE LADY. In the happy marriage scenes of Part III we recognise reminiscences from the wedding of Strindberg, then fifty-two, and the twenty-three-year-old actress Harriet Bosse, whose marriage to him lasted from 1901 until 1904.

The character of THE LADY in Parts I and II is chiefly drawn from recollections—fairly recent when the drama was written—of Frida Uhl and his life with her. From the very beginning her marriage to Strindberg had been most troublous. In the autumn of 1892 Strindberg moved from the Stockholm skerries to Berlin, where he lived a rather hectic Bohemian life among the artists collecting in the little tavern 'Zum Schwarzen Ferkel.' He made the acquaintance of Frida Uhl in the beginning of the year 1893, and after a good many difficulties was able to arrange for a marriage on the 2nd May on Heligoland Island, where English marriage laws, less rigorous than the German, applied. Strindberg's nervous temperament would not tolerate a quiet and peaceful honeymoon; quite soon the couple departed to Gravesend via Hamburg. Strindberg was too restless to stay there and moved on to London. There he left his wife to try to negotiate for the production of his plays, and journeyed alone to Sellin, on the island of Rügen, after having first been compelled to stop in Hamburg owing to lack of money. Strindberg stayed on Rügen during the month of July, and then left for the home of his parents-in-law at Mondsee, near Salzburg in Austria, where he was to meet his wife. But when she was delayed a few days on the journey from London, Strindberg impatiently departed for Berlin, where Frida Uhl followed shortly after. About the same time an action was brought for the suppression of the German version of *Le Plaidoyer d'un Fou* as being immoral. This book gives an undisguised, intensely personal picture of Strindberg's first marriage, and was intended by him for publication only after his death as a defence against accusations directed against him for his behaviour towards Siri von Essen. Strindberg was acquitted after a time, but before that his easily fired imagination had given him a thorough shake-up, which could only hasten the crisis which seemed to be approaching. After a trip to Brünn, where Strindberg wrote his scientific work *Antibarbarus*, the couple arrived in November at the home of Frida Uhl's grandparents in the little village of Dornach, by the Upper Danube; here the wanderings of 1893 at last came to an end. For a few months comparative peace reigned in the artists' little home, but the birth of a daughter, Kerstin, in May, brought this tranquillity to a sudden end. Strindberg, who had lived in a state of nervous depression since the 1880's, felt himself put on one side by the child, and felt ill at ease in an environment of, as he put it in the autobiographical *The Quarantine Master*, 'articles of food, excrements, wet-nurses treated like milch-cows, cooks and decaying vegetables.' He longed for cleanliness and peace, and in letters to an artist friend he spoke of entering a monastery. He even thought of founding one himself in the Ardennes and drew up detailed schemes for rules, dress, and food. The longing to get away and common interests with his Parisian friend (a musician named Leopold Littmansson) attracted Strindberg to Paris, where he settled down in the beginning of the autumn 1894. His wife joined him, but left again at the close of the autumn. In reality Strindberg was at this time almost impossible to live with. Persecution mania and hallucinations took possession of him and his morbid suspicions knew no bounds. In spite of this he was half conscious that there was something wrong with his mental faculties, and in the beginning of 1895, assisted by the Swedish Minister, he went by his own consent to the St. Louis Hospital in Paris. During his chemical experiments, in which among other things he tried to produce gold, he had burnt his hands, so that he had to seek medical attention on that account also. He wrote about this in a letter:

'I am going to hospital because I am ill, because my doctor has sent me there, and because I need to be looked after like a child, because I am ruined. . . . And it torments me and grieves me, my nervous system is rotten, paralytic, hysterical. . . . '

Never before had Strindberg lived in such distress as at this period, both physically and mentally. With shattered nerves, sometimes over the verge of insanity, without any means of existence other than what friends managed to scrape together, separated from his second wife, who had opened proceedings for divorce, far from his native land and without any prospects for the future, he was brought to a profound religious crisis. With almost incredible fortitude he succeeded in fighting his way through this difficult period, with the remarkable result that the former Bohemian, atheist, and scoffer was gradually able to emerge with the firm assurance of a prophet, and even enter a new creative period, perhaps mightier than before. One cannot help reflecting that a man capable of overcoming a crisis of such a formidable character and of several years' duration, as this one of Strindberg's had been, with reason intact and even with increased creative power, in reality, in spite of his hypersensitive nervous system, must have been an unusually strong man both physically and mentally.

Upon trying to define more closely what actual relation the play has to those events of Strindberg's restless life, of which we have given a rough outline, we find that for the most part the author has undoubtedly made use of his own experiences, but has adapted, combined and added to them still more, so that the result is a mixture of real experience and imagination, all moulded into a carefully worked out artistic form.

If to begin with, we dwell for a while on Part I it is evident that the hurried wanderings of THE STRANGER and THE LADY between the street corner, the room in the hotel, the sea and the Rose Room with the mother-in-law, have their foundation—often in detail—in Strindberg's rovings with Frida Uhl. I will give a few examples. In a book by Frida Uhl about her marriage to the Swedish genius (splendid in parts but not very reliable) she recalls that the month before her marriage she took rooms at Neustädtische Kirchstrasse 1, in Berlin, facing a Gothic church in Dorotheenstrasse, situated at the cross-roads between the post office in

Dorotheenstrasse and the café 'Zum Schwarzen Ferkel' in Wilhelmstrasse. This Berlin environment appears to be almost exactly reproduced in the introductory scene of Part I, where THE STRANGER and THE LADY meet outside a little Gothic church with a post office and café adjoining. The happy scenes by the sea are, of course, pleasant recollections from Heligoland, and the many discussions about money matters in the midst of the honeymoon are quite explicable when we know how the dramatist was continually haunted by money troubles, even if occasionally he received a big fee, and that this very financial insecurity was one of the chief reasons why Frida Uhl's father opposed the marriage. Again, the country scenes which follow in Part I, shift to the hilly country round the Danube, with their Catholic Calvaries and expiation chapels, where Strindberg lived with his parents-in-law in Mondsee and with his wife's grandparents in Dornach and the neighbouring village Klam, with its mill, its smithy, and its gloomy ravine. The Rose Room was the name he gave to the room in which he lived during his stay with his mother-in-law and his daughter Kerstin in Klam in the autumn of 1896, as he has himself related in one of his autobiographical books *Inferno*. In this way we could go on, showing how the localities which are to be met with in the drama often correspond in detail to the places Strindberg had visited in the course of his pilgrimage during the years 1893-1898. Space prevents us, however, from entering on a more detailed analysis in this respect.

That THE STRANGER represents Strindberg's *alter ego* is evident in many ways, even apart from the fact that THE STRANGER'S wanderings from place to place, as we have already seen, bear a direct relation to those of Strindberg himself. THE STRANGER is an author, like Strindberg; his childhood of hate is Strindberg's own; other details—such as for instance that THE STRANGER has refused to attend his father's funeral, that the Parish Council has wanted to take his child away from him, that on account of his writings he has suffered lawsuits, illness, poverty, exile, divorce; that in the police description he is characterised as a person without a permanent situation, with uncertain income; married, but had deserted his wife and left his children; known as entertaining subversive opinions on social questions (by *The Red Room, The New Realm* and other works Strindberg became the great standard-bearer of the Swedish Radicals in their campaign against conventionalism and bureaucracy); that he gives the impression of not being in full possession of his senses; that he is sought by his children's guardian because of unpaid maintenance allowance—everything corresponds to the experiences of the unfortunate Strindberg himself, with all his bitter defeats in life and his triumphs in the world of letters.

Those scenes where THE STRANGER is uncertain whether the people he sees before him are real or not—he catches hold of THE BEGGAR'S arm to feel whether he is a real, live person—or those occasions when he appears as a visionary or thought-reader—he describes the kitchen in his wife's parental home without ever having seen it, and knows her thoughts before she has expressed them—have their deep foundation in Strindberg's mental make-up, especially as it was during the period of tension in the middle of the 1890's, termed the Inferno period, because at that time Strindberg thought that he lived in hell. Our most prominent student of Strindberg, Professor Martin Lamm, wrote about this in his work on Strindberg's dramas:

'In order to understand the first part of *The Road to Damascus* we must take into consideration that the author had not yet shaken off his terrifying visions and persecutionary hallucinations. He can play with them artistically, sometimes he feels tempted to make a joke of them, but they still retain for him their "terrifying semi-reality." It is this which makes the drama so bewildering, but at the same time so vigorous and affecting. Later, when depicting dream states, he creates an artful blend of reality and poetry. He produces more exquisite works of art, but he no longer gives the same anguished impression of a soul striving to free itself from the meshes of his *idées fixes*.'

With his hypersensitive nervous system Strindberg, like THE STRANGER, really gives the impression of having been a visionary. For instance, his author friend Albert Engström, has told how one evening during a stay far out in the Stockholm skerries, far from all civilisation, Strindberg suddenly had a feeling that his little daughter was ill, and wanted to return to town at once. True enough, it turned out that the girl had fallen ill just at the time when Strindberg had felt the warning. As regards thought-reading, it appears that at the slightest change in expression and often for no perceptible reason at all, Strindberg would draw the most definite conclusions, as definite as from an uttered word or an action. This we have to keep in mind, for instance, when judging Strindberg's accusations against his wife in *Le Plaidoyer d'un Fou*, the book which THE LADY in *The Road to Damascus* is tempted to read, in spite of having been forbidden by THE STRANGER, with tragic results. In Part III of the drama Strindberg lets THE STRANGER discuss this thought-reading problem with his first wife. THE STRANGER says:

'We made a mistake when we were living together, because we accused each other of wicked thoughts before they'd become actions; and lived in mental reservations instead of realities. For instance, I once noticed how you enjoyed the defiling gaze of a strange man, and I accused you of unfaithfulness'; to which THE LADY, to Strindberg's satisfaction, has to reply:

'You were wrong to do it, and right. Because my thoughts were sinful.'

As regards the other figures in the gallery of characters in Part I, we have already shown THE LADY as the identical counterpart in all essentials of Strindberg's second wife, Frida Uhl. Like the latter THE LADY is a Catholic, has a grandfather, Dr. Cornelius Reisch—called THE OLD MAN in the drama—whose passion is shooting; and a mother, Maria Uhl, with a predilection for religious discourses in Strindberg's own style; another detail, the fact that she was eighteen years old before she crossed to the other shore to see what had shimmered dimly in the distant haze, corresponds with Frida Uhl's statement that she had been confined in a convent until she was eighteen and a half years old. On the other hand, the chief female character of the drama does not correspond to her real life counterpart in that she is supposed to have been married to a doctor before eloping with THE STRANGER, Strindberg. Here reminiscences from Strindberg's first marriage play a part. Siri von Essen, Strindberg's first wife, was married to an officer, Baron Wrangel, and both the Wrangels received Strindberg kindly in their home as a friend. Love quickly flared up between Siri von Essen-Wrangel and Strlndberg. She obtained a divorce from her husband and married Strindberg. Baron von Wrangel shortly afterwards married again, a cousin of Siri von Essen. Knowing these matrimonial complications we understand how Strindberg must have felt when, on the point of leaving for Heligoland to marry Frida Uhl, he met his former wife's (Siri von Essen) first husband, Baron Wrangel, on Lehrter Station in Berlin, and found that, like Strindberg himself, he was on a lover's errand. Knowing all this we need not be surprised at the extremely complicated matrimonial relations in *The Road to Damascus*, where, for example, for the sake of THE STRANGER, THE DOCTOR obtains a divorce from THE LADY in order to marry THE STRANGER'S first wife. In addition to Baron Wrangel a doctor in the town of Ystad, in the south of Sweden—Dr. Eliasson who attended Strindberg during his most difficult period—has stood as a model for THE DOCTOR. We note in particular that the description of the doctor's house enclosing a courtyard on three sides, tallies with a type of building which is characteristic of the south of Sweden. When THE DOCTOR ruthlessly explains to THE STRANGER that the asylum, 'The Good Help,' was not a hospital but a lunatic asylum, he expresses Strindberg's own misgivings that the St. Louis Hospital, of which, as mentioned above, Strindberg was an inmate in the beginning of the year 1895, was really to be regarded as a lunatic asylum.

Even minor characters, such as CAESAR and THE BEGGAR have their counterparts in real life, even though in the main they are fantastic creations of his imagination. The guardian of his daughter, Kerstin, a relative of Frida Uhl's, was called Dr. Cäsar R. v. Weyr. Regarding THE BEGGAR it may be enough to quote Strindberg's feelings when confronted with the collections made by his Paris friends:

'I am a beggar who has no right to go to cafés. Beggar! That is the right word; it rings in my ears and brings a burning blush to my cheeks, the blush of shame, humiliation, and rage!

'To think that six weeks ago I sat at this table! My theatre manager addressed me as Dear Master; journalists strove to interview me, the photographer begged to be allowed to sell my portrait. And now: a beggar, a branded man, an outcast from society!'

After this we can understand why Strindberg in *The Road to Damascus* apparently in such surprising manner is seized by the suspicion that he is himself the beggar.

We have thus seen that Part I of *The Road to Damascus* is at the same time a free creation of fantasy and a drama of portrayal. The elements of realism are starkly manifest, but they are moulded and hammered into a work of art by a force of combinative imagination rising far above the task of mere descriptive realism. The scenes unroll themselves in calculated sequence up to the central asylum picture, from there to return in reverse order through the second half of the drama, thus symbolising life's continuous repetition of itself, Kierkegaard's *Gentagelse*. The first part of *The Road to Damascus* is the one most frequently produced on the stage. This is understandable, having regard to its firm structure and the consistency of its faith in a Providence directing the fortunes and misfortunes of man, whether the individual rages in revolt or submits in quiet resignation.

The second part of *The Road to Damascus* is dominated by the scenes of the great alchemist banquet which, in all its fantastic oddity, is one of the most suggestive ever created on the ancient theme of the fickleness of fortune. It was suggested above that there were two factors beyond all others binding Strindberg to the world and making him hesitate before the monastery; one was woman, from whom he sets himself free in Part II, after the birth of a child—precisely as in his marriage to Frida Uhl—the other was scientific honour, in its highest phase equivalent, to Strindberg, to the power to produce gold. Countless were the experiments for this purpose made by Strindberg in his primitive laboratories, and countless his failures. To the world-famous author, literary honour meant little as opposed to the slightest prospect of being acknowledged as a prominent scientist. Harriet Bosse has told me that Strindberg seldom said anything about his literary work, never was interested in what other people thought of them, or troubled to read the reviews; but on the other hand he would often, with sparkling eyes and childish pride, show her strips of paper, stained at one end with some golden-brown substance. 'Look,' he said, 'this is pure gold, and I have made it!' In face of the stubborn scepticism of scientific experts Strindberg was, however, driven to despair as to his ability, and felt his dreams of fortune shattered, as did THE STRANGER at the macabre banquet given in his honour—a banquet which was, as a matter of fact, planned by his Paris friends, not, as Strindberg would have liked to believe, in honour of the great scientist, but to the great author.

In Part I of *The Road to Damascus*, THE STRANGER replies with a hesitating 'Perhaps' when THE LADY wants to lead him to the protecting Church; and at the end of Part II he exclaims: 'Come, priest, before I change my mind'; but in Part III his decision is final, he enters the monastery. The reason is that not even THE LADY in her third incarnation had shown herself capable of reconciling him to life. The wedding day scenes just before, between Harriet Bosse and the ageing author, form, however, the climax of Part III and are among the most poetically moving that Strindberg has ever written.

Besides having his belief in the rapture of love shattered, THE STRANGER also suffers disappointment at seeing his child fall short of expectations. The meeting between the daughter Sylvia and THE STRANGER probably refers to an episode from the summer of 1899, when Strindberg, after long years of suffering in foreign countries, saw his beloved Swedish skerries again, and also his favourite daughter Greta, who had come over from Finland to meet him. Contrary to the version given in the drama, the reunion of father and daughter seems to have been very happy and cordial. However, it is typical of the fate-oppressed

Strindberg that in his work even the happiest summer memories become tinged with black. Once and for all the dark colours on his palette were the most intense.

The final entry into the monastery was more a symbol for the struggling author's dream of peace and atonement than a real thing in his life. It is true he visited the Benedictine monastery, Maredsous, in Belgium in 1898, and its well stocked library came to play a certain part In the drama, but already he realised, after one night's sojourn there, that he had no call for the monastic life.

Seen as a whole the trilogy marks a turning point in Strindberg's dramatic production. The logical, calculated concentration of his naturalistic work of the 1880's has given way to a freer form of composition, in which the atmosphere has come to mean more than the dialogue, the musical and dreamlike qualities more than conciseness. *The Road to Damascus* abounds with details from real life, reproduced in sharply naturalistic manner, but these are not, as things were in his earlier works viewed by the author *a priori* as reality but become wrapped in dreamlike mystery. Just as with *Lady Julia* and *The Father* Strindberg ushered in the naturalistic drama of the 1880's, so in the years around the turn of the century he was, with his symbolist cycle *The Road to Damascus*, to break new ground for European drama which had gradually become stuck in fixed formulas. *The Road to Damascus* became a landmark in world literature both as a brilliant work of art and as bearer of new stage technique.

GUNNAR OLLÉN

Translated by
ESTHER JOHANSON

PART I

CHARACTERS

THE STRANGER
THE LADY
THE BEGGAR
THE DOCTOR
HIS SISTER
AN OLD MAN
A MOTHER
AN ABBESS
A CONFESSOR

less important figures
FIRST MOURNER
SECOND MOURNER
THIRD MOURNER
LANDLORD
CAESAR
WAITER

non-speaking
A SMITH
MILLER'S WIFE
FUNERAL ATTENDANTS

SCENES

PART ONE

English Version by
GRAHAM RAWSON

First Performance in England by the Stage Society at the Westminster Theatre, 2nd May 1937

CAST

THE STRANGER	Francis James
THE LADY	Wanda Rotha
THE BEGGAR	Alexander Sarner
FIRST MOURNER	George Cormack
SECOND MOURNER	Kenneth Bell
THIRD MOURNER	Peter Bennett
FOURTH MOURNER	Bryan Sears
FIFTH MOURNER	Michael Boyle
SIXTH MOURNER	Stephen Patrick
THE LANDLORD	Stephen Jack

THE DOCTOR	Neil Porter
HIS SISTER	Olga Martin
CAESAR	Peter Land
A WAITER	Peter Bennett
AN OLD MAN	A. Corney Grain
A MOTHER	Frances Waring
THE SMITH	Norman Thomas
THE MILLER'S WIFE	Julia Sandham
AN ABBESS	Natalia Moya
A CONFESSOR	Tristan Rawson
PRODUCER	Carl H. Jaffe
ASSISTANT PRODUCER	Ossia Trilling

SCENE I

STREET CORNER

[Street Corner with a seat under a tree; the side-door of a small Gothic Church nearby; also a post office and a café with chairs outside it. Both post office and café are shut. A funeral march is heard off, growing louder sand then fainter. A STRANGER is standing on the edge of the pavement and seems uncertain which way to go. A church clock strikes: first the four quarters and then the hour. It is three o'clock. A LADY enters and greets the STRANGER. She is about to pass him, but stops.]

STRANGER. It's you! I almost knew you'd come.

LADY. You wanted me: I felt it. But why are you waiting here?

STRANGER. I don't know. I must wait somewhere.

LADY. Who are you waiting for?

STRANGER. I wish I could tell you! For forty years I've been waiting for something: I believe they call it happiness; or the end of unhappiness. (Pause.) There's that terrible music again. Listen! But don't go, I beg you. I'll feel afraid, if you do.

LADY. We met yesterday for the first time; and talked for four hours. You roused my sympathy, but you mustn't abuse my kindness on that account.

27

STRANGER. I know that well enough. But I beg you not to leave me. I'm a stranger here, without friends; and my few acquaintances seem more like enemies.

LADY. You have enemies everywhere. You're lonely everywhere. Why did you leave your wife and children?

STRANGER. I wish I knew. I wish I knew why I still live; why I'm here now; where I should go and what I should do! Do you believe that the living can be damned already?

LADY. No.

STRANGER. Look at me.

LADY. Hasn't life brought you a single pleasure?

STRANGER. Not one! If at any time I thought so, it was merely a trap to tempt me to prolong my miseries. If ripe fruit fell into my hand, it was poisoned or rotten at the core.

LADY. What is your religion—if you'll forgive the question?

STRANGER. Only this: that when I can bear things no longer, I shall go.

LADY. Where?

STRANGER. Into annihilation. If I don't hold life in my hand, at least I hold death. . . . It gives me an amazing feeling of power.

LADY. You're playing with death!

STRANGER. As I've played with life. (Pause.) I was a writer. But in spite of my melancholy temperament I've never been able to take anything seriously—not even my worst troubles. Sometimes I even doubt whether life itself has had any more reality than my books. (A De Profundis is heard from the funeral procession.) They're coming back. Why must they process up and down these streets?

LADY. Do you fear them?

STRANGER. They annoy me. The place might be bewitched. No, it's not death I fear, but solitude; for then one's not alone. I don't know who's there, I or another, but in solitude one's not alone. The air grows heavy and seems to engender invisible beings, who have life and whose presence can be felt.

LADY. You've noticed that?

STRANGER. For some time I've noticed a great deal; but not as I used to. Once I merely saw objects and events, forms and colours, whilst now I perceive ideas and meanings. Life, that once had no meaning, has begun to have one. Now I discern intention where I used to see nothing but chance. (Pause.) When I met you yesterday it struck me you'd been sent across my path, either to save me, or destroy me.

LADY. Why should I destroy you?

STRANGER. Because it may be your destiny.

LADY. No such idea ever crossed my mind; it was largely sympathy I felt for you. . . . Never, in all my life, have I met anyone like you. I have only to look at you for the tears to start to my eyes. Tell me, what have you on your conscience? Have you done something wrong, that's never been discovered or punished?

STRANGER. You may well ask! No, I've no more sins on my conscience than other free men. Except this: I determined that life should never make a fool of me.

LADY. You must let yourself be fooled, more or less, to live at all.

STRANGER. That would seem a kind of duty; but one I wanted to get out of. (Pause.) I've another secret. It's whispered in the family that I'm a changeling.

LADY. What's that?

STRANGER. A child substituted by the elves for the baby that was born.

LADY. Do you believe in such things?

STRANGER. No. But, as a parable, there's something to be said for it. (Pause.) As a child I was always crying and didn't seem to take to life in this world. I hated my parents, as they hated me. I brooked no constraint, no conventions, no laws, and my longing was for the woods and the sea.

LADY. Did you ever see visions?

STRANGER. Never. But I've often thought that two beings were guiding my destiny. One offers me all I desire; but the other's ever at hand to bespatter the gifts with filth, so that they're useless to me and I can't touch them. It's true that life has given me all I asked of it—but everything's turned out worthless to me.

LADY. You've had everything and yet are not content?

STRANGER. That is the curse. . . .

LADY. Don't say that! But why haven't you desired things that transcend this life, that can never be sullied?

STRANGER. Because I doubt if there is a beyond.

30

LADY. But the elves?

STRANGER. Are merely a fairy story. (Pointing to a seat.) Shall we sit down?

LADY. Yes. Who are you waiting for?

STRANGER. Really, for the post office to open. There's a letter for me—it's been forwarded on but hasn't reached me. (They sit down.) But tell me something of yourself now. (The Lady takes up her crochet work.)

LADY. There's nothing to tell.

STRANGER. Strangely enough, I should prefer to think of you like that. Impersonal, nameless—I only do know one of your names. I'd like to christen you myself—let me see, what ought you to be called? I've got it. Eve! (With a gesture towards the wings.) Trumpets! (The funeral march is heard again.) There it is again! Now I must invent your age, for I don't know how old you are. From now on you are thirty-four—so you were born in sixty-four. (Pause.) Now your character, for I don't know that either. I shall give you a good character, your voice reminds me of my mother—I mean the idea of a mother, for my mother never caressed me, though I can remember her striking me. You see, I was brought up in hate! An eye for an eye—a tooth for a tooth. You see this scar on my forehead? That comes from a blow my brother gave me with an axe, after I'd struck him with a stone. I never went to my father's funeral, because he turned me out of the house when my sister married. I was born out of wedlock, when my family were bankrupt and in mourning for an uncle who had taken his life. Now you know my family! That's the stock I come from. Once I narrowly escaped fourteen years' hard labour—so I've every reason to thank the elves, though I can't be altogether pleased with what they've done.

LADY. I like to hear you talk. But don't speak of the elves: it makes me sad.

STRANGER. Frankly, I don't believe in them; yet they're always making themselves felt. Are these elves the souls of the unhappy, who still await redemption? If so, I am the child of an evil spirit. Once I believed I was near redemption—through a woman. But no mistake could have been greater: I was plunged into the seventh hell.

LADY. You must be unhappy. But this won't go on always.

STRANGER. Do you think church bells and Holy Water could comfort me? I've tried them; they only made things worse. I felt like the Devil when he sees the sign of the cross. (Pause.) Let's talk about you now.

LADY. There's no need. (Pause.) Have you been blamed for misusing your gifts?

STRANGER. I've been blamed for everything. In the town I lived in no one was so hated as I. Lonely I came in and lonely I went out. If I entered a public place people avoided me. If I wanted to rent a room, it would be let. The priests laid a ban on me from the pulpit, teachers from their desks and parents in their homes. The church committee wanted to take my children from me. Then I blasphemously shook my fist . . . at heaven!

LADY. Why did they hate you so?

STRANGER. How should I know! Yet I do! I couldn't endure to see men suffer. So I kept on saying, and writing, too: free yourselves, I will help you. And to the poor I said: do not let the rich exploit you. And to the women: do not allow yourselves to be enslaved by the men. And—worst of all—to the children: do not obey your parents, if they are unjust.

32

What followed was impossible to foresee. I found that everyone was against me: rich and poor, men and women, parents and children. And then came sickness and poverty, beggary and shame, divorce, law-suits, exile, solitude, and now. . . . Tell me, do you think me mad?

LADY. No.

STRANGER. You must be the only one. But I'm all the more grateful.

LADY (rising). I must leave you now.

STRANGER. You, too?

LADY. And you mustn't stay here.

STRANGER. Where should I go?

LADY. Home. To your work.

STRANGER. But I'm no worker. I'm a writer.

LADY. I know. But I didn't want to hurt you. Creative power is something given you, that can also taken away. See you don't forfeit yours.

STRANGER. Where are you going?

LADY. Only to a shop.

STRANGER (after a pause). Tell me, are you a believer?

LADY. I am nothing.

STRANGER. All the better: you have a future. How I wish I were your old blind father, whom you could lead to the market place to sing for his bread. My tragedy is I cannot grow old that's what happens to children of the elves, they have big heads and never only cry. I wish I were someone's dog. I could follow him and never be alone again. I'd get a meal sometimes, a kick now and then, a pat perhaps, a blow often. . . .

LADY. Now I must go. Good-bye. (She goes out.)

STRANGER (absent-mindedly). Good-bye. (He remains on the seat. He takes off his hat and wipes his forehead. Then he draws on the ground with his stick. A BEGGAR enters. He has a strange look and is collecting objects from the gutter.) White are you picking up, beggar?

BEGGAR. Why call me that? I'm no beggar. Have I asked you for anything?

STRANGER. I beg your pardon. It's so hard to judge men from appearances.

BEGGAR. That's true. For instance, can you guess who I am?

STRANGER. I don't intend to try. It doesn't interest me.

BEGGAR. No one can know that in advance. Interest commonly comes afterwards—when it's too late. Virtus post nummos!

STRANGER. What? Do beggars know Latin?

BEGGAR. You see, you're interested already. Omne tulit punctum qui miscuit utile dulci. I have always succeeded in everything I've undertaken, because I've never attempted anything. I should like to call myself Polycrates, who found the gold ring in the fish's stomach. Life has given me all I asked of it. But I never asked anything; I grew tired of success and threw the ring away. Yet, now I've grown old I regret it. I search for it in the gutters; but as the search takes time, in default of my gold ring I don't disdain a few cigar stumps. . . .

STRANGER. I don't know whether this beggar's cynical or mad.

BEGGAR. I don't know either.

STRANGER. Do you know who I am?

BEGGAR. No. And it doesn't interest me.

STRANGER. Well, interest commonly comes afterwards. . . . You see you tempt me to take the words out of your mouth. And that's the same thing as picking up other people's cigars.

BEGGAR. So you won't follow my example?

STRANGER. What's that scar on your forehead?

BEGGAR. I got it from a near relation.

STRANGER. Now you frighten me! Are you real? May I touch you? (He touches his arm.) There's no doubt of it. . . . Would you deign to accept a small coin in return for a promise to seek Polycrates' ring in another part of the town? (He hands him a coin.) Post nummos virtus. . . . Another echo. You must go at once.

BEGGAR. I will. But you've given me far too much. I'll return three-quarters of it. Now we owe one another nothing but friendship.

STRANGER. Friendship! Am I a friend of yours?

BEGGAR. Well, I am of yours. When one's alone in the world one can't be particular.

STRANGER. Then let me tell you you forget yourself . . .

BEGGAR. Only too pleased! But when we meet again I'll have a word of welcome for you. (Exit.)

STRANGER (sitting down again and drawing in the dust with his stick). Sunday afternoon! A long, dank, sad time, after the usual Sunday dinner of roast beef, cabbage and watery potatoes. Now the older people are testing, the younger playing chess and smoking. The servants have gone to church and the shops are shut. This frightful afternoon, this day of rest, when there's nothing to engage the soul, when it's as hard to meet a friend as to get into a wine shop. (The LADY comes back again, she is noun wearing a flower at her breast.) Strange! I can't speak without being contradicted at once!

LADY. So you're still here?

STRANGER. Whether I sit here, or elsewhere, and write in the sand doesn't seem to me to matter—as long so I write in the sand.

LADY. What are you writing? May I see?

STRANGER. I think you'll find: Eve 1864. . . . No, don't step on it.

LADY. What happens then?

STRANGER. A disaster for you . . . and for me.

LADY. You know that?

STRANGER. Yes, and more. That the Christmas rose you're wearing is a mandragora. Its symbolical meaning is malice and calumny; but it was once used in medicine for the healing of madness. Will you give it me?

LADY (hesitating). As medicine?

36

STRANGER. Of course. (Pause.) Have you read my books?

LADY. You know I have. And that it's you I have to thank for giving me freedom and a belief in human rights and human dignity.

STRANGER. Then you haven't read the recent ones?

LADY. No. And if they're not like the earlier ones I don't want to.

STRANGER. Then promise never to open another book of mine.

LADY. Let me think that over. Very well, I promise.

STRANGER. Good! But see you keep your promise. Remember what happened to Bluebeard's wife when curiosity tempted her into the forbidden chamber. . . .

LADY. You see, already you make demands like those of a Bluebeard. What you don't see, or have long since forgotten, is that I'm married, and that my husband's a doctor, and that he admires your work. So that his house is open to you, if you wish to be made welcome there.

STRANGER. I've done all I can to forget it. I've expunged it from my memory so that it no longer has any reality for me.

LADY. If that's so, will you come home with me tonight?

STRANGER. No. Will you come with me?

LADY. Where?

STRANGER. Anywhere! I have no home, only a trunk. Money I sometimes have—though not often. It's the one thing life has capriciously refused me, perhaps because I never desired it intensely enough. (The LADY shakes her head.) Well? What are you thinking?

LADY. I'm surprised I'm not angry with you. But you're not serious.

STRANGER. Whether I am or not's all one to me. Ah! There's the organ! It won't be long now before the drink shops open.

LADY. Is it true *you* drink?

STRANGER. Yes. A great deal! Wine makes my soul from her prison, up into the firmament, where she what has never yet been seen, and hears what men never yet heard. . . .

LADY. And the day after?

STRANGER. I have the most delightful scruples of conscience! I experience the purifying emotions of guilt and repentance. I enjoy the sufferings of the body, whilst my soul hovers like smoke about my head. It is as if one were suspended between Life and Death, when the spirit feels that she has already opened her pinions and could fly aloft, if she would.

LADY. Come into the church for a moment. You'll hear no sermon, only the beautiful music of vespers.

STRANGER. No. Not into church! It depresses me because I feel I don't belong there. . . . That I'm an unhappy soul and that it's as impossible for me to re-enter as to become a child again.

LADY. You feel all that . . . already?

STRANGER. Yes. I've got that far. I feel as if I lay hacked in pieces and were being slowly melted in Medea's cauldron. Either I shall be sent to the soap-boilers, or arise renewed from my own dripping! It depends on Medea's skill!

LADY. That sounds like the word of an oracle. We must see if you can't become a child again.

STRANGER. We should have to start with the cradle; and this time with the right child.

LADY. Exactly! Wait here for me whilst I go into the church. If the café were open I'd ask you please not to drink. But luckily it's shut.

(The LADY exits. The STRANGER sits down again and draws in the sand. Enter six funeral attendants in brown with some mourners. One of them carries a banner with the insignia of the Carpenters, draped in brown crêpe; another a large axe decorated with spruce, a third a cushion with a chairman's mallet. They stop outside the café and wait.)

STRANGER. Excuse me, whose funeral have you been attending?

FIRST MOURNER. A house-breaker's. (He imitates the ticking of a clock.)

STRANGER. A real house-breaker? Or the insect sort, that lodges in the woodwork and goes 'tick-tick'?

FIRST MOURNER. Both—but mainly the insect sort. What do they call them?

STRANGER (to himself). He wants to fool me into saying the death-watch beetle. So I won't. You mean a burglar?

SECOND MOURNER. No. (The clock is again heard ticking.)

STRANGER. Are you trying to frighten me? Or does the dead man work miracles? In that case I'd better explain that my nerves are good, and that I don't believe in miracles. But I do find it strange that the mourners wear brown. Why not black? It's cheap and suitable.

THIRD MOURNER. To us, in our simplicity, it looks black; but if Your Honour wishes it, it shall look brown to you.

STRANGER. A queer company! They give me an uneasy feeling I'd like to ascribe to the wine I drank yesterday. If I were to ask if that were spruce, you'd probably say—well what?

FIRST MOURNER. Vine leaves.

STRANGER. I thought it would not be spruce! The café's opening, at last! (The Café opens, the STRANGER sits at a table and is served with wine. The MOURNERS sit at the other tables.) They must have been glad to be rid of him, if the mourners start drinking as soon as the funeral's over.

FIRST MOURNER. He was a good-for-nothing, who couldn't take life seriously.

STRANGER. And who probably drank?

SECOND MOURNER. Yes.

THIRD MOURNER. And let others support his wife and children.

STRANGER. He shouldn't have done so. Is that why his friends speak so well of him now? Please don't shake my table when I'm drinking.

SECOND MOURNER. When I'm drinking, I don't mind.

40

STRANGER. Well, I do. There's a great difference between us! (The MOURNERS whisper together. The BEGGAR comes back.) Here's the beggar again!

BEGGAR (sitting down at a table). Wine. Moselle!

LANDLORD (consulting a police last). I can't serve you: you've not paid your taxes. Here's your name, age and profession, and the decision of the court.

BEGGAR. Omnia serviliter pro dominatione! I'm a free man with a university education. I refused to pay taxes because I didn't want to become a member of parliament. Moselle!

LANDLORD. You'll get free transport to the poor house, if you don't get out.

STRANGER. Couldn't you gentlemen settle this somewhere else. You're disturbing your patrons.

LANDLORD. You can witness I'm in the right.

STRANGER. No. The whole thing's too distressing. Even without paying taxes he has the right to enjoy life's small pleasures.

LANDLORD. So you're the kind who'd absolve vagabonds from their duties?

STRANGER. This is too much! I'd have you know that I'm a famous man. (The LANDLORD and MOURNERS laugh.)

LANDLORD. Infamous, probably! Let me look at the police list, and see if the description tallies: thirty-eight, brown hair, moustache, blue eyes; no settled employment, means unknown; married, but has deserted his wife and children; well known for revolutionary views on social questions: gives impression he is not in full possession of his faculties. . . . It fits!

STRANGER (rising, pale and taken aback). What?

LANDLORD. Yes. It fits all right.

BEGGAR. Perhaps he's on the list. And not me!

LANDLORD. It looks like it. In any case, both of you had better clear out.

BEGGAR (to the STRANGER). Shall we?

STRANGER. We? This begins to look like a conspiracy.

(The church bells are heard. The sun comes out and illuminates the coloured rose window above the church door, which is now opened, disclosing the interior. The organ is heard and the choir singing Ave Maris Stella.)

LADY (coming from the church). Where are you? What are you doing? Why did you call me? Must you hang on a woman's skirts like a child?

STRANGER. I'm afraid now. Things are happening that have no natural explanation.

LADY. But you were afraid of nothing. Not even death!

STRANGER. Death . . . no. But of something else, the unknown.

LADY. Listen. Give me your hand. You're ill, I'll take you to a doctor. Come!

STRANGER. If you like. But tell me: is this carnival, or . . . reality?

LADY. It's real enough.

STRANGER. This beggar must be a wretched fellow. Is it true he resembles me?

LADY. He will, if you go on drinking. Now go to the post office and get your letter. And then come with me.

STRANGER. No, I won't. It'll only be about lawsuits.

LADY. If not?

STRANGER. Malicious gossip.

LADY. Well, do as you wish. No one can escape his fate. At this moment I feel a higher power is sitting in judgment on us and has made a decision.

STRANGER. You feel that, too! I heard the hammer fall just now; and the chairs being pushed back. The clerk's being sent to find me! Oh, the suspense! No, I can't follow you.

LADY. Tell me, what have you done to me? In the church I found I couldn't pray. A light on the altar was extinguished and an icy wind blew in my face when I heard you call me.

STRANGER. I didn't call you. But I wanted you.

LADY. You're not as weak as you pretend. You have great strength; and I'm afraid of you. . . .

STRANGER. When I'm alone I've no strength at all; but if I can find a single companion I grow strong. I shall be strong now; and so I'll follow you.

LADY. Perhaps you can free me from the werewolf.

STRANGER. Who's he?

LADY. That's what I call him.

STRANGER. Count on me. Killing dragons, freeing princesses, defeating werewolves—that is Life!

LADY. Then come, my liberator!

(She draws her veil over her face, kisses him on the mouth and hurries out. The STRANGER stands where he is for a moment, surprised and stunned. A loud chord sung by women's voices, rather like a cry, is heard from the church. The rose window suddenly grows dark and the tree above the seat is shaken by the wind. The MOURNERS rise and look at the sky, as if they could see something terrifying. The STRANGER hurries out after the LADY.)

SCENE II

DOCTOR'S HOUSE

[Courtyard enclosed on three sides by a single-storied house with a tiled roof. Small windows in all three façades. Right, verandah with glass doors. Left, climbing roses and bee-hives outside the windows. In the middle of the courtyard a woodpile in the form of a cupola. A well beside it. The top of a walnut tree is seen above the central façade of the house. In the corner, right, a garden gate. By the well a large tortoise. On right, entrance below to a wine-cellar. An ice-chest and dust-bin. The DOCTOR'S SISTER enters from the verandah with a telegram.]

SISTER. Now misfortune will fall on your house.

DOCTOR. When has it not, my dear sister?

SISTER. This time. . . . Ingeborg's coming and bringing . . . guess whom?

DOCTOR. Wait! I know, because I've long foreseen this, even desired it, for he's a writer I've always admired. I've learnt much from him and often wished to meet him. Now he's coming, you say. Where did Ingeborg meet him?

SISTER. In town, it seems. Probably in some literary *salon.*

DOCTOR. I've often wondered whether this man was the boy of the same name who was my friend at school. I hope not; for he seemed one

45

that fortune would treat harshly. And in a life-time he'll have given his unhappy tendencies full scope.

SISTER. Don't let him come here. Go out. Say you're engaged.

DOCTOR. No. One can't escape one's fate.

SISTER. But you've never bowed your head to anyone! Why crawl before this spectre, and call him fate?

DOCTOR. Life has taught me to. I've wasted time and energy in fighting the inevitable.

SISTER. But why allow your wife to behave like this? She'll compromise you both.

DOCTOR. You think so? Because, when I made her break off her engagement I held out false hopes to her of a life of freedom, instead of the slavery she'd known. Besides, I could never love her if I were in a position to give her orders.

SISTER. You'd be friends with your enemy?

DOCTOR. Oh . . . !

SISTER. Will you let her bring someone into the house who'll destroy you? If you only knew how I hate that man.

DOCTOR. I do. His last book's terrible; and shows a certain lack of mental balance.

SISTER. They ought to shut him up.

DOCTOR. Many people have said so, but I don't think him bad enough.

SISTER. Because you're eccentric yourself, and live in daily contact with a woman who's mad.

DOCTOR. I admit abnormality has always had a strong attraction for me, and originality is at least not commonplace. (The syren of a steamer is heard.) What was that?

SISTER. Your nerves are on edge. It's only the steamer. (Pause.) Now, I implore you, go away!

DOCTOR. I ought to want to; but I'm held fast. (Pause.) From here I can see his portrait in my study. The sunlight throws a shadow on it that changes it completely. It makes him look like. . . . Horrible! You see what I mean?

HATER. The devil! Come away!

DOCTOR. I can't.

SISTER. Then at least defend yourself.

DOCTOR. I always do. But this time I feel a thunder storm gathering. How often have I tried to fly, and not been able to. It's as if the earth were iron and I a compass needle. If misfortune comes, it's not of my fee choice. They've come in at the door.

SISTER. I heard nothing.

DOCTOR. I did! Now I can see them, too! He *is* the friend of my boyhood. He got into trouble at school; but I was blamed and punished. He was nick-named Caesar, I don't know why.

SISTER. And this man. . . .

DOCTOR. That's what always happens. Caesar! (The LADY comes in.)

LADY. I've brought a visitor.

DOCTOR. I know, and he's welcome.

LADY. I left him in the house, to wash.

DOCTOR. Well, are you satisfied with your conquest?

LADY. I think he's the unhappiest man I ever met.

DOCTOR. That's saying a great deal.

LADY. Yes, there's enough unhappiness for all of us.

DOCTOR. There is! (To his SISTER.) Would you ask him to come out here? (His SISTER goes out.) Have you had an interesting time?

LADY. Yes. I met a number of strange people. Have you had many patients?

DOCTOR. No. The consulting room's empty this morning. I think the practice is going down.

LADY (kindly). I'm sorry. Tell me, oughtn't that woodpile to be taken into the house? It only draws the damp.

DOCTOR (without reproach). Yes, and the bees should be killed, too; and the fruit in the garden picked. But I've no time to do it.

LADY. You're tired.

DOCTOR. Tired of everything.

LADY (without bitterness). And you've a wife who can't even help you.

DOCTOR (kindly). You mustn't say that, if I don't think so.

LADY (turning towards the verandah). Here he is!

(The STRANGER comes in through the verandah, dressed in a way that makes him look younger than before. He has an air of forced candour. He seems to recognise the doctor, and shrinks back, but recovers himself.)

DOCTOR. You're very welcome.

STRANGER. It's kind of you.

DOCTOR. You bring good weather with you. And we need it; for it's rained for six weeks.

STRANGER. Not for seven? It usually rains for seven if it rains on St. Swithin's. But that's later on—how foolish of me!

DOCTOR. As you're used to town life I'm afraid you'll find the country dull.

STRANGER. Oh no. I'm no more at home there than here. Excuse me asking, but haven't we met before—when we were boys?

DOCTOR. Never.

(The LADY has sat down at the table and is crocheting.)

STRANGER. Are you sure?

DOCTOR. Perfectly. I've followed your literary career from the first with great interest; as I know my wife has told you. So that if we *had* met I'd certainly have remembered your name. (Pause.) Well, now you can see how a country doctor lives!

STRANGER. If you could guess what the life of a so-called liberator's like, you wouldn't envy him.

DOCTOR. I can imagine it; for I've seen how men love their chains. Perhaps that's as it should be.

STRANGER (listening). Strange. Who's playing in the village?

DOCTOR. I don't know. Do you, Ingeborg?

LADY. No.

STRANGER. Mendelssohn's Funeral March! It pursues me. I never know whether I've heard it or not.

DOCTOR. Do you suffer from hallucinations?

STRANGER. No. But I'm pursued by trivial incidents. Can't you hear anyone playing?

DOCTOR. Yes.

LADY. Someone *is* playing. Mendelssohn.

DOCTOR. Not surprising.

STRANGER. No. But that it should be played precisely at the right place, at the right time . . . . (He gets up.)

DOCTOR. To reassure you, I'll ask my sister. (Exit through the verandah.)

STRANGER (to the LADY). I'm stifling here. I can't pass a night under this roof. Your husband looks like a werewolf and in his presence you turn into a pillar of salt. Murder has been done in this house; the place is haunted. I shall escape as soon as I can find an excuse.

(The DOCTOR comes back.)

DOCTOR. It's the girl at the post office.

STRANGER (nervously). Good. That's all right. You've an original house. That pile of wood, for instance.

DOCTOR. Yes. It's been struck by lightning twice.

STRANGER. Terrible! And you still keep it?

DOCTOR. That's why. I've made it higher out of defiance; and to give shade in summer. It's like the prophet's gourd. But in the autumn it must go into the wood shed.

STRANGER (looking round). Christmas roses, too! Where did you get them? They're flowering in summer! Everything's upside down here.

DOCTOR. They were given me by a patient. He's not quite sane.

STRANGER. Is he staying in the house?

DOCTOR. Yes. He's a quiet soul, who ponders on the purposelessness of nature. He thinks it foolish for hellebore to grow in the snow and freeze; so he puts the plants in the cellar and beds them out in the spring.

STRANGER. But a madman . . . in the house. Most unpleasant!

DOCTOR. He's very harmless.

STRANGER. How did he lose his wits?

DOCTOR. Who can tell. It's a disease of the mind, not the body.

STRANGER. Tell me—is he here—now?

DOCTOR. Yes. He's free to wander in the garden and arrange creation. But if his presence disquiets you, we can shut him up.

STRANGER. Why aren't such poor devils put out of—their misery?

DOCTOR. It's hard to know whether they're ripe. . . .

STRANGER. What for?

DOCTOR. For what's to come.

STRANGER. There *is* nothing. (Pause.)

DOCTOR. Who knows!

STRANGER. I feel strangely uneasy. Have you medical material . . . specimens . . . dead bodies?

DOCTOR. Oh yes. In the ice-box—for the authorities, you know. (He pulls out an arm and leg.) Look here.

STRANGER. No. Too much like Bluebeard!

DOCTOR (sharply). What do you mean by that? (Looking at the LADY.) Do you think I kill my wives?

STRANGER. Oh no. It's clear you don't. Is this house haunted, too?

DOCTOR. Oh yes. Ask my wife.(He disappears behind the wood pile where neither the STRANGER nor the LADY can see him.)

LADY. You needn't whisper, my husband's deaf. Though he can lip read.

STRANGER. Then let me say that I've never known a more painful half-hour. We exchange the merest commonplaces, because none of us has the courage to say what he thinks. I suffered so that the idea came to me of opening my veins to get relief. But now I'd like to tell him the truth and have done with it. Shall we say to his face that we mean to go away, and that you've had enough of his foolishness?

LADY. If you talk like that I'll begin to hate you. You must behave under any circumstances.

STRANGER. How well brought up you are! (The DOCTOR now becomes visible to the STRANGER and the LADY, who continue their conversation.) Come away with me, before the sun goes down. (Pause.) Tell me, why did you kiss me yesterday?

LADY. But. . . .

STRANGER. Supposing he could hear what we say! I don't trust him.

DOCTOR. What shall we do to amuse our guest?

LADY. He doesn't care much for amusement. His life's not been happy.

(The DOCTOR blows a whistle. The MADMAN comes into the garden. He wears a laurel wreath and his clothes are curious.)

DOCTOR. Come here, Caesar.

STRANGER (displeased). What? Is he called Caesar?

DOCTOR. No. It's a nickname I gave him, to remind me of a boy I was at school with.

STRANGER (disturbed). Oh?

DOCTOR. He was involved in a strange incident, and I got all the blame.

LADY (to the STRANGER). You'd never believe a boy could have been so corrupt.

(The STRANGER looks distressed. The MADMAN comes nearer.)

DOCTOR. Caesar, come and make your bow to our famous writer.

CAESAR. Is this the great man?

LADY (to the DOCTOR). Why did you let him come, if it annoys our guest?

DOCTOR. Caesar, you must behave. Or I shall have to whip you.

CAESAR. Yes. He is Caesar, but he's not great. He doesn't even know which came first, the hen or the egg. But I do.

STRANGER (to the LADY). I shall go. Is this a trap? What am I to think? In a minute he'll unloose his bees to amuse me.

LADY. Trust me . . . whatever happens! And turn your face away when you speak.

STRANGER. This werewolf never leaves us.

DOCTOR (looking at his watch). You must excuse me for about an hour. I've a patient to visit. I hope the time won't hang on your hands.

STRANGER. I'm used to waiting, for what never comes. . . .

DOCTOR (to the MADMAN). Come along, Caesar. I must lock you up in the cellar. (He goes out with the MADMAN.)

STRANGER (to the LADY). What does that mean? Someone's pursuing me! You told me your husband was well disposed towards me, and I believed you. But he can't open his mouth without wounding me. Every word pricks like a goad. Then this funeral march . . . it's really being played! And here, once more, Christmas roses! Why does everything follow in an eternal round? Dead bodies, beggars, madmen, human destinies and childhood memories? Come away. Let me free you from this hell.

LADY. That's why I brought you here. Also that it could never be said you'd stolen the wife of another. But one thing I must ask you: can I put my trust in you?

STRANGER. You mean in my feelings?

LADY. I don't speak of them. We're taking them for granted. They'll endure as long as they'll endure.

STRANGER. You mean in my position? Large sums are owed me. All I have to do is to write or telegraph. . . .

LADY. Then I will trust you. (Putting away her work.) Now go straight out of that door. Follow the syringa hedge till you find a gate. We'll meet in the next village.

STRANGER (hesitating). I don't like leaving the back way. I'd rather have fought it out with him here.

LADY. Quick!

STRANGER. Won't you come with me?

LADY. Yes. But then I must go first. (She turns and blows a kiss towards the verandah.) My poor werewolf!

SCENE III

ROOM IN AN HOTEL

[The STRANGER enters followed by the LADY. A WAITER.]

STRANGER (who is carrying a suitcase). Is no other room free?

WAITER. No.

STRANGER. I don't want this one.

LADY. But it's the only one: the other hotels are all full.

STRANGER (to the WAITER). You can go. (The LADY sinks on to a chair without taking off her hat and coat.) What is it you want?

LADY. I wish you'd kill me.

STRANGER. I don't wonder! Thrown out of hotels, because we're not married, and pestered by the police, we're forced to come to this place, the last I'd have wished. To this very room, number eight. . . . Someone must be against me!

LADY. Is this eight?

STRANGER. What? Have you been here before?

LADY. Have you?

STRANGER. Yes.

LADY. Then let's get away. Onto the road, into the woods. It doesn't matter where.

STRANGER. I should like to. But after this terrible time I'm as tired as you are. I felt this was to be our journey's end. I resisted, I tried to go in the opposite direction, but trains were late, or we missed them, and we had to come here. To this room! The devil's in it—at least what I call the devil. But I'll be even with him yet.

LADY. It seems we'll never find peace on earth again.

STRANGER. Nothing's been changed. The dying Christmas roses. (Looking at two pictures.) There he is again. And that's the Hotel Breuer in Montreux. I've stayed there, too.

LADY. Did you go to the post office?

STRANGER. I thought you'd ask me that. I did. And as an answer to five letters and three telegrams I found a telegram saying that my publisher had gone away for a fortnight.

LADY. Then we're lost.

STRANGER. Very nearly.

LADY. The waiter will be back in five minutes and ask for our passports. Then the landlord will come up and tell us to go.

STRANGER. Then only one course remains.

LADY. Two.

STRANGER. The second's impossible.

LADY. What is the second?

STRANGER. To go to your parents in the country.

LADY. You're beginning to read my thoughts.

STRANGER. We no longer have any secrets from one another.

LADY. Then the whole dream's at an end.

STRANGER. It maybe.

LADY. You must telegraph again.

STRANGER. I ought to, I know. But I can't stir from here. I no longer believe that what I do can succeed. Someone's paralysed me.

LADY. And me! We decided never to speak of the past and yet we drag it with us. Look at this carpet. Those flowers seem to form. . . .

STRANGER. Him! It's him. He's everywhere. How many hundred times has he. . . . Yet I see someone else in the pattern of the table cloth. No, it's an illusion! Any moment now I'll hear my funeral march—then everything will be complete. (Listening.) There!

LADY. I hear nothing.

STRANGER. Am I . . . am I. . . .

LADY. Shall we go home?

STRANGER. The last place. The worst of all! To arrive like an adventurer, a beggar. Impossible!

LADY. Yes, I know, but. . . . No, it would be too much. To bring shame, disgrace and sorrow to the old people, and to see you humiliated, and you me! We could never respect one another again.

STRANGER. It would be worse than death. Yet I feel it's inevitable, and I begin to long for it, to get it over quickly, if it must be.

LADY (taking out her work). But I don't want to be reviled in your presence. We must find another way. If only we were married—and divorce would be easy, because my former marriage isn't recognised by the laws of the country in which it was contracted. . . . All we need do is to go away and be married by the same priest . . . but that would be wounding for you!

STRANGER. It would match the rest! For this honeymoon's becoming a pilgrimage!

LADY. You're right! The landlord will be here in five minutes to turn us out. There's only one way to end such humiliations. Of our own free will we must accept the worst. . . . I can hear footsteps!

STRANGER. I've foreseen this and am ready. Ready for everything. If I can't overcome the unseen, I can show you how much I can endure. . . . You must pawn your jewellery. I can buy it back when my publisher gets home, if he's not drowned bathing or killed in a railway accident. A man as ambitious as I must be ready to sacrifice his honour first of all.

LADY. As we're agreed, wouldn't it be better to give up this room? Oh, God! He's coming now.

60

STRANGER. Let's go. We'll run the gauntlet of waiters, maids and servants. Red with shame and pale with indignation. Animals have their lairs to hide in, but we are forced to flaunt our shame. (Pause.) Let down your veil.

LADY. So this is freedom!

STRANGER. And I . . . am the liberator. (Exeunt.)

SCENE IV

BY THE SEA

[A hut on a cliff by the sea. Outside it a table with chairs. The STRANGER and the LADY are dressed in less sombre clothing and look younger than in the previous scene. The LADY is doing crochet work.]

STRANGER. Three peaceful happy days at my wife's side, and anxiety returns!

LADY. What do you fear?

STRANGER. That this will not last long.

LADY. Why do you think so?

STRANGER. I don't know. I believe it must end suddenly, terribly. There's something deceptive even the sunshine and the stillness. I feel that happiness if not part of my destiny.

LADY. But it's all over! My parents are resigned to what we've done. My husband understands and has written a kind letter.

STRANGER. What does that matter? Fate spins the web; once more I hear the mallet fall and the chairs being pushed back from the table— judgment has been pronounced. Yet that must have happened before

I was born, because even in childhood I began to serve my sentence. There's no moment in my life on which can look back with happiness.

LADY. Unfortunate man! Yet you've had everything you wished from life!

STRANGER. Everything. Unluckily I forgot to wish for money.

LADY. You're thinking of that again.

STRANGER. Are you surprised?

LADY. Quiet!

STRANGER. What is it you're always working at? You sit there like one of the Fates and draw the threads through your fingers. But go on. The most beautiful of sights is a woman bending over her work, or over her child. What are you making?

LADY. Nothing. Crochet work.

STRANGER. It looks like a network of nerves and knots on which you've fixed your thoughts. The brain must look like that—from within.

LADY. If only I thought of half the things you imagine. . . . But I think of nothing.

STRANGER. Perhaps that's why I feel so contented when I'm with you. Why, I find you so perfect that I can no longer imagine life without you! Now the clouds have blown away. Now the sky is clear! The wind soft— feel how it caresses us! This is Life! Yes, now I live. And I feel my spirit growing, spreading, becoming tenuous, infinite. I am everywhere, in the ocean which is my blood, in the rocks that are my bones, in the trees, in the flowers; and my head reaches up to the heavens. I can survey the whole universe. I *am* the universe. And I feel the power of the Creator within me, for I am He! I wish I could grasp the all in my hand and refashion it into something more perfect, more lasting, more beautiful. I want all creation and created beings to be happy, to be born without pain, live without suffering, and die in quiet content. Eve! Die with me now! This moment, for the next will bring sorrow again.

LADY. I'm not ready to die.

STRANGER. Why not?

LADY. I believe there are things I've not yet done. Perhaps I've not suffered enough.

STRANGER. Is that the purpose of life?

LADY. It seems to be. (Pause.) Now I want to ask one thing of you.

STRANGER. Well?

LADY. Don't blaspheme against heaven again, or compare yourself with the Creator, for then you remind me of Caesar at home.

STRANGER (excitedly). Caesar! How can you say that . . . ?

LADY. I'm sorry if I've said anything I shouldn't. It was foolish of me to say 'at home.' Forgive me.

STRANGER. You were thinking that Caesar and I resemble one another in our blasphemies?

LADY. Of course not.

STRANGER. Strange. I believe you when you say you don't mean to hurt me; yet you *do* hurt me, as all the others do. Why?

LADY. Because you're over-sensitive.

STRANGER. You say that again! Do you think I've sensitive hidden places?

LADY. No. I didn't mean that. And now the spirits of suspicion and discord are coming between us. Drive them away—at once.

STRANGER. You mustn't say I blaspheme if I use the well-known words: See, we are like unto the gods.

LADY. But if that's so, why can't you help yourself, or us?

STRANGER. Can't I? Wait. As yet we've only seen the beginning.

LADY. If the end is like it, heaven help us!

STRANGER. I know what you fear; and I meant to hold back a pleasant surprise. But now I won't torment you longer. (He takes out a registered letter, not yet opened.) Look!

LADY. The money's come!

STRANGER. This morning. Who can destroy me now?

LADY. Don't speak like that. You know who could.

STRANGER. Who?

LADY. He who punishes the arrogance of men.

STRANGER. And their courage. That especially. This was my Achilles' heel; I bore with everything, except this fearful lack of money.

LADY. May I ask how much they've sent?

STRANGER. I don't know. I've not opened the letter. But I do know about how much to expect. I'd better look and see. (He opens the letter.) What? Only an account showing I'm owed nothing! There's something uncanny in this.

LADY. I begin to think so, too.

STRANGER. I know I'm damned. But I'm ready to hurl the curse back at him who so nobly cursed me. . . . (He throws up the letter.) With a curse of my own.

LADY. Don't. You frighten me.

STRANGER. Fear me, so long as you don't despise me! The challenge has been thrown down; now you shall see a conflict between two great opponents. (He opens his coat and waistcoat and looks threateningly aloft.) Strike me with your lightning if you dare! Frighten me with your thunder if you can!

LADY. Don't speak like that.

STRANGER. I will. Who dares break in on my dream of love? Who tears the cup from my lips; and the woman from my arms? Those who envy me, be they gods or devils! Little bourgeois gods who parry sword thrusts with pin-pricks from behind, who won't stand up to their man, but strike at him with unpaid bills. A backstairs way of discrediting a master before his servants. They never attack, never draw, merely soil and decry! Powers, lords and masters! All are the same!

LADY. May heaven not punish you.

STRANGER. Heaven's blue and silent. The ocean's silent and stupid. Listen, I can hear a poem—that's what I call it when an idea begins to germinate in my mind. First the rhythm; this time like the thunder of hooves and the jingle of spurs and accoutrements. But there's a fluttering too, like a sail flapping. . . . Banners!

LADY. No. It's the wind. Can't you hear it in the trees?

STRANGER. Quiet! They're riding over a bridge, a wooden bridge. There's no water in the brook, only pebbles. Wait! Now I can hear them, men and women, saying a rosary. The angels' greeting. Now I can see— on what you're working—a large kitchen, with white-washed walls, it has three small latticed windows, with flowers in them. In the left-hand corner a hearth, on the right a table with wooden seats. And above the table, in the corner, hangs a crucifix, with a lamp burning below. The ceiling's of blackened beams, and dried mistletoe hangs on the wall.

LADY (frightened). Where can you see all that?

STRANGER. On your work.

LADY. Can you see people there?

STRANGER. A very old man's sitting at the table, bent over a game bag, his hands clasped in prayer. A woman, so longer young, kneels on the floor. Now once more I hear the angels' greeting, as if far away. But those two in the kitchen are as motionless as figures of wax. A veil shrouds everything. . . . No, that was no poem! (Waking.) It was something else.

LADY. It was reality! The kitchen at home, where you've never set foot. That old man was my grandfather, the forester, and the woman my mother! They were praying for us! It was six o'clock and the servants were saying a rosary outside, as they always do.

STRANGER. You make me uneasy. Is this the beginning of second sight? Still, it was beautiful. A snow-white room, with flowers and mistletoe. But why should they pray for us?

LADY. Why indeed! Have we done wrong?

STRANGER. What is wrong?

LADY. I've read there's no such thing. And yet . . . I long to see my mother; not my father, for he turned me out as he did her.

STRANGER. Why should he have turned your mother out?

LADY. Who can say? The children least of all. Let us go to my home. I long to.

STRANGER. To the lion's den, the snake pit? One more or less makes no matter. I'll do it for you, but not like the Prodigal Son. No, you shall see that I can go through fire and water for your sake.

LADY. How do you know . . . ?

STRANGER. I can guess.

LADY. And can you guess that the path to where my parents live in the mountains is too steep for carts to use?

STRANGER. It sounds extraordinary, but I read or dreamed something of the kind.

LADY. You may have. But you'll see nothing that's not natural, though perhaps unusual, for men and women are a strange race. Are you ready to follow me?

STRANGER. I'm ready—for anything!

(The LADY kisses him on the forehead and makes the sign of the cross simply, timidly and without gestures.)

LADY. Then come!

SCENE V

ON THE ROAD

[A landscape with hills; a chapel, right, in the far distance on a rise. The road, flanked by fruit trees, winds across the background. Between the trees hills can be seen on which are crucifixes, chapels and memorials to the victims of accidents. In the foreground a sign post with the legend, 'Beggars not allowed in this parish.' The STRANGER and the LADY.]

LADY. You're tired.

STRANGER. I won't deny it. But it's humiliating to confess I'm hungry, because the money's gone. I never thought that would happen to me.

LADY. It seems we must be prepared for anything, for I think we've fallen into disfavour. My shoe's split, and I could weep at our having to go like this, looking like beggars.

STRANGER (pointing to the signpost). And beggars are not allowed in this parish. Why must that be stuck up in large letters here?

LADY. It's been there as long as I can remember. Think of it, I've not been back since I was a child. And In those days I found the way short and the hills lower. The trees, too, were smaller, and I think I used to hear birds singing.

STRANGER. Birds sang all the year for you then! Now they only sing in the spring—and autumn's not far off. But in those days you used to dance along this endless way of Calvaries, plucking flowers at the feet of the crosses. (A horn in the distance.) What's that?

LADY. My grandfather coming back from shooting. A good old man. Let's go on and reach the house by dark.

STRANGER. Is it still far?

LADY. No. Only across the hills and over the river.

STRANGER. Is that the river I hear?

LADY. The river by which I was born and brought up. I was eighteen before I crossed over to this bank, to see what was in the blue of the distance. . . . Now I've seen.

STRANGER. You're weeping!

LADY. Poor old man! When I got into the boat, he said: My child, beyond lies the world. When you've seen enough, come back to your mountains, and they will hide you. Now I've seen enough. Enough!

STRANGER. Let's go. It's beginning to grow dusk already. (They pick up their travelling capes and go on.)

SCENE VI

IN A RAVINE

[Entrance to a ravine between steep cliffs covered with pines. In the foreground a wooden shanty, a broom by the door with a ramshorn hanging from its handle. Left, a smithy, a red glow showing through its open door. Right, a flourmill. In the background the road through the ravine with mill-stream and footbridge. The rock formations look like giant profiles.]

[On the rise of the curtain the SMITH is at the smithy door and the MILLER'S WIFE at the door of the mill. When the LADY enters they sign to one another and disappear. The clothing of both the LADY and the STRANGER is torn and shabby.]

STRANGER. They're hiding, from us, probably.

LADY. I don't think so.

STRANGER. What a strange place! Everything seems conspire to arouse disquiet. What's that broom there? And the horn with ointment? Probably because it's their usual place, but it makes me think of witchcraft. Why is the smithy black and the mill white? Because one's sooty and the other covered with flour; yet when I saw the blacksmith by the light of his forge and the white miller's wife, it reminded me of an old poem. Look at those giant faces. . . . There's your werewolf from whom I saved you. There he is, in profile, see!

LADY. Yes, but it's only the rock.

STRANGER. Only the rock, and yet it's he.

LADY. Shall I tell you why we can see him?

STRANGER. You mean—it's our conscience? Which pricks us when we're hungry and tired, and is silent when we've eaten and rested. It's horrible to arrive in rags. Our clothes are torn from climbing through the brambles. Someone's fighting against me.

LADY. Why did you challenge him?

STRANGER. Because I want to fight in the open; not battle with unpaid bills and empty purses. Anyhow: here's my last copper. The devil take it, if there is one! (He throws it into the brook.)

LADY. Oh! We could have paid the ferry with it. Now we'll have to talk of money when we reach home.

STRANGER. When can we talk of anything else?

LADY. That's because you've despised it.

STRANGER. As I've despised everything. . . .

LADY. But not everything's despicable. Some things are good.

STRANGER. I've never seen them.

LADY. Then follow me and you will.

STRANGER. I'll follow you. (He hesitates when passing the smithy.)

LADY (who has gone on ahead). Are you frightened of fire?

STRANGER. No, but . . . (The horn is heard in the distance. He hurries past the smithy after the LADY.)

SCENE VII

IN A KITCHEN

[A large kitchen with whitewashed walls. Three windows in the corner, right, so arranged that two are at the back and one in the right wall. The windows are small and deeply recessed; in the recesses there are flower pots. The ceiling is beamed and black with soot. In the left corner a large range with utensils of copper, iron and tin, and wooden vessels. In the corner, right, a crucifix with a lamp. Beneath it a four-cornered table with benches. Bunches of mistletoe on the walls. A door at the back. The Poorhouse can be seen outside, and through the window at the back the church. Near the fire bedding for dogs and a table with food for the poor.]

[The OLD MAN is sitting at the table beneath the crucifix, with his hands clasped and a game bag before him. He is a strongly-built man of over eighty with white hair and along beard, dressed as a forester. The MOTHER is kneeling on the floor; she is grey-haired and nearly fifty; her dress is of black-and-white material. The voices of men, women and children can be clearly heard singing the last verse of the Angels' Greeting in chorus. 'Holy Mary, Mother of God, pray for us poor sinners, now and in the hour of death. Amen.']

OLD MAN and MOTHER. Amen!

MOTHER. Now I'll tell you, Father. They saw two vagabonds by the river. Their clothing was torn and dirty, for they'd been in the water. And when it came to paying the ferryman, they'd no money. Now they're drying their clothes in the ferryman's hut.

OLD MAN. Let them stay there.

MOTHER. Don't forbid a beggar your house. He might be an angel.

OLD MAN. True. Let them come in.

MOTHER. I'll put food for them on the table for the poor. Do you mind that?

OLD MAN. No.

MOTHER. Shall I give them cider?

OLD MAN. Yes. And you can light the fire; they'll be cold.

MOTHER. There's hardly time. But I will, if you wish it, Father.

OLD MAN (looking out of the window). I think you'd better.

MOTHER. What are you looking at?

OLD MAN. The river; it's rising. And I'm asking myself, as I've done for seventy years—when I shall reach the sea.

MOTHER. You're sad tonight, Father.

OLD MAN. . . . et introibo ad altare Dei: ad Deum qui laetificat juventutem meam. Yes. I do feel sad. . . . Deus, Deus meus: quare tristis es anima mea, et quare conturbas me.

MOTHER. Spera in Deo. . . .

(The Maid comes in, and signs to the MOTHER, who goes over to her. They whisper together and the maid goes out again.)

OLD MAN. I heard what you said. O God! Must I bear that too!

MOTHER. You needn't see them. You can go up to your room.

OLD MAN. No. It shall be a penance. But why come like this: as vagabonds?

MOTHER. Perhaps they lost their way and have had much to endure.

OLD MAN. But to bring her husband! Is she lost to shame?

MOTHER. You know Ingeborg's queer nature. She thinks all she does is fitting, if not right. Have you ever seen her ashamed, or suffer from a rebuff? I never have. Yet she's not without shame; on the contrary. And everything she does, however questionable, seems natural when she does it.

OLD MAN. I've always wondered why one could never be angry with her. She doesn't feel herself responsible, or think an insult's directed at her. She seems impersonal; or rather two persons, one who does nothing but ill whilst the other gives absolution. . . . But this man! There's no one I've hated from afar so much as he. He sees evil everywhere; and of no one have I heard so much ill.

MOTHER. That's true. But it may be Ingeborg's found some mission in this man's life; and he in hers. Perhaps they're meant to torture each other into atonement.

OLD MAN. Perhaps. But I'll have nothing to do with at seems to me shameful. This man, under my roof! Yet I must accept it, like everything else. For I've deserved no less.

MOTHER. Very well then. (The LADY and the STRANGER come in.) You're welcome.

LADY. Thank you, Mother. (She looks over to the OLD MAN, who rises and looks at the STRANGER.) Peace, Grandfather. This is my husband. Give him your hand.

OLD MAN. First let me look at him. (He goes to the STRANGER, puts his hands on his shoulders and looks him in the eyes.) What motives brought you here?

STRANGER (simply). None, but to keep my wife company, at her earnest desire.

OLD MAN. If that's true, you're welcome! I've a long and stormy life behind me, and at last I've found a certain peace in solitude. I beg you not to trouble it.

STRANGER. I haven't come here to ask favours. I'll take nothing with me when I go.

OLD MAN. That's not the answer I wanted; for we all need one another. I perhaps need you. No one can know, young man.

LADY. Grandfather!

OLD MAN. Yes, my child. I shan't wish you happiness, for there's no such thing; but I wish you strength to bear your destiny. Now I'll leave you for a little. Your mother will look after you. (He goes out.)

LADY (to her mother). Did you lay that table for us, Mother?

MOTHER. No, it's a mistake, as you can imagine.

LADY. I know we look wretched. We were lost in the mountains, and if grandfather hadn't blown his horn . . .

MOTHER. Your grandfather gave up hunting long ago.

LADY. Then it was someone else. . . . Listen, Mother, I'll go up now to the 'rose' room, and get it straight.

MOTHER. Do. I'll come in a moment.

(The LADY would like to say something, cannot, and goes out.)

STRANGER (to the MOTHER). I've seen this room already.

MOTHER. And I've seen you. I almost expected you.

STRANGER. As one expects a disaster?

MOTHER. Why say that?

STRANGER. Because I sow devastation wherever I go. But as I must go somewhere, and cannot change my fate, I've lost my scruples.

MOTHER. Then you're like my daughter—she, too, has no scruples and no conscience.

STRANGER. What?

MOTHER. You think I'm speaking ill of her? I couldn't do that of my own child. I only draw the comparison, because you know her.

STRANGER. But I've noticed what you speak of in Eve.

MOTHER. Why do you call Ingeborg Eve?

STRANGER. By inventing a name for her I made her mine. I wanted to change her. . . .

MOTHER. And remake her in your image? (Laughing.) I've been told that country wizards carve images of their victims, and give them the names of those they'd bewitch. That was your plan: by means of this Eve, that you yourself had made, you intended to destroy the whole Sex!

STRANGER (looking at the MOTHER in surprise). Those were damnable words! Forgive me. But you have religious beliefs: how can you think such things?

MOTHER. The thoughts were yours.

STRANGER. This begins to be interesting. I imagined an idyll in the forest, but this is a witches' cauldron.

MOTHER. Not quite. You've forgotten, or never knew, that a man deserted me shamefully, and that you're a man who also shamefully deserted a woman.

STRANGER. Frank words. Now I know where I am.

MOTHER. I'd like to know where I am. Can you support two families?

STRANGER. If all goes well.

MOTHER. All doesn't—in this life. Money can be lost.

STRANGER. But my talent's capital I can never lose.

80

MOTHER. Really? The greatest of talents has been known to fail . . . gradually, or suddenly.

STRANGER. I've never met anyone who could so damp one's courage.

MOTHER. Pride should be damped. Your last book was much weaker.

STRANGER. You read it?

MOTHER. Yes. That's why I know all your secrets. So don't try to deceive me; it won't go well with you. (Pause.) A trifle, but one that does us no good here: why didn't you pay the ferryman?

STRANGER. My heel of Achilles! I threw my last coin away. Can't we speak of something else than money in this house?

MOTHER. Oh yes. But in this house we do our duty before we amuse ourselves. So you came on foot because you had no money?

STRANGER (hesitating). Yes. . . .

MOTHER (smiling). Probably nothing to eat?

STRANGER (hesitating). No. . . .

MOTHER. You're a fine fellow!

STRANGER. In all my life I've never been in such a predicament.

MOTHER. I can believe it. It's almost a pity. I could laugh at the figure you cut, if I didn't know it would make you weep, and others with you. (Pause.) But now you've had your will, hold fast to the woman who loves you; for if you leave her, you'll never smile again, and soon forget what happiness was.

STRANGER. Is that a threat?

MOTHER. A warning. Go now, and have your supper.

STRANGER (pointing at the table for the poor). There?

MOTHER. A poor joke; which might become reality. I've seen such things.

STRANGER. Soon I'll believe anything can happen—this is the worst I've known.

MOTHER. Worse yet may come. Wait!

STRANGER (cast down). I'm prepared for anything.

(Exit. A moment later the OLD MAN comes in.)

OLD MAN. It was no angel after all.

MOTHER. No good angel, certainly.

OLD MAN. Really! (Pause.) You know how superstitious people here are. As I went down to the river I heard this: a farmer said his horse shied at 'him'; another that the dogs got so fierce he'd had to tie them up. The ferryman swore his boat drew less water when 'he' got in. Superstition, but. . . .

MOTHER. But what?

OLD MAN. It was only a magpie that flew in at her window, though it was closed. An illusion, perhaps.

MOTHER. Perhaps. But why does one often see such things at the right time?

OLD MAN. This man's presence is intolerable. When he looks at me I can't breathe.

MOTHER. We must try to get rid of him. I'm certain he won't care to stay for long.

OLD MAN. No. He won't grow old here. (Pause.) Listen, I got a letter tonight warning me about him. Among other things he's wanted by the courts.

MOTHER. The courts?

OLD MAN. Yes. Money matters. But, remember, the laws of hospitality protect beggars and enemies. Let him stay a few days, till he's got over this fearful journey. You can see how Providence has laid hands on him, how his soul is being ground in the mill ready for the sieve. . . .

MOTHER. I've felt a call to be a tool in the hands of Providence.

OLD MAN. Don't confuse it with your wish for vengeance.

MOTHER. I'll try not to, if I can.

OLD MAN. Well, good-night.

MOTHER. Do you think Ingeborg has read his last book?

OLD MAN. It's unlikely. If she had she'd never have married a man who held such views.

MOTHER. No, she's not read it. But now she must.

SCENE VIII

THE 'ROSE' ROOM

[A simple, pleasantly furnished room in the forester's house. The walls are colour-washed in red; the curtains are of thin rose-coloured muslin. In the small latticed windows there are flowers. On right, a writing-table and bookshelf. Left, a sofa with rose-coloured curtains above in the form of a baldachino. Tables and chairs in Old German style. At the back, a door. Outside the country can be seen and the poorhouse, a dark, unpleasant building with black, uncurtained windows. Strong sunlight. The LADY is sitting on the sofa working.]

MOTHER (standing with a book bound in rose-coloured cloth in her hand.) You won't read your husband's book?

LADY. Not that one. I promised not to.

MOTHER. You don't want to know the man to whom you've entrusted your fate?

LADY. What would be the use? We're all right as we are.

MOTHER. You make no great demands on life?

LADY. Why should I? They'd never be fulfilled.

MOTHER. I don't know whether you were born full of worldly wisdom, or foolishness.

LADY. I don't know myself.

MOTHER. If the sun shines and you've enough to eat, you're content.

LADY. Yes. And when it goes in, I make the best of it.

MOTHER. To change the subject: did you know your husband was being pressed by the courts on account of his debts?

LADY. Yes. It happens to all writers.

MOTHER. Is he mad, or a rascal?

LADY. He's neither. He's no ordinary man; and it's a pity I can tell him nothing he doesn't know already. That's why we don't speak much; but he's glad to have me near him; and so am I to be near him.

MOTHER. You've reached calm water already? Then it can't be far to the mill-race! But don't you think you'd have more to talk of, if you read what he has written?

LADY. Perhaps. You can leave me the book, if you like.

MOTHER. Take it and hide it. It'll be a surprise if you can quote something from his masterpiece.

LADY (hiding the book in her bag). He's coming. If he's spoken of he seems to feel it from afar.

MOTHER. If he could only feel how he makes others suffer—from afar. (Exit left.)

(The LADY, alone for an instant, looks at the book and seems taken aback. She hides it in her bag.)

STRANGER (entering). Your mother was here? You were speaking of me, of course. I can almost hear her ill-natured words. They cut the air and darken the sunshine. I can almost divine the impression of her body in the atmosphere of the room, and she leaves an odour like that of a dead snake.

LADY. You're irritable today.

STRANGER. Fearfully. Some fool has restrung my nerves out of tune, and plays on them with a horse-hair bow till he sets my teeth on edge. . . . You don't know what that is! There's someone here who's stronger than I! Someone with a searchlight who shines it at me, wherever I may be. Do they use the black art in this place?

LADY. Don't turn your back on the sunlight. Look at this lovely country; you'll feel calmer.

STRANGER. I can't bear that poorhouse. It seems to have been built there solely for me. And a demented woman always stands there beckoning.

LADY. Do you think they treat you badly here?

STRANGER. In a way, no. They feed me with tit-bits, as if I were to be fattened for the butcher. But I can't eat because they grudge it me, and I feel the cold rays of their hate. To me it seems there's an icy wind everywhere, although it's still and hot. And I can hear that accursèd mill. . . .

LADY. It's not grinding now.

STRANGER. Yes. Grinding . . . grinding.

LADY. Listen. There's no hate here. Pity, at most.

STRANGER. Another thing. . . . Why do people I meet cross themselves?

LADY. Only because they're used to praying in silence. (Pause.) You had an unwelcome letter this morning?

STRANGER. Yes. The kind that makes your hair rise from the scalp, so that you want to curse at fate. I'm owed money, but can't get paid. Now the law's being set in motion against me by . . . the guardians of my children, because I've not paid alimony. No one has ever been in such a dishonourable position. I'm blameless. I could pay my way; I want to, but am prevented! Not my fault; yet my shame! It's not in nature. The devil's got a hand in it.

LADY. Why?

STRANGER. Why? Why is one born into this world an ignoramus, knowing nothing of the laws, customs and usage one inadvertently breaks? And for which one's punished. Why does one grow into a youth full of high ambition only to be driven into vile actions one abhors? Why, why?

LADY (who has secretly been looking at the book: absent-mindedly). There must be a reason, even if we don't know it.

STRANGER. If it's to humble one, it's a poor method. It only makes me more arrogant. Eve!

LADY. Don't call me that.

STRANGER (starting). Why not?

LADY. I don't like it. You'd feel as I do, if I called you Caesar.

87

STRANGER. Have we got back to that?

LADY. To what?

STRANGER. Did you mention that name for any reason?

LADY. Caesar? No. But I'm beginning to find things out.

STRANGER. Very well! Then I may as well fall honourably by my own hand. I am Caesar, the school-boy, for whose escapade your husband, the werewolf, was punished. Fate delights in making links for eternity. A noble sport! (The LADY, uncertain what to do, does not reply.) Say something!

LADY. I can't.

STRANGER. Say that he became a werewolf because, as a child, he lost his belief in the justice of heaven, owing to the fact that, though innocent, he was punished for the misdeeds of another. But if you say so, I shall reply that I suffered ten times as much from my conscience, and that the spiritual crisis that followed left me so strengthened that I've never done such a thing again.

LADY. No. It's not that.

STRANGER. Then what is it? Do you respect me no longer?

LADY. It's not that either.

STRANGER. Then it's to make me feel my shame before you! And it would be the end of everything between us.

LADY. No!

STRANGER. Eve.

LADY. You rouse evil thoughts.

STRANGER. You've broken your vow: you've been reading my book!

LADY. I have.

STRANGER. Then you've done wrong.

LADY. My intention was good.

STRANGER. The results even of your good intentions are terrible! You've blown me into the air with my own petard. Why must all our misdeeds come home to roost—both boyish escapades and really evil action? It's fair enough to reap evil where one has sown it. But I've never seen a good action get its reward. Never! It's a disgrace to Him who records all sins, however black or venial. No man could do it: men would forgive. The gods . . . never!

LADY. Don't say that. Say rather *you* forgive.

STRANGER. I'm not small-minded. But what have I forgive you?

LADY. More than I can say.

STRANGER. Say it. Perhaps then we'll be quits.

LADY. He and I used to read the curse of Deutertonomy over you . . . for you'd ruined his life.

STRANGER. What curse is that?

LADY. From the fifth book of Moses. The priests chant it in chorus when the fasts begin.

STRANGER. I don't remember it. What does it matter—a curse more or less?

LADY. In my family those whom we curse, are struck.

STRANGER. I don't believe it. But I do believe that evil emanates from this house. May it recoil upon it! That is my prayer! Now, according to custom, it would be my duty to shoot myself; but I can't, so long as I have other duties. You see, I can't even die, and so I've lost my last treasure—what, with reason, I call my religion. I've heard that man can wrestle with God, and with success; but not even job could fight against Satan. (Pause.) Let's speak of you. . . .

LADY. Not now. Later perhaps. Since I've got to know your terrible book—I've only glanced at it, only read a few lines here and there—I feel as if I'd eaten of the tree of knowledge. My eyes are opened and I know what's good and what's evil, as I've never known before. And now I see how evil you are, and why I am to be called Eve. She was a mother and brought sin into the world: it was another mother who brought expiation. The curse of mankind was called down on us by the first, a blessing by the second. In me you shall not destroy my whole sex. Perhaps I have a different mission in your life. We shall see!

STRANGER. So you've eaten of the tree of knowledge? Farewell.

LADY. You're going away?

STRANGER. I can't stay here.

90

LADY. Don't go.

STRANGER. I must. I must clear up everything. I'll take leave of the old people now. Then I'll come back. I shan't be long. (Exit.)

LADY (remains motionless, then goes to the door and looks out. She sinks to her knees). No! He won't come back!

Curtain.

SCENE IX

CONVENT

[The refectory of an ancient convent, resembling a simple whitewashed Romanesque church. There are damp patches on the walls, looking like strange figures. A long table with bowls; at the end a desk for the Lector. At the back a door leading to the chapel. There are lighted candles on the tables. On the wall, left, a painting representing the Archangel Michael killing the Fiend.]

[The STRANGER is sitting left, at a refectory table, dressed in the white clothing of a patient, with a bowl before him. At the table, right, are sitting: the brown-clad mourners of Scene I. The BEGGAR. A woman in mourning with two children. A woman who resembles the Lady, but who is not her and who is crocheting instead of eating. A Man very like the Doctor, another like the Madman. Others like the Father, Mother, Brother. Parents of the 'Prodigal Son,' etc. All are dressed in white, but over this are wearing costumes of coloured crêpe. Their faces are waxen and corpse-like, their whole appearance queer, their gestures strange. On the rise of the curtain all are finishing a Paternoster, except the STRANGER.]

STRANGER (rising and going to the ABBESS, who is standing at a serving table). Mother. May I speak to you?

ABBESS (in a black-and-white Augustinian habit). Yes, my son. (They come forward.)

STRANGER. First, where am I?

ABBESS. In a convent called 'St. Saviour.' You were found on the hills above the ravine, with a cross you'd broken from a calvary and with which you were threatening someone in the clouds. Indeed, you thought you could see him. You were feverish and had lost your foothold. You were picked up, unhurt, beneath a cliff, but in delirium. You were brought to the hospital and put to bed. Since then you've spoken wildly, and complained of a pain in your hip, but no injury could be found.

STRANGER. What did I speak of?

ABBESS. You had the usual feverish dreams. You reproached yourself with all kinds of things, and thought you could see your victims, as you called them.

STRANGER. And then?

ABBESS. Your thoughts often turned to money matters. You wanted to pay for yourself in the hospital. I tried to calm you by telling you no payment would be asked: all was done out of charity. . . .

STRANGER. I want no charity.

ABBESS. It's more blessed to give than to receive; yet a noble nature can accept and be thankful.

STRANGER. I want no charity.

ABBESS. Hm!

STRANGER. Tell me, why will none of those people sit at the same table with me? They're getting up . . . going. . . .

ABBESS. They seem to fear you.

STRANGER. Why?

ABBESS. You look so. . . .

STRANGER. I? But what of them? Are they real?

ABBESS. If you mean true, they've a terrible reality. It may be they look strange to you, because you're still feverish. Or there may be another reason.

STRANGER. I seem to know them, all of them! I see them as if in a mirror: they only make as if they were eating. . . . Is this some drama they're performing? Those look like my parents, rather like . . . (Pause.) Hitherto I've feared nothing, because life was useless to me. . . . Now I begin to be afraid.

ABBESS. If you don't believe them real, I'll ask the Confessor to introduce you. (She signs to the CONFESSOR who approaches.)

CONFESSOR (dressed in a black-and-white habit of Dominicans). Sister!

ABBESS. Tell the patient who are at that table.

CONFESSOR. That's soon done.

STRANGER. Permit a question first. Haven't we met already?

CONFESSOR. Yes. I sat by your bedside, when you were delirious. At your desire, I heard your confession.

94

STRANGER. What? My confession?

CONFESSOR. Yes. But I couldn't give you absolution; because it seemed that what you said was spoken in fever.

STRANGER. Why?

CONFESSOR. There was hardly a sin or vice you didn't take upon yourself—things so hateful you'd have had to undergo strict penitence before demanding absolution. Now you're yourself again I can ask whether there are grounds for your self-accusations.

(The ABBESS leaves them.)

STRANGER. Have you the right?

CONFESSOR. No. In truth, no right. (Pause.) But you want to know in whose company you are! The very best. There, for instance, is a madman, Caesar, who lost his wits through reading the works of a certain writer whose notoriety is greater than his fame. There's a beggar, who won't admit he's a beggar, because he's learnt Latin and is free. There, a doctor, called the werewolf, whose history's well known. There, two parents, who grieved themselves to death over a son who raised his hand against theirs. He must be responsible for refusing to follow his father's bier and desecrating his mother's grave. There's his unhappy sister, whom he drove out into the snow, as he himself recounts, with the best intentions. Over there's a woman who's been abandoned with her two children, and there's another doing crochet work. . . . All are old acquaintances. Go and greet them!

(The STRANGER has turned his back on the company: he now goes to the table, left, and sits down with his back to them. He raises his head, sees the picture of the Archangel Michael and lowers his eyes. The

95

CONFESSOR stands behind the STRANGER. A Catholic Requiem can be heard from the chapel. The CONFESSOR speaks to the STRANGER in a low voice while the music goes on.)

> Quantus tremor est futurus
> Quando judex est venturus
> Cuncta stricte discussurus,
> Tuba mirum spargens sonum
> Per sepulchra regionum
> Coget omnes ante thronum.
> Mors stupebit et natura,
> Cum resurget creatura
> Judicanti responsura
> Liber scriptus proferetur
> In quo totum continetur
> Unde mundus judicetur.
> Judex ergo cum sedebit
> Quidquid latet apparebit
> Nil inultum remanebit.

(He goes to the desk by the table, right, and opens his breviary. The music ceases.)

We will continue the reading. . . . 'But if thou wilt not hearken unto the voice of the Lord thy God all these curses shall overtake thee. Cursèd shalt thou be in the city, and cursèd shalt thou be in the field; cursèd shalt thou be when thou comest in, and cursèd when thou goest out.'

OMNES (in a low voice). Cursèd!

CONFESSOR. 'The Lord shall send upon thee vexation and rebuke in all that thou settest thy hand for to do, until thou be destroyed, and until thou perish quickly, because of the wickedness of thy doings, whereby thou hast forsaken me.'

OMNES (loudly). Cursèd!

CONFESSOR. 'The Lord shall cause thee to be smitten before thine enemies: thou shalt go out one way against them, and flee seven ways before them, and shalt be moved into all the kingdoms of the earth. And thy carcase shall be meat unto all fowls of the air, and unto the beasts of the earth, and no man shall fray them away. The Lord will smite thee with the botch of Egypt, the scab and the itch, with madness and blindness, that thou shalt grope at noonday, as the blind gropeth in darkness. Thou shalt not prosper in thy ways, and thou shalt be only oppressed and spoiled evermore, and no man shall save thee. Thou shalt betroth a wife, and another man shall lie with her: thou shalt build an house, and thou shalt not dwell therein: thou shalt plant a vineyard, and shalt not gather the grapes thereof. Thy sons and thy daughters shall be given unto another people, and thine eyes fail with longing for them; and there shall be no might in thy hand. And thou shalt find no ease on earth, neither shall the sole of thy foot have rest: the Lord shall give thee a trembling heart, and failing of eyes and sorrow of mind. And thy life shall hang in doubt before thee; and thou shalt fear day and night. In the morning thou shalt say, would God it were even! And at even thou shalt say, would God it were morning! And because thou servedst not the Lord thy God when thou livedst in security, thou shalt serve him in hunger, in thirst, in nakedness and in want; and He shall put a yoke of iron upon thy neck, until He have destroyed thee!'

OMNES. Amen!

(The CONFESSOR has read the above loudly and rapidly, without turning to the STRANGER. All those present, except the LADY, who

97

is working, have been listening and have joined in the curse, though they have feigned not to notice the STRANGER, who has remained with his back to them, sunk in himself. The STRANGER now rises as if to go. The CONFESSOR goes towards him.)

STRANGER. What was that?

CONFESSOR. The Book of Deuteronomy.

STRANGER. Of course. But I seem to remember blessings in it, too.

CONFESSOR. Yes, for those who keep His commandments.

STRANGER. Hm. . . . I can't deny that, for a moment, I felt shaken. Are they temptations to be resisted, or warnings to be obeyed? (Pause.) Anyhow I'm certain now that I have fever. I must go to a real doctor.

CONFESSOR. See he *is* the right one!

STRANGER. Of course!

CONFESSOR. Who can heal 'delightful scruples of conscience'!

ABBESS. Should you need charity again, you now know where to find it.

STRANGER. No. I do not.

ABBESS (in a low voice). Then I'll tell you. In a 'rose' room, near a certain running stream.

STRANGER. That's the truth! In a 'rose' room. Wait; how long have I been here?

ABBESS. Three months today.

STRANGER. Three months! Have I been sleeping? Or where have I been? (Looking out of the window.) It's autumn. The trees are bare; the clouds look cold. Now it's coming back to me! Can you hear a mill grinding? The sound of a horn? The rushing of a river? A wood whispering—and a woman weeping? You're right. Only there can charity be found. Farewell. (Exit.)

CONFESSOR (to the Abbess). The fool! The fool!

Curtain.

SCENE X

THE 'ROSE' ROOM

[The curtains have been taken down. The windows gape into the darkness outside. The furniture has been covered in brown loose-covers and pulled forward. The flowers have been taken away, and the large black stove lit. The MOTHER is standing ironing white curtains by the light of a single lamp. There is a knock at the door.]

MOTHER. Come in!

STRANGER (doing so). Where's my wife?

MOTHER. Where do you come from?

STRANGER. I think, from hell. But where's my wife?

MOTHER. Which of them do you mean?

STRANGER. The question's justified. Everything is, except to me.

MOTHER. There may be a reason: I'm glad you've seen it. Where have you been?

STRANGER. Whether in a poorhouse, a madhouse or a hospital, I don't know. I should like to think it all a feverish dream. I've been ill: I lost my memory and can't believe three months have passed. But where's my wife?

MOTHER. I ought to ask you that. When you deserted her, she went away—to look for you. Whether she's tired of looking, I can't say.

STRANGER. Something's amiss here. Where's the Old Man?

MOTHER. Where there's no more suffering.

STRANGER. You mean he's dead?

MOTHER. Yes. He's dead.

STRANGER. You say it as if you wanted to add him to my victims.

MOTHER. Perhaps I'm right to do so.

STRANGER. He didn't look sensitive: he was capable of steady hatred.

MOTHER. No. He hated only what was evil, in himself and others.

STRANGER. So I'm wrong there, too! (Pause.)

MOTHER. What do you want here?

STRANGER. Charity!

MOTHER. At last! How was it at the hospital! Sit down and tell me.

STRANGER (sitting). I don't want to think of it. I don't even know if it *was* a hospital.

MOTHER. Strange. Tell me what happened after you left here.

STRANGER. I fell in the mountains, hurt my hip and lost consciousness. If you'll speak kindly to me you shall know more.

MOTHER. I will.

STRANGER. When I woke I was in a red iron bedstead. Three men were pulling a cord that ran through two blocks. Every time they pulled I felt I grew two feet taller. . . .

MOTHER. They were putting in your hip.

STRANGER. I hadn't thought of that. Then . . . I lay watching my past life unroll before me like a panorama, through childhood, youth. . . . And when the roll was finished it began again. All the time I heard a mill grinding. . . . I can hear it still. Yes, here too!

MOTHER. Those were not pleasant visions.

STRANGER. No. At last I came to the conclusion . . . that I was a thoroughgoing scamp.

MOTHER. Why call yourself that?

STRANGER. I know you'd like to hear me say I was a scoundrel. But that would seem to me like boasting. It would imply a certainty about myself to which I've not attained.

MOTHER. You're still in doubt?

STRANGER. Of a great deal. But I've begun to have an inkling.

MOTHER. That. . . . ?

STRANGER. That there are forces which, till now, I've not believed in.

MOTHER. You've come to see that neither you, nor any other man, directs your destiny?

STRANGER. I have.

MOTHER. Then you've already gone part of the way.

STRANGER. But I myself have changed. I'm ruined; for I've lost all aptitude for writing. And I can't sleep at night.

MOTHER. Indeed!

STRANGER. What are called nightmares stop me. Last and worst: I daren't die; for I'm no longer sure my miseries will end, with *my* end.

MOTHER. Oh!

STRANGER. Even worse: I've grown so to loathe myself that I'd escape from myself, if I knew how. If I were a Christian, I couldn't obey the first commandment, to love my neighbour as myself, for I should have to hate him as I hate myself. It's true that I'm a scamp. I've always suspected it; and because I never wanted life to fool me, I've observed 'others' carefully. When I saw they were no better than I, I resented their trying to browbeat me.

MOTHER. You've been wrong to think it a matter between you and others. You have to deal with Him.

STRANGER. With whom?

MOTHER. The Invisible One, who guides your destiny.

STRANGER. Would I could see Him.

MOTHER. It would be your death.

STRANGER. Oh no!

MOTHER. Where do you get this devilish spirit of rebellion? If you won't bow your neck like the rest, you must be broken like a reed.

STRANGER. I don't know where this fearful stubbornness comes from. It's true an unpaid bill can make me tremble; but if I were to climb Mount Sinai and face the Eternal One, I should not cover my face.

MOTHER. Jesus and Mary! Don't say such things. You'll make me think you're a child of the Devil.

STRANGER. Here that seems the general opinion. But I've heard that those who serve the Evil One get honours, goods and gold as their reward. Gold especially. Do you think me suspect?

MOTHER. You'll bring a curse on my house.

STRANGER. Then I'll leave it.

MOTHER. And go into the night. Where?

STRANGER. To seek the only one that I don't hate.

MOTHER. Are you sure she'll receive you?

STRANGER. Quite sure.

MOTHER. I'm not.

STRANGER. I am.

MOTHER. Then I must raise your doubts.

104

STRANGER. You can't.

MOTHER. Yes, I can.

STRANGER. It's a lie.

MOTHER. We're no longer speaking kindly. We must stop. Can you sleep in the attic?

STRANGER. I can't sleep anywhere.

MOTHER. Still, I'll say good-night to you, whether you think I mean it, or not.

STRANGER. You're sure there are no rats in the attic? I don't fear ghosts, but rats aren't pleasant.

MOTHER. I'm glad you don't fear ghosts, for no one's slept a whole night there . . . whatever the cause may be.

STRANGER (after a moment's hesitation). Never have I met a more wicked woman than you. The reason is: you have religion.

MOTHER. Good-night!

Curtain.

SCENE XI

IN THE KITCHEN

[It is dark, but the moon outside throws moving shadows of the window lattices on to the floor, as the storm clouds race by. In the corner, right, under the crucifix, where the OLD MAN used to sit, a hunting horn, a gun and a game bag hang on the wall. On the table a stuffed bird of prey. As the windows are open the curtains are flapping in the wind; and kitchen cloths, aprons and towels, that are hung on a line by the hearth, move in the wind, whose sighing can be heard. In the distance the noise of a waterfall. There is an occasional tapping on the wooden floor.]

STRANGER (entering, half-dressed, a lamp in his hand). Is anyone here? No. (He comes forward with a light, which makes the play of shadow less marked.) What's moving on the floor? Is anyone here? (He goes to the table, sees the stuffed bird and stands riveted to the spot.) God!

MOTHER (coming in with a lamp). Still up?

STRANGER. I couldn't sleep.

MOTHER (gently). Why not, my son?

STRANGER. I heard someone above me.

MOTHER. Impossible. There's nothing over the attic.

STRANGER. That's why I was uneasy! What's moving on the floor like snakes?

MOTHER. Moonbeams.

STRANGER. Yes. Moonbeams. That's a stuffed bird. And those are cloths. Everything's natural; that's what makes me uneasy. Who was knocking during the night? Was anyone locked out?

MOTHER. It was a horse in the stable.

STRANGER. Why should it make that noise?

MOTHER. Some animals have nightmares.

STRANGER. What are nightmares?

MOTHER. Who knows?

STRANGER. May I sit down?

MOTHER. Do. I want to speak seriously to you. I was malicious last night; you must forgive me. It's because of that I need religion; just as I need the penitential garment and the stone floor. To spare you, I'll tell you what nightmares are to me. My bad conscience! Whether I punish myself or another punishes me, I don't know. I don't permit myself to ask. (Pause.) Now tell me what you saw in your room.

STRANGER. I hardly know. Nothing. When I went in I felt as if someone were there. Then I went to bed. But someone started pacing up and down above me with a heavy tread. Do you believe in ghosts?

MOTHER. My religion won't allow me to. But I believe our sense of right and wrong will find a way to punish us.

STRANGER. Soon I felt cold air on my breast—it reached my heart and forced me to get up.

MOTHER. And then?

STRANGER. To stand and watch the whole panorama of my life unroll before me. I saw everything—that was the worst of it.

MOTHER. I know. I've been through it. There's no name for the malady, and only one cure.

STRANGER. What is it?

MOTHER. You know what children do when they've done wrong?

STRANGER. What?

MOTHER. First ask forgiveness!

STRANGER. And then?

MOTHER. Try to make amends.

STRANGER. Isn't it enough to suffer according to one's deserts?

MOTHER. No. That's revenge.

STRANGER. Then what must one do?

MOTHER. Can you mend a life you've destroyed? Undo a bad action?

STRANGER. Truly, no. But I was forced into it! Forced to take, for no one gave me the right. Accursèd be He who forced me! (Putting his hand to his heart.) Ah! He's here, in this room. He's plucking out my heart!

MOTHER. Then bow your head.

STRANGER. I cannot.

MOTHER. Down on your knees.

STRANGER. I will not.

MOTHER. Christ have mercy! Lord have mercy on you! On your knees before Him who was crucified! Only He can wipe out what's been done.

STRANGER. Not before Him! If I were forced, I'll recant ... afterwards.

MOTHER. On your knees, my son!

STRANGER. I cannot bow the knee. I cannot. Help me, God Eternal. (Pause.)

MOTHER (after a hasty prayer). Do you feel better?

STRANGER. Yes. . . . It was not death. It was annihilation!

MOTHER. The annihilation of the Divine. We call it spiritual death.

STRANGER. I see. (Without irony.) I begin to understand.

MOTHER. My son! You have left Jerusalem and are on the road to Damascus. Go back the same way you came. Erect a cross at every station, and stay at the seventh. For you, there are not fourteen, as for Him.

STRANGER. You speak in riddles.

MOTHER. Then go your way. Search out those to whom you have something to say. First, your wife.

STRANGER. Where is she?

MOTHER. You must find her. On your way don't forget to call on him you named the werewolf.

STRANGER. Never!

MOTHER. You'd have said that, as you came here. As you know, I expected your coming.

STRANGER. Why?

MOTHER. For no one reason.

STRANGER. Just as I saw this kitchen . . . in a trance. . . .

MOTHER. That's why I now regret trying to separate you and Ingeborg. Go and search for her. If you find her, well and good. If not, perhaps that too has been ordained. (Pause.) Dawn's now at hand. Morning has come and the night has passed.

STRANGER. Such a night!

MOTHER. You'll remember it.

STRANGER. Not all of it . . . yet something.

MOTHER (looking out of the window, as if to herself). Lovely morning star—how far from heaven have you fallen!

110

STRANGER (after a pause). Have you noticed that, before the sun rises, a feeling of awe takes hold of mankind? Are we children of darkness, that we tremble before the light?

MOTHER. Will you never be tired of questioning?

STRANGER. Never. Because I yearn for light.

MOTHER. Go then, and search. And peace be with you!

SCENE XII

IN THE RAVINE

[The same landscape as before, but in autumn colouring. The trees have lost their leaves. Work is going on at the smithy and the mill. The SMITH stands, left, in the doorway; the MILLER'S wife, right. The LADY dressed in a jacket with a hat of patent leather; but she is in mourning. The STRANGER is in Bavarian alpine kit: short jacket of rough material, knickers, heavy boots and alpenstock, green hat with heath-cock feather. Over this he wears a brown cloak with a cape and hood.]

LADY (entering tired and dispirited). Did a man pass here in a long cloak, with a green hat? (The SMITH and the MILLER'S WIFE shake their heads.) Can I lodge here for the night? (The SMITH and the MILLER'S WIFE again shake their heads: to the SMITH.) May I stand in the doorway for a moment and warm myself? (The SMITH pushes her away.) God reward you according to your deserts!

(Exit. She reappears on the footbridge, and exit once more.)

STRANGER (entering). Has a lady in a coat and skirt crossed the brook? (The SMITH and MILLER'S WIFE shake their heads.) Will you give me some bread? I'll pay for it. (The MILLER'S WIFE refuses the money.) No charity!

ECHO (imitating his voice from afar). Charity.

(The SMITH and the MILLER'S WIFE laugh so loudly and so long that, at length, ECHO replies.)

STRANGER. Good! An eye for an eye—a tooth for a tooth. It helps to lighten my conscience! (He enters the ravine.)

SCENE XIII

ON THE ROAD

[The same landscape as before; but autumn. The BEGGAR is sitting outside a chapel with a lime twig and a bird cage, in which is a starling. The STRANGER enters wearing the same clothes as in the preceding scene.]

STRANGER. Beggar! Have you seen a lady in a coat and skirt pass this way?

BEGGAR. I've seen five hundred. But, seriously, I must ask you not to call me beggar now. I've found work!

STRANGER. Oh! So it's you!

BEGGAR. Ille ego qui quondam. . . .

STRANGER. What kind of work have you?

BEGGAR. I've a starling, that whistles and sings.

STRANGER. You mean, *he* does the work?

BEGGAR. Yes. I'm my own master now.

STRANGER. Do you catch birds?

BEGGAR. No. The lime twig's merely for appearances.

STRANGER. So you still cling to such things?

BEGGAR. What else should I cling to? What's within us is nothing but pure . . . nonsense.

STRANGER. Is that the final conclusion of your whole philosophy of life?

BEGGAR. My complete metaphysic. The view mad be rather out of date, but . . .

STRANGER. Can you be serious for a moment? Tell me about your past.

BEGGAR. Why unravel that old skein? Twist it up rather. Twist it up. Do you think I'm always so merry? Only when I meet you: you're so damnably funny!

STRANGER. How can you laugh, with a wrecked life behind you?

BEGGAR. Now he's getting personal! (Pause.) If you can't laugh at adversity, not even that of others, you're begging of life itself. Listen! If you follow this wheel track you'll come, at last, to the ocean, and there the path will stop. If you sit down there and rest, you'll begin to take another view of things. Here there are so many accidents, religious themes, disagreeable memories that hinder thought as it flies to the 'rose' room. Only follow the track! If it's muddy here and there, spread your wings and flutter. And talking of fluttering: I once heard a bird that sang of Polycrates and his ring; how he'd become possessed of all the marvels of this world, but didn't know what to do with them. So he sent tidings east and west of the great Nothing he'd helped to fashion from the empty universe. I wouldn't assert you were the man, unless I believed it so firmly I could take my oath on it. Once I asked you whether you knew who I was, and you said it didn't interest you. In return I offered you my friendship, but you refused it rudely. However, I'm not sensitive or resentful, so I'll give you good advice on your way. Follow the track!

STRANGER (avoiding him). You don't deceive me.

BEGGAR. You believe nothing but evil. That's why you get nothing but evil. Try to believe what is good. Try!

STRANGER. I will. But if I'm deceived, I've the right to. . . .

BEGGAR. You've no right to do that.

STRANGER (as if to himself). Who is it reads my secret thoughts, turns my soul inside out, and pursues me? Why do you persecute me?

BEGGAR. Saul! Saul! Why persecutest thou Me?

(The STRANGER goes out with a gesture of horror. The chord of the funeral march is heard again. The LADY enters.)

LADY. Have you seen a man pass this way in a long cloak, with a green hat?

BEGGAR. There was a poor devil here, who hobbled off. . . .

LADY. The man I'm searching for's not lame.

BEGGAR. Nor was he. It seems he'd hurt his hip; and that made him walk unsteadily. I mustn't be malicious. Look here in the mud.

LADY. Where?

BEGGAR (pointing). There! At that rut. In it you can see the impression of a boot, firmly planted. . . .

LADY (looking at the impression). It's he! His heavy tread. . . . Can I catch him up?

BEGGAR. Follow the track!

LADY (taking his hand and kissing it). Thank you, my friend. (Exit.)

SCENE XIV

BY THE SEA

[The same landscape as before, but now winter. The sea is dark blue, and on the horizon great clouds take on the shapes of huge heads. In the distance three bare masts of a wrecked ship, that look like three white crosses. The table and seat are still under the tree, but the chairs have been removed. There is snow on the ground. From time to time a bell-buoy can be heard. The STRANGER comes in from the left, stops a moment and looks out to sea, then goes out, right, behind the cottage. The LADY enters, left, and appears to be following the STRANGER'S footsteps on the snow; she exits in front of the cottage, right. The STRANGER re-enters, right, notices the footprints of the LADY, pauses, and looks back, right. The LADY re-enters, throws herself into his arms, but recoils.]

LADY. You thrust me away.

STRANGER. No. It seems there's someone between us.

LADY. Indeed there is! (Pause.) What a meeting!

STRANGER. Yes. It's winter; as you see.

LADY. I can feel the cold coming from you.

STRANGER. I got frozen in the mountains.

LADY. Do you think the spring will ever come?

STRANGER. Not to us! We've been driven from the garden, and must wander over stones and thistles. And when our hands and feet are bruised, we feel we must rub salt in the wounds of the . . . other one. And then the mill starts grinding. It'll never stop; for there's always water.

LADY. No doubt what you say is true.

STRANGER. But I'll not yield to the inevitable. Rather than that we should lacerate each other I'll gash myself as a sacrifice to the gods. I'll take the blame upon me; declare it was I who taught you to break your chains. I who tempted you! Then you can lay all the blame on me: for what I did, and what happened after.

LADY. You couldn't bear it.

STRANGER. Yes, I could. There are moments when I feel as if I bore all the sin and sorrow, all the filth and shame of the whole world. There are moments when I believe we are condemned to sin and do bad actions as a punishment! (Pause.) Not long ago I lay sick of a fever, and amidst all that happened to me, I dreamed that I saw a crucifix without the Crucified. And when I asked the Dominican—for there was a Dominican among many others—what it could mean, he said: 'You will not allow Him to suffer for you. Suffer then yourself!' That's why mankind have grown so conscious of their own sufferings.

LADY. And why consciences grow so heavy, if there's no one to help to bear the burden.

STRANGER. Have you also come to think so?

LADY. Not yet. But I'm on the way.

STRANGER. Put your hand in mine. From here let us go on together.

LADY. Where?

STRANGER. Back! The same way we came. Are you weary?

LADY. Now no longer.

STRANGER. Several times I sank exhausted. But I met a strange beggar—perhaps you remember him: he was thought to be like me. And he begged me, as an experiment, to believe his good intentions. I did believe—as an experiment—and . . . .

LADY. Well?

STRANGER. It went well with me. And since then I feel I've strength to go on my way. . . .

LADY. Let's go together!

STRANGER (turning to the sea). Yes. It's growing dark and the clouds are gathering.

LADY. Don't look at the clouds.

STRANGER. And below there? What's that?

LADY. Only a wreck.

STRANGER (whispering). Three crosses! What new Golgotha awaits us?

LADY. They're white ones. That means good fortune.

STRANGER. Can good fortune ever come to us?

LADY. Yes. But not yet.

STRANGER. Let's go!

SCENE XV

ROOM IN AN HOTEL

[The room is as before. The LADY is sitting by the side of the STRANGER, crocheting.]

LADY. Do say something.

STRANGER. I've nothing but unpleasant things to say, since we came here.

LADY. Why were you so anxious to have this terrible room?

STRANGER. I don't know. It was the last one I wanted. I began to long for it, in order to suffer.

LADY. And are you suffering?

STRANGER. Yes. I can no longer listen to singing, or look at anything beautiful. During the day I hear the mill and see that great panorama now expanding to embrace the universe. . . . And, at night . . .

LADY. Why did you cry out in your sleep?

STRANGER. I was dreaming.

LADY. A real dream?

STRANGER. Terribly real. But you see what a curse is on me. I feel I must describe it, and to no one else but you. Yet I daren't tell you, for it would be rattling at the door of the locked chamber. . . .

LADY. The past!

STRANGER. Yes.

LADY (simply). It's foolish to have any such secret place.

STRANGER. Yes. (Pause.)

LADY. And now tell me!

STRANGER. I'm afraid I must. I dreamed your first husband was married to my first wife.

LADY. Only you could have thought of such a thing!

STRANGER. I wish it were so. (Pause.) I saw how he ill-treated my children. (Getting up.) I put my hands to his throat. . . . I can't go on. . . . But I shall never rest till I know the truth. And to know it, I must go to him in his own house.

LADY. It's come to that?

STRANGER. It's been coming for some time. Nothing can now prevent it. I must see him.

LADY. But if he won't receive you?

STRANGER. I'll go as a patient, and tell him of my sickness. . . .

LADY (frightened). Don't do that!

STRANGER. You think he might be tempted to shut me up as mad! I must risk it. I want to risk everything—life, freedom, welfare. I need an emotional shock, strong enough to bring myself into the light of day. I demand this torture, that my punishment may be in just proportion to my sin, so that I shall not be forced to drag myself along under the burden of my guilt. So down into the snake pit, as soon as may be!

LADY. Could I come with you?

STRANGER. There's no need. My sufferings will be enough for both.

LADY. Then I'll call you my deliverer. And the curse I once laid on you will turn into a blessing. Look! It's spring once more.

STRANGER. So I see. The Christmas rose there has begun to wither.

LADY. But don't you feel spring in the air?

STRANGER. The cold within isn't so great.

LADY. Perhaps the werewolf will heal you altogether.

STRANGER. We shall see. Perhaps he's not so dangerous, after all.

LADY. He's not so cruel as you.

STRANGER. But my dream. . . .

LADY. Let's hope it was only a dream. Now my wool's finished; and with it, my useless work. It's grown soiled in the making.

STRANGER. It can be washed.

LADY. Or dyed.

STRANGER. Rose red.

LADY. Never!

STRANGER. It's like a roll of manuscript.

LADY. With our story on it.

STRANGER. In the filth of the roads, in tears and in blood.

LADY. But the story's nearly done. Go and write the last chapter.

STRANGER. Then we'll meet at the seventh station. Where we began!

SCENE XVI

THE DOCTOR'S HOUSE

[The scene is more or less as before. But half the wood-pile has been taken away. On a seat near the verandah surgical instruments, knives, saws, forceps, etc. The DOCTOR is engaged in cleaning these.]

SISTER (coming from the verandah). A patient to see you.

DOCTOR. Do you know who it is?

SISTER. I've not seen him. Here's his card.

DOCTOR (reading it). This outdoes everything!

SISTER. Is it he?

DOCTOR. Yes. Courage I respect; but this is cynicism. A kind of challenge. Still, let him come in.

SISTER. Are you serious?

DOCTOR. Perfectly. But, if you care to talk to him a little, in that straightforward way of yours. . . .

SISTER. I'd like to.

126

DOCTOR. Very well. Do the heavy work, and leave the final polish to me.

SISTER. You can trust me. I'll tell him everything your kindness forbids you to say.

DOCTOR. Enough of my kindness! Make haste, or I'll get impatient. Shut the doors. (His SISTER goes out.) What are you doing at that dustbin, Caesar? (CAESAR comes in.) Listen, Caesar, if your enemy were to come and lay his head in your lap, what would you do?

CAESAR. Cut it off!

DOCTOR. That's not what I've taught you.

CAESAR. No; you said, heap coals of fire on it. But I think that's a shame.

DOCTOR. I think so, too; it's more cruel and more cunning. (Pause.) Isn't it better to take some revenge? It heartens the other person, lifts the burden off him.

CAESAR. As you know more about it than I, why ask?

DOCTOR. Quiet! I'm not speaking to you. (Pause.) Very well. First cut off his head, and then. . . . We'll see.

CAESAR. It all depends on how he behaves.

DOCTOR. Yes. On how he behaves. Quiet. Get along.

(The STRANGER comes from the verandah: he seems excited but his manner betrays a certain resignation. CAESAR has gone out.)

STRANGER. You're surprised to see me here?

DOCTOR (seriously). I've long given up being surprised. But I see I must begin again.

STRANGER. Will you permit me to speak to you?

DOCTOR. About anything decent people may discuss. Are you ill?

STRANGER (hesitating). Yes.

DOCTOR. Why did you come to me—of all people?

STRANGER. You must guess!

DOCTOR. I refuse to. (Pause.) What do you complain of?

STRANGER (with uncertainty). Sleeplessness.

DOCTOR. That's not a disease, but a symptom. Have you already seen a doctor?

STRANGER. I've been lying ill in an . . . institution. I was feverish. I've a strange malady.

DOCTOR. What was so strange about it?

STRANGER. May I ask this? Can one go about as usual; and yet be delirious?

DOCTOR. If you're mad; not otherwise. (The STRANGER lets up, but then sits down again.) What was the hospital called?

STRANGER. St. Saviour.

DOCTOR. That's not a hospital.

STRANGER. A convent, then.

DOCTOR. No. It's an asylum. (The STRANGER gets up, the DOCTOR does so, too, and calls.) Sister! Shut the front door. And the gate leading to the road. (To the STRANGER.) Won't you sit down? I have to keep the doors here locked. There are so many tramps.

STRANGER (calms himself). Be frank with me: do you think me . . . insane?

DOCTOR. No one ever gets a frank answer to that question, as you know. And no one who suffers in that way ever believes what he's told. So my opinion must be a matter of indifference to you. (Pause.) But if it's your soul, go to a spiritual healer.

STRANGER. Could you take his place for a moment?

DOCTOR. I haven't the vocation.

STRANGER. But . . .

DOCTOR (interrupting). Or the time. We're getting ready for a wedding here!

STRANGER. I dreamed it!

DOCTOR. It may ease your mind to know that I've consoled myself, as it's called. You may be pleased, it would be natural . . . but I see, on the contrary, it makes you suffer more. There must be a reason. Why, should you be upset at my marrying a widow?

STRANGER. With two children?

DOCTOR. Two children! Now we have it! A damnable supposition worthy of you. If there were a hell, you should be hell's overseer, for your skill in finding means of punishment exceeds my wildest inventions. Yet I'm called a werewolf!

STRANGER. It might happen that . . .

DOCTOR (cutting him short). For a long time, I hated you, because by an unforgiveable action you cheated me of my good name. But when I grew older and wiser I saw that, although the punishment wasn't earned, I deserved it for other things that had never been discovered. Besides, you were a boy with enough conscience to be able to punish yourself. So you need worry no more about the whole thing. Is that what you wanted to speak of?

STRANGER. Yes.

DOCTOR. Then you'll be content, if I let you go? (The STRANGER is about to ask a question.) Did you think I'd shut you up? Or cut you in pieces with those instruments? Kill you? 'Perhaps such poor devils ought to be put out of their misery!' (The STRANGER looks at his watch.) You can still catch the boat.

STRANGER. Will you give me your hand?

DOCTOR. Impossible. And what is the use of my forgiving you, if you lack the strength to forgive yourself? (Pause.) Some things can only be cured by making them undone. So this never can be.

STRANGER. St. Saviour . . .

DOCTOR. Helped you. You challenged destiny and were broken. There's no shame in losing such a fight. I did the same; but, as you see, I've got rid of my woodpile. I want no thunder in my home. And I shall play no more with the lightning.

STRANGER. One station more, and I shall reach my goal.

DOCTOR. You'll never reach your goal. Farewell!

STRANGER. Farewell!

SCENE XVII

A STREET CORNER

[The same as Scene I. The STRANGER is sitting on the seat beneath the tree, drawing in the sand.]

LADY (entering). What are you doing?

STRANGER. Writing in the sand . . . still.

LADY. Can you hear singing?

STRANGER (pointing to the church). Yes. But from there! I've been unjust to someone, unwittingly.

LADY. I think our wanderings must be over, now we've come back here.

STRANGER. Where we began . . . at the street corner, between the inn, the church and the post office. By the way . . . isn't there a registered letter for me there, that I never fetched?

LADY. Yes. Because there was nothing but unpleasantness in it.

STRANGER. Or legal matters. (Striking his forehead.) Then that's the explanation.

LADY. Fetch it then. In the belief that what it contains is good.

STRANGER (ironically). Good!

LADY. Believe it. Imagine it!

STRANGER (going to the post office). I'll make the attempt.

(The LADY waits on the pavement. The STRANGER comes back with a letter.)

LADY. Well?

STRANGER. I feel ashamed of myself. It's the money.

LADY. You see! All these sufferings, all these tears . . . in vain!

STRANGER. Not in vain! It looks like spite, what happens here, but it's not that. I wronged the Invisible when I mistook . . .

LADY. Enough! No accusations.

STRANGER. No. It was my own stupidity or wickedness. I didn't want to be made a fool of by life. That's why I was! It was the elves . . .

LADY. Who made the change in you. Come. Let's go.

STRANGER. And hide ourselves and our misery in the mountains.

LADY. Yes. The mountains will hide us! (Pause.) But first I must go and light a candle to my good Saint Elizabeth. Come. (The STRANGER shakes his head.) Come!

STRANGER. Very well. I'll go through that way. But I can't stay.

LADY. How can you tell? Come. In there you shall hear new songs.

(The STRANGER follows her to the door of the church.)

STRANGER. It may be!

LADY. Come!

THE END.

PART II

CHARACTERS

CHARACTERS
THE STRANGER
THE LADY
THE MOTHER
THE FATHER
THE CONFESSOR
THE DOCTOR
CAESAR

less important figures
MAID
PROFESSOR
RAGGED PERSON
ANOTHER RAGGED PERSON
FIRST WOMAN
SECOND WOMAN
WAITRESS
POLICEMAN

SCENES

ACT I

OUTSIDE THE HOUSE

[On the right a terrace, on which the house stands. Below it a road runs towards the back, where there is a thick pine wood with heights beyond, whose outlines intersect. On the left there is a suggestion of a river bank, but the river itself cannot be seen. The house is white and has small, mullioned windows with iron bars. On the wall vines and climbing roses. In front of the house, on the terrace, a well; at the end of the terrace pumpkin plants, whose large yellow flowers hang dozen over the edge. Fruit trees are planted along the road, and a memorial cross can be seen erected at a spot where an accident occurred. Steps lead down from the terrace to the road, and there are flower-pots on the balustrade. In front of the steps there is a seat. The road reaches the foreground from the right, curving past the terrace, which projects like a promontory, and then loses itself in the background. Strong sunlight from the left. The MOTHER is sitting on the seat below the steps. The DOMINICAN is standing in front of her.]

DOMINICAN [Note: The same character as the CONFESSOR and BEGGAR.]. You called me to discuss a family matter of importance to you. Tell me what it is.

MOTHER. Father, life has treated me hardly. I don't know what I've done to be so frowned upon by Providence.

DOMINICAN. It's a mark of favour to be tried by the Eternal One, and triumph awaits the steadfast.

MOTHER. That's what I've often said to myself; but there are limits to the suffering one can bear. . . .

DOMINICAN. There are no limits. Suff'ering's as boundless as grace.

MOTHER. First my husband leaves me for another woman.

DOMINICAN. Then let him go. He'll come crawling back again on his bare knees!

MOTHER. And as you know, Father, my only daughter was married to a doctor. But she left him and came home with a stranger, whom she presented to me as her new husband.

DOMINICAN. That's not easy to understand. Divorce isn't recognised by our religion.

MOTHER. No. But they'd crossed the frontier, to a land where there are other laws. He's an Old Catholic, and he found a priest to marry them.

DOMINICAN. That's no real marriage, and can't be dissolved because it never existed. But it can be nullified. Who is your present son-in-law?

MOTHER. Truly, I wish I knew! One thing I do know, and that's enough to fill my cup of sorrow. He's been divorced and his wife and children live in wretched circumstances.

DOMINICAN. A difficult case. But we'll find a way to put it right. What does he do?

MOTHER. He's a writer; said to be famous at home.

DOMINICAN. Godless, too, I suppose?

MOTHER. Yes. At least he used to be; but since his second marriage he's not known a happy hour. Fate, as he calls it, seized him with an iron hand and drove him here in the shape of a ragged beggar. Ill-fortune struck him blow after blow, so that I pitied him at the very moment he fled from here. Then he wandered in the woods and, later, lay out in the fields where he fell, till he was found by merciful folk and taken to a convent. There he lay ill for three months, without our knowing where he was.

DOMINICAN. Wait! Last year a man was brought to the Convent of St. Saviour, where I'm Confessor, under the circumstances you describe. Whilst he was feverish he opened his heart to me, and there was scarcely a sin of which he didn't confess his guilt. But when he came to himself again, he said he remembered nothing. So to prove him in heart and reins I used the secret apostolic powers that are given us; and, as a trial, employed the lesser curse. For when a crime's been done in secret, the curse of Deuteronomy is read over the suspected man. If he's innocent, he goes his way unscathed. But if he's struck by it, then, as Paul relates, 'he is delivered unto Satan for the destruction of the flesh, that his spirit may be saved.'

MOTHER. O God! It must be he!

DOMINICAN. Yes, it is he. Your son-in-law! The ways of Providence are inscrutable. Was he heavily struck by the curse?

MOTHER. Yes. That night he slept here, and was torn from his sleep by an unexplained power that, as he told me, turned his heart to ice. . . .

DOMINICAN. Did he have fearful visions?

MOTHER. Yes.

139

DOMINICAN. And was he harried by those terrible thoughts, of which Job says, 'When I say, my bed shall comfort me, then Thou scarest me with dreams and terrifiest me with visions; so that my soul chooseth strangling, and death rather than life.' That's as it should be. Did it open his eyes?

MOTHER. Yes. But only so that his sight was blinded. For his sufferings grew so great that he could no longer find a natural explanation for them, and as no doctor could cure him, he began to see that he was fighting higher conscious powers.

DOMINICAN. Powers that meant him ill, and were therefore themselves evil. That's the usual course of things. And then?

MOTHER. He came upon books that taught him that such evil powers could be fought.

DOMINICAN. Oh! So he looked for what's hidden, and should remain so! Did he succeed in exorcising the spirits that chastised him?

MOTHER. He says he did. And it seems now that he can sleep again.

DOMINICAN. Yes, and he believes what he says. Yet, since he hasn't truly accepted the love of truth, God will trouble him with great delusion, so that he'll believe what is false.

MOTHER. The fault's his own. But he's changed my daughter: in other days she was neither hot nor cold; but now she's on the way to becoming evil.

DOMINICAN. How do the two of them get on?

MOTHER. Half the time, happily; the other half they plague one another like devils.

DOMINICAN. That's the way they must go. Plague one another till they come to the Cross.

MOTHER. If they don't part again.

DOMINICAN. What? Have they done so?

MOTHER. They've left one another four times, but have always come back. It seems as if they're chained together. It would be a good thing if they were, for a child's on the way.

DOMINICAN. Let the child come. Children bring gifts that are refreshing to tired souls.

MOTHER. I hope it may be so. But it looks as if this one will be an apple of discord. They're already quarrelling over its name; they're quarrelling over its baptism; and the mother's already jealous of her husband's children by his first wife. He can't promise to love this child as much as the others, and the mother absolutely insists that he shall! So there's no end to their miseries.

DOMINICAN. Oh yes, there is. Wait! He's had dealings with higher powers, so that we've gained a hold on him; and our prayers will be more, powerful than his resistance. Their effect is as extraordinary as it is mysterious. (The STRANGER appears on the terrace. He is in hunting costume and wears a tropical helmet. In his hand he has an alpenstock.) Is that him, up there?

MOTHER. Yes. That's my present son-in-law.

DOMINICAN. Singularly like the first! But watch how he's behaving. He hasn't seen me yet, but he feels I'm here. (He makes the sign of the cross in the air.) Look how troubled he grows. . . . Now he stiffens like an icicle. See! In a moment he'll cry out.

STRANGER (who has suddenly stopped, grown rigid, and clutched his heart). Who's down there?

MOTHER. I am.

STRANGER. You're not alone.

MOTHER. No. I've someone with me.

DOMINICAN (making the sign of the cross). Now he'll say nothing; but fall like a felled tree. (The STRANGER crumples up and falls to the ground.) Now I shall go. It would be too much for him if he were to see me, But I'll come back soon. You'll see, he's in good hands! Farewell and peace be with you. (He goes out.)

STRANGER (raising himself and coming down the steps). Who was that?

MOTHER. A traveller. Sit down; you look so pale.

STRANGER. It was a fainting fit.

MOTHER. You've always new names for it; but they mean nothing fresh. Sit down here, on the seat.

STRANGER. No; I don't like sitting there. People are always passing.

MOTHER. Yet I've been sitting here since I was a child, watching life glide past as the river does below. Here, on the road, I've watched the children of men go by, playing, haggling, begging, cursing and dancing. I love this seat and I love the river below, though it does much damage every year and washes away the property we inherited. Last spring it carried our whole hay crop off, so that we had to sell our beasts. The property's lost half its value in the last few years, and when the lake in the mountains has reached its new level and the swamp's been drained into the river, the water will rise till it washes the house away. We've been at law about it for ten years, and we've lost every appeal; so we shall be destroyed. It's as inevitable as fate.

STRANGER. Fate's not inevitable.

MOTHER. Beware, if you think to fight it.

STRANGER. I've done so already.

MOTHER. There you go again! You learn nothing from the chastisement of Providence.

STRANGER. Oh yes. I've learned to hate. Can one love what does evil?

MOTHER. I've little learning, as you know; but I read yesterday in an encyclopaedia that the Eumenides are not evilly disposed.

STRANGER. That's true; but it's a lie they're friendly. I only know one friendly fury. My own!

MOTHER. Can you call Ingeborg a fury?

STRANGER. Yes. She is one; and as a fury, she's remarkable. Her talent for making me suffer excels my most infernal inventions; and if I escape from her hands with my life, I'll come out of the fire as pure as gold.

MOTHER. You've got what you deserve. You wanted to mould her as you wished, and you've succeeded.

STRANGER. Completely. But where is this fury?

MOTHER. She went down the road a few minutes ago.

STRANGER. Down there? Then I'll go to meet my own destruction. (He goes towards the back.)

MOTHER. So you can still joke about it? Wait! (The MOTHER is left alone for a moment, until the STRANGER has disappeared. The LADY then enters from the right. She is wearing a summer frock, and is carrying a post bag and some opened letters in her hand.)

LADY. Are you alone, Mother?

MOTHER. I've just been left alone.

LADY. Here's the post. This is for job.

MOTHER. What? Do you open his letters?

LADY. All of them, because I want to know who it is I've linked my life to. And I want to suppress everything that might minister to his pride. In a word, I isolate him, so that he has to keep his own electricity and run the danger of being broken to pieces.

MOTHER. How learnèd you've grown?

LADY. Yes. If he's unwise enough to confide almost everything to me, I'll soon hold his fate in my hand. Now, if you please, he's making electrical experiments and claims he'll be able to harness the lightning, so that it'll give him light, warmth and power. Well, let him do as he likes! From a letter that came today I see he's even corresponding with alchemists.

MOTHER. Does he want to make gold? Is the man sane?

144

LADY. That's the important question. Whether he's a charlatan doesn't matter so much.

MOTHER. Do you suspect it?

LADY. I'd believe any evil of him, and any good, on the same day.

MOTHER. Is there any other news?

LADY. The plans my divorced husband made for a new marriage have gone wrong; he's grown melancholic, abandoned his practice and is tramping the roads.

MOTHER. Oh! He was always my son-in-law. He had a kind heart under his rough manner.

LADY. Yes. I only called him a werewolf in his rôle as my husband and master. As long as I knew he was at peace, and on the way to find consolation, I was content. But now he'll torment me like a bad conscience.

MOTHER. Have you a conscience?

LADY. I never used to have one. But my eyes have been opened since I read my husband's works, and I know the difference between good and evil.

MOTHER. But he forbade you to read them, and never foresaw you wouldn't obey him.

LADY. Who can foresee all the results of any action?

MOTHER. Have you more bad news in your pocket, Pandora?

LADY. The worst of all! Think of it, Mother, his divorced wife's going to marry again.

MOTHER. That ought to be reassuring, to you and to him.

LADY. Didn't you know it was his worst nightmare? That his wife would marry again and his children have a stepfather?

MOTHER. If he can bear that alone, I shall think him a strange man.

LADY. You believe he's too sensitive? But didn't he say himself that an educated man of the world at the end of the nineteenth century never lets himself be put out of countenance!

MOTHER. It's easy to say so; but when things really happen. . . .

LADY. Yet there was a gift at the bottom of Pandora's box that was no misfortune. Look, Mother! A portrait of his six-year-old son.

MOTHER (looking at the picture). A lovely child.

LADY. It does one good to see such a charming and expressive picture. Tell me, do you think my child will be as beautiful? Well, what do you say? Answer, or I'll be unhappy! I love this boy already, but I feel I'd hate him if my child's not as lovely as he. Yes, I'm jealous already.

MOTHER. When you came here after your unlucky honeymoon, I'd hoped you'd have got over the worst. But now I see it was only a foretaste of what was to come.

LADY. I'm ready for anything; and I don't think this knot can ever be undone. It must be cut!

MOTHER. But you're only making more difficulties for yourself by suppressing his letters.

LADY. In days gone by, when I went through life like a sleep-walker, everything seemed easy to me, but I begin to be uncertain now he's started to waken thoughts in me. (She puts the letters into the post-bag.) Here he is. 'Sh!

MOTHER. One thing more. Why do you let him wear that suit of your first husband's?

LADY. I like torturing and humiliating him. I've persuaded him it fits him and belonged to my father. Now, when I see him in the werewolf's things, I feel I've got both of them in my clutches.

MOTHER. Heaven defend us! How spiteful you've grown!

LADY. Perhaps that was my rôle, if I have one in this man's life!

MOTHER. I sometimes wish the river would rise and carry us all away whilst we're asleep at night. If it were to flow here for a thousand years perhaps it would wash out the sin on which this house is built.

LADY. Then it's true that my grandfather, the notary, illegally seized property not his own? It's said this place was built with the heritage of widows and orphans, the funds of ruined men, the property of dead ones and the bribes of litigants.

MOTHER. Don't speak of it any more. The tears of those still living have run together and formed a lake. And it's that lake, people say, that's being drained now, and that'll cause the river to wash us away.

LADY. Can't it be stopped by taking legal action? Is there no justice on earth?

MOTHER. Not on earth. But there is in heaven. And heaven will drown us, for we're the children of evildoers. (She goes up the steps.)

LADY. Isn't it enough to put up with one's own tears? Must one inherit other people's?

(The STRANGER comes back.)

STRANGER. Did you call me?

LADY. No. I only tried to draw you to me, without really wanting you.

STRANGER. I felt you meddling with my destiny in a way that made me uneasy. Soon you'll have learnt all I know.

LADY. And more.

STRANGER. But I must ask you not to lay rough hands on my fate. I am Cain, you see, and am under the ban of mysterious powers, who permit no mortals to interfere with their work of vengeance. You see this mark on my brow? (He removes his hat.) It means: Revenge is mine, saith the Lord.

LADY. Does your hat press. . . .

STRANGER. No. It chafes me. And so does the coat. If it weren't that I wanted to please you, I'd have thrown them all into the river. When I walk here in the neighbourhood, do you know that people call me the doctor? They must take me for your husband, the werewolf. And I'm unlucky. If I ask who planted some tree: they say, the doctor. If I ask to whom the green fish basket belongs: they say, the doctor. And if it isn't his then it belongs to the doctor's wife. That is, to you! This confusion between him and me makes my visit unbearable. I'd like to go away. . . .

LADY. Haven't you tried in vain to leave this place six times?

STRANGER. Yes. But the seventh, I'll succeed.

LADY. Then try!

STRANGER. You say that as if you were convinced I'd fail.

LADY. I am.

STRANGER. Plague me in some other way, dear fury.

LADY. Well, I can.

STRANGER. A new way! Try to say something ill-natured that 'the other one's' not said already.

LADY. Your first wife's 'the other one.' How tactful to remind me of her.

STRANGER. Everything that lives and moves, everything that's dead and cold, reminds me of what's gone. . . .

LADY. Until the being comes, who can wipe out the darkness of the past and bring light.

STRANGER. You mean the child we're expecting!

LADY. Our child!

STRANGER. Do you love it?

LADY. I began to today.

STRANGER. Today? Why, what's happened? Five months ago you wanted to run off to the lawyers and divorce me; because I wouldn't take you to a quack who'd kill your unborn child.

LADY. That was some time ago. Things have changed now.

STRANGER. Why now? (He looks round as if expecting something.) Now? Has the post come?

LADY. You're still more cunning than I am. But the pupil will outstrip the master.

STRANGER. Were there any letters for me?

LADY. No.

STRANGER. Then give me the wrapper?

LADY. What made you guess?

STRANGER. Give the wrapper, if your conscience can make such fine distinctions between it and the letter.

LADY (picking up the letter-bag, which she has hidden behind the seat). Look at this! (The STRANGER takes the photograph, looks at it carefully, and puts it in his breast-pocket.) What was it?

STRANGER. The past.

LADY. Was it beautiful?

STRANGER. Yes. More beautiful than the future can ever be.

LADY (darkly). You shouldn't have said that.

STRANGER. No, I admit it. And I'm sorry. . . .

LADY. Tell me, are you capable of suffering?

STRANGER. Now, I suffer twice; because I feel when you're suffering. And if I wound you in self-defence, it's I who gets fever from the wound.

LADY. That means you're at my mercy?

STRANGER. No. Less now than ever, because you're protected by the innocent being you carry beneath your heart.

LADY. He shall be my avenger.

STRANGER. Or mine!

LADY (tearfully). Poor little thing. Conceived in sin and shame, and born to avenge by hate.

STRANGER. It's a long time since I've heard you speak like that.

LADY. I dare say.

STRANGER. That was the voice that first drew me to you; it was like that of a mother speaking to her child.

LADY. When you say 'mother' I feel I can only believe good of you; but a moment after I say to myself: it's only one more of your ways of deceiving me.

STRANGER. What ill have I ever really done you? (The LADY is uncertain what to reply.) Answer me. What ill have I done you?

LADY. I don't know.

STRANGER. Then invent something. Say to me: I hate you, because I can't deceive you.

LADY. Can't I? Oh, I'm sorry for you.

STRANGER. You must have poison in the pocket of your dress.

LADY. Well, I have!

STRANGER. What can it be? (Pause.) Who's that coming down the road?

LADY. A harbinger.

STRANGER. Is it a man, or a spectre?

LADY. A spectre from the past.

STRANGER. He's wearing a black coat and a laurel crown. But his feet are bare.

LADY. It's Caesar.

STRANGER (confused). Caesar? That was my nickname at school.

LADY. Yes. But it's also the name of the madman whom my . . . first husband used to look after. Forgive me speaking of him like that.

STRANGER. Has this madman got away?

LADY. It looks like it, doesn't it?

(CAESAR comes in from the back; he wears a black frock coat and is without a collar; he has a laurel crown on his head and his feet are bare. His general appearance is bizarre.)

CAESAR. Why don't you greet me? You ought to say: Ave, Caesar! For now I'm the master. The werewolf, you must know, has gone out of his mind since the Great Man went off with his wife, whom he himself snatched from her first lover, or bridegroom, or whatever you call him.

STRANGER (to the LADY). That was strychnine for two adults! (To CAESAR) Where's your master now—or your slave, or doctor, or warder?

CAESAR. He'll be here soon. But you needn't be frightened of him. He won't use daggers or poison. He only has to show himself, for all living things to fly from him; for trees to drop their leaves, and the very dust of the highway to run before him in a whirlwind like the pillar of cloud before the Children of Israel. . . .

STRANGER. Listen. . . .

CAESAR. Quiet, whilst I'm speaking. . . . Sometimes he believes himself to be a werewolf, and says he'd like to eat a little child that's not yet born, and that's really his according to the right of priority. . . . (He goes on his way.)

LADY (to the STRANGER). Can you exorcise this demon?

STRANGER. I can do nothing against devils who brave the sunshine.

LADY. Yesterday you made an arrogant remark, and now you shall have it back. You said it wasn't fair for invisible ones to creep in by night and strike in the darkness, they should come by day when the sun's shining. Now they've come!

STRANGER. And that pleases you!

LADY. Yes. Almost.

STRANGER. What a pity it gives me no pleasure when it's you who's struck! Let's sit down on the seat—the bench for the accused. For more are coming.

LADY. I'd rather we went.

STRANGER. No, I want to see how much I can bear. You see, at every stroke of the lash I feel as if a debit entry had been erased from my ledger.

LADY. But I can stand no more. Look, there he comes himself. Heavens! This man, whom I once thought I loved!

STRANGER. Thought? Yes, because everything's merely delusion. And that means a great deal. You go! I'll take the duty on myself of confronting him alone.

(The LADY goes up the steps, but does not reach the toy before the DOCTOR becomes visible at the back of the stage. The DOCTOR comes in, his grey hair long and unkempt. He is wearing a tropical helmet and a hunting coat, which are exactly similar to the clothes of the STRANGER. He behaves as though he doesn't notice the STRANGER'S presence, and sits down on a stone on the other side of the road, opposite the STRANGER, who is sitting on the seat. He takes of his hat and mops the sweat from his brow. The STRANGER grows impatient.) What do you want?

154

DOCTOR. Only to see this house again, where my happiness once dwelt and my roses blossomed. . . .

STRANGER. An intelligent man of the world would have chosen a time when the present inhabitants of the house were away for a short while; even on his own account, so as not to make himself ridiculous.

DOCTOR. Ridiculous? I'd like to know which of us two's the more ridiculous?

STRANGER. For the moment, I suppose I am.

DOCTOR. Yes. But I don't think you know the whole extent of your wretchedness.

STRANGER. What do you mean?

DOCTOR. That you want to possess what I used to possess.

STRANGER. Well, go on.

DOCTOR. Have you noticed that we're wearing similar clothes? Good! Do you know the reason? It's this: you're wearing the things I forgot to fetch when the catastrophe took place. No intelligent man of the world at the end of the nineteenth century would ever put himself into such a position.

STRANGER (throwing down his hat and coat). Curse the woman!

DOCTOR. You needn't complain. Cast-off male attire has always been fatal ever since the celebrated shirt of Nessus. Go in now and change. I'll sit out here and watch, and listen, how you settle the matter alone with that accursèd woman. Don't forget your stick! (The LADY, who is hurrying towards the house, trips in front of the steps. The STRANGER stays where he is in embarrassment.) The stick! The stick!

STRANGER. I don't ask mercy for the woman's sake, but for the child's.

DOCTOR (wildly). So there's a child, too. Our house, our roses, our clothes, the bed-clothes not forgotten, and now our child! I'm within your doors, I sit at your table, I lie in your bed; I exist in your blood; in your lungs, in your brain; I am everywhere and yet you can't get hold of me. When the pendulum strikes the hour of midnight, I'll blow cold, on your heart, so that it stops like a clock that's run down. When you sit at your work, I shall come with a poppy, invisible to you, that will put your thoughts to sleep, and confuse your mind, so that you'll see visions you can't distinguish from reality. I shall lie like a stone in your path, so that you stumble; I shall be the thorn that pricks your hand when you go to pluck the rose. My soul shall spin itself about you like a spider's web; and I shall guide you like an ox by means of the woman you stole from me. Your child shall be mine and I shall speak through its mouth; you shall see my look in its eyes, so that you'll thrust it from you like a foe. And now, belovèd house, farewell; farewell, 'rose' room—where no happiness shall dwell that I could envy. (He goes out. The STRANGER has been sitting on the seat all this time, without being able to answer, and has been listening as if he were the accused.)

Curtain.

ACT II

SCENE I
LABORATORY

[A Garden Pavilion in rococo style with high windows. In the middle of the room there is a large writing desk on which are various pieces of chemical and physical apparatus. Two copper wires are suspended from the ceiling to an electroscope that is standing on the middle of the table and which is provided with a number of bells, intended to record the tension of atmospheric electricity.]

[On the table to the left a large old-fashioned frictional electric generating machine, with glass plates, brass conductors, and Leyden battery. The stands are lacquered red and white. On the right a large old-fashioned open fireplace with tripods, crucibles, pincers, bellows, etc.]

[In the background a door with a view of the country beyond; it is dark and cloudy weather, but the red rays of the sun occasionally shine into the room. A brown cloak with a cape and hood is hanging up by the fireplace; nearby a travelling bag and an alpenstock. The STRANGER and the MOTHER are discovered together.]

STRANGER. Where is . . . Ingeborg?

MOTHER. You know that better than I.

STRANGER. With the lawyer, arranging a divorce. . . .

157

MOTHER. Why?

STRANGER. I told you. No, it's so far-fetched, you'll think I'm lying to you.

MOTHER. Well, tell me!

STRANGER. She wants a divorce, because I've refused to turn this man out, although he's deranged. She says it's cowardly of me. . . .

MOTHER. I don't believe it.

STRANGER. You see! You only believe what you wish; all the rest is lies. Well, can you find it in accordance with your interests to believe that she's been stealing my letters?

MOTHER. I know nothing of that.

STRANGER. I'm not asking you whether you know of it, but whether you believe it.

MOTHER (changing the subject). What are you trying to do here?

STRANGER. I'm making experiments concerning atmospheric electricity.

MOTHER. And that's the lighting conductor, that you've connected to the desk!

STRANGER. Yes. But there's no danger; for the bells would ring if there were an atmospheric disturbance.

MOTHER. That's blasphemy and black magic. Take care! And what are you doing there, in the fireplace?

158

STRANGER. Making gold.

MOTHER. You think it possible?

STRANGER. You take it for granted I'm a charlatan? I shan't blame you for that; but don't judge too quickly. At any moment I expect to get a sworn statement of analysis.

MOTHER. I dare say. But what are you going to do if Ingeborg doesn't come back?

STRANGER. She will, this time. Later, perhaps, when the child's here, she'll cut herself adrift.

MOTHER. You seem very sure.

STRANGER. Yes. As I said, I still am. So long as the bond's not broken you can feel it. When it is, you'll feel that unpleasantly clearly, too.

MOTHER. But when you've parted from one another, you may yet both be bound to the child. You can't tell in advance.

STRANGER. I've been providing against that by a great interest, that I hope will fill my empty life.

MOTHER. You mean gold. And honour!

STRANGER. Precisely! For a man the most enduring of all illusions.

MOTHER. So you'd build on illusions?

STRANGER. On what else should I build, when everything's illusion?

MOTHER. If you ever awake from your dream, you'll find a reality of which you've never been able to dream.

STRANGER. Then I'll wait till that happens.

MOTHER. Wait then. Now I'll go and shut the window, before the thunderstorm breaks.

STRANGER (going towards the back of the stage). That's going to be interesting. (A hunting horn is heard in the distance.) Who's sounding that horn?

MOTHER. No one knows; and it means nothing good. (She goes out.)

STRANGER (busying himself with the electroscope, and turning his back on the open window as he does so; then taking up a book and reading aloud.) 'When Adam's race of giants had increased enough for them to consider their number sufficient to risk an attack on those above, they began to build a tower that was to reach up to Heaven. Those above were then seized with fear and, in order to protect themselves, broke up the assembled multitude by so confusing their tongues and their minds that two people who met could not understand one another, even if they spoke the same language Since then, those above rule by discord: divide and rule. And the discord is upheld by the belief that the truth has been found; but when one of the prophets is believed, he is a lying prophet. If on the other hand a mortal succeeds in penetrating the secret of those above, no one believes him, and he is struck with madness so that no one ever shall. Since then mortals have been more or less demented, particularly those who are held to be wise, but madmen are in reality the only wise men; for they can see, hear and feel the invisible, the inaudible and the intangible, though they cannot relate their experiences to others.' Thus Zohar, the wisest of all the books of wisdom, and therefore one that no one believes. I shall build no tower of Babel, but I shall tempt the Powers into my mousetrap, and send them to the Powers below, the subterranean ones, so that they can be neutralised. It is the higher Schedim, who have come between mortal men and the Lord Zabaoth; and that is why joy, peace and happiness have vanished from the earth.

LADY (coming back in despair, throwing herself down in front of the STRANGER and putting her arms round his feet and her head on the ground.) Help me! Help me! And forgive me.

STRANGER. Get up. In God's name! Get up. Don't do that. What's happened?

LADY. In my anger I've behaved foolishly. I've been caught in my own net.

STRANGER (lifting her up). Stand up, foolish child; and tell me what's happened.

LADY. I went to the public prosecutor.

STRANGER. . . . and asked for a divorce. . . .

LADY. . . . that was my intention; but when I got there, I laid information against the werewolf for a breach of the peace and attempted murder.

STRANGER. But he's guilty of neither!

LADY. No, but I laid the information all the same. . . . And when I was there, he came himself to lay information against me for bearing false witness. Then I went to the lawyer and he told me that I could expect a sentence of at least a month. Think of it, my child will be born in prison! How can I escape from that? Help me. You can. Speak!

STRANGER. Yes, I can help you. But, if I do, don't revenge yourself on me afterwards.

LADY. How little you know me. But tell me quickly.

STRANGER. I must take the blame on myself, and say I sent you.

LADY. How generous you are! Am I rid of the whole business now?

STRANGER. Dry your eyes, my child, and take comfort. But tell me about something else, that's nothing to do with this. Did you leave this purse here? (The LADY is embarrassed.) Tell me!

LADY. Has such a thing ever happened before?

STRANGER. Yes. The 'other one' wanted to discover, in this way, whether I stole. The first time it happened I wept, because I was still young and innocent.

LADY. Oh no!

STRANGER. Now you seem to me the most wretched creature on earth.

LADY. Is that why you love me?

STRANGER. No. You've been stealing my letters, too! Answer, yes! And that's why you wanted to prove me a thief with this purse.

LADY. What have you got there, on the table.

STRANGER. Lightning!

(There is a flash of lightning, but no thunder.)

LADY. Aren't you afraid?

162

STRANGER. Yes, sometimes; but not of what you fear.

(The contorted face of the DOCTOR appears outside the window.)

LADY. Is there a cat in the room? I feel uneasy.

STRANGER. I don't think so. Yet I too have a feeling that there's someone here.

LADY (turning and seeing the DOCTOR's face; then screaming and hurrying to the STRANGER for protection.) Oh! There he is!

STRANGER. Where? Who?

(The DOCTOR'S face disappears.)

LADY. There, at the window. It's he!

STRANGER. I can see no one. You must be wrong.

LADY. No, I saw him. The werewolf! Can't we be rid of him?

STRANGER. Yes, we could. But it'd be useless, because he has an immortal soul, which is bound to yours.

LADY. If I'd only known that before!

STRANGER. It's surely in the Catechism.

LADY. Then let us die!

STRANGER. That was once my religion; but as I no longer believe that death's the end, nothing remains but to bear everything—to fight, and to suffer!

LADY. For how long must we suffer?

STRANGER. As long as he suffers and our consciences plague us.

LADY. Then we must try and justify ourselves to our consciences; find excuses for our frivolous actions, and discover his weaknesses.

STRANGER. Well, you can try!

LADY. You say that! Since I've known he's unhappy I can see nothing but his qualities, and you lose when I compare you with him.

STRANGER. See how well it's arranged! His sufferings sanctify him, but mine make me abhorrent and laughable! We must face the immutable. We've destroyed a soul, so we are murderers.

LADY. Who is to blame?

STRANGER. He who's so mismanaged the fate of men.

(There is a flash of lightning; the electric bells begin to ring.)

LADY. O God! What's that?

STRANGER. The answer.

LADY. Is there a lightning conductor here?

STRANGER. The priest of Baal wishes to coax the lightning from heaven. . . .

LADY. Now I'm frightened, frightened of you. You're terrifying.

STRANGER. You see!

164

LADY. Who are you to defy Heaven, and to dare to play with the destinies of men?

STRANGER. Get up and collect your thoughts. Listen to me, believe me, and pay me the respect that's my due; and I'll lift both of us high above this frog pond, to which we've both descended. I'll breathe on your sick conscience so that it heals like a wound. Who am I? A man who has done what no one else has ever done; who will overthrow the Golden Calf and upset the tables of the money-changers. I hold the fate of the world in my crucible; and in a week I can make the richest of the rich a poor man. Gold, the most false of all standards, has ceased to rule; every man will now be as poor as his neighbour, and the children of men will hurry about like ants whose heap has been disturbed.

LADY. What good will that be to us?

STRANGER. Do you think I'll make gold in order to enrich ourselves and others? No. I'll do it to paralyse the present order, to disrupt it, as you'll see! I am the destroyer, the dissolver, the world incendiary; and when all lies in ashes, I shall wander hungrily through the heaps of ruins, rejoicing at the thought that it is all my work: that I have written the last page of world history, which can then be held to be ended.

(The face of the DOMINICAN appears at the open window, without being seen by those on the stage.)

LADY. Then that was the real meaning of your last book! It was no invention!

STRANGER. No. But in order to write it, I had to link myself with the self of another, who could take everything from me that fettered my soul. So that my spirit could once more find a fiery blast, on which to mount to the ether, elude the Powers, and reach the Throne, in order to lay the lamentations of mankind at the feet of the Eternal One. . . . (The DOMINICAN makes the sign of the cross in the air and disappears.) Who's here? Who is the Terrible One who follows me and cripples my thoughts? Did you see no one?

LADY. No. No one.

STRANGER. But I can feel his presence. (He puts his hand to his heart.) Can't you hear, far, far away, someone saying a rosary?

LADY. Yes, I can hear it. But it's not the Angels' Greeting. It's the Curse of Deuteronomy! Woe unto us!

STRANGER. Then it must be in the convent of St. Saviour.

LADY. Woe! Woe!

STRANGER. Beloved. What is it?

LADY. Belovèd! Say that word again.

STRANGER. Are you ill?

LADY. No, but I'm in pain, and yet glad at the same time. Go and ask my mother to make up my bed. But first give me your blessing.

STRANGER. Shall I . . . ?

LADY. Say you forgive me; I may die, if the child takes my life. Say that you love me.

STRANGER. Strange: I can't get the word to cross my lips.

LADY. Then you don't love me?

STRANGER. When you say so, it seems so to me. It's terrible, but I fear I hate you.

LADY. Then at least give me your hand; as you'd give it to someone in distress.

STRANGER. I'd like to, but I can't. Someone in me takes pleasure in your agony; but it's not I. I'd like to carry you in my arms and bear your suffering for you. But I may not. I cannot!

LADY. You're as hard as stone.

STRANGER (with restrained emotion). Perhaps not. Perhaps not.

LADY. Come to me!

STRANGER. I can't stir from here. It's as if someone had taken possession of my soul; and I'd like to kill myself so as to take the life of the other.

LADY. Think of your child with joy. . . .

STRANGER. I can't even do that, for it'll bind me to earth.

LADY. If we've sinned, we've been punished! Haven't we suffered enough?

STRANGER. Not yet. But one day we shall have.

LADY (sinking down). Help me. Mercy! I shall faint!

(The STRANGER extends his hand, as if he had recovered from a cramp. The LADY kisses it. The STRANGER lifts her up and leads her to the door of the house.)

Curtain.

167

SCENE II
THE 'ROSE' ROOM

[A room with rose-coloured walls; it has small windows with iron lattices and plants in pots. The curtains are rose red; the furniture is white and red. In the background a door leading to a white bed-chamber; when this door is opened, a large bed can be seen with a canopy and white hangings. On the right the door leading out of the house. On the left a fireplace with a coal fire. In front of it a bath tub, covered with a white towel. A cradle covered with white, rose-coloured and light-blue stuff. Baby clothes are spread out here and there. A green dress hangs on the right-hand wall. Four Sisters of Mercy are on their knees, facing the door at the back, dressed in the black and white of Augustinian nuns. The midwife, who is in black, is by the fireplace. The child's nurse wears a peasant's dress, of black and white, from Brittany. The MOTHER is standing listening by the door at the back. The STRANGER is sitting on a chair right and is trying to read a book. A hat and a brown cloak with a cape and hood hang nearby, and on the floor there is a small travelling bag. The Sisters of Mercy are singing a psalm. The others join in from time to time, but not the STRANGER.]

SISTERS.   Salve, Regina, mater misericordiae;

Vita, dulcedo, et spes nostra, salve.

Ad to clamamus, exules filii Evae;

Ad to suspiramus gementes et flentes

In hac lacrymarum valle.

(The STRANGER rises and goes to the MOTHER.)

MOTHER. Stay where you are! A human being's coming into the world; another's dying. It's all the same to you.

STRANGER. I'm not so sure! If I want to go in, I'm not allowed to. And when I don't want to, you wish it. I'd like to now.

MOTHER. She doesn't want to see you. Besides, presence here's no longer needed. The child matters most now.

STRANGER. For you, yes; but I'm still of most importance to myself.

MOTHER. The doctor's forbidden anyone to go in, whoever they may be, because she's in danger.

STRANGER. What doctor?

MOTHER. So your thoughts are there again!

STRANGER. Yes. And it's you who led them! An hour ago you gave me to understand that the child couldn't be mine. With that you branded your daughter a whore; but that means nothing to you, if you can only strike me to the heart! You are almost the most contemptible creature I know!

MOTHER (to the SISTERS). Sisters! Pray for this unhappy man.

STRANGER. Make way for me to go in. For the last time—out of the way.

MOTHER. Leave this room, and this house too.

STRANGER. If I were to do as you ask, in ten minutes you'd send the police after me, for abandoning my wife and child!

MOTHER. I'd only do that to have you taken to a convent you know of.

MAID (entering at the back). The Lady's asking you to do something for her.

STRANGER. What is it?

MAID. There's supposed to be a letter in the dress she left hanging here.

STRANGER (looks round and notices the green dress; he goes over to it and takes a letter from the pocket). This is addressed to me, and was opened two days ago. Broken open! That's good!

MOTHER. You must forgive someone who's as ill as your wife.

STRANGER. She wasn't ill two days ago.

MOTHER. No. But she is now.

STRANGER. But not two days ago! (Reading the letter.) Well, I'll forgive her now, with the magnanimity of the victor.

MOTHER. Of the victor?

STRANGER. Yes. For I've done something no one's ever done before.

MOTHER. You mean the gold. . . . ?

STRANGER. Here's a certificate from the greatest living authority. Now I'll go and see him myself.

MOTHER. Now!

STRANGER. At your request.

MAID (to the STRANGER). The Lady asks you to come in.

MOTHER. You hear?

STRANGER. No, now I don't want to! You've made your own daughter, my wife, into a whore; and branded my unborn child a bastard. You can keep them both. You've murdered my honour. There's nothing for me to do but to revive it elsewhere.

MOTHER. You can never forgive!

STRANGER. I can. I forgive you—and I shall leave you. (He puts on the brown cloak and hat, picks up his stick and travelling bag.) For if I were to stay, I'd soon grow worse than I am now. The innocent child, whose mission was to ennoble our warped relationship, has been defiled by you in his mother's womb and made an apple of discord and a source of punishment a revenge. Why should I stay here to be torn to pieces?

MOTHER. For you, duties don't exist.

STRANGER. Oh yes, they do! And the first of them's this: To protect myself from total destruction. Farewell!

Curtain.

ACT III

SCENE I
THE BANQUETING HALL

[Room in a hotel prepared for a banquet. There are long tables laden with flowers and candelabra. Dishes with peacocks, pheasants in full plumage, boars' heads, entire lobsters, oysters, salmon, bundles of asparagus, melons and grapes. There is a musicians' gallery with eight players in the right-hand corner at the back.]

[At the high table: the STRANGER in a frock coat; next to him a Civil Uniform with orders; a professorial Frock Coat with an order; and other black Frock Coats with orders of a more or less striking kind. At the second table a few Frock Coats between black Morning Coats. At the third table clean every-day costumes. At the fourth table dirty and ragged figures of strange appearance.]

[The tables are so arranged that the first is furthest to the left and the fourth furthest to the right, so that the people sitting at the fourth table cannot be seen by the STRANGER. At the fourth table CAESAR and the DOCTOR are seated, in shabby clothes. They are the farthest down stage. Dessert has just been handed round and the guests have golden goblets in front of them. The band is playing a passage in the middle of Mendelssohn's Dead March pianissimo. The guests are talking to one another quietly.]

DOCTOR (to CAESAR). The company seems rather depressed and the dessert came too soon!

172

CAESAR. By the way, the whole thing look's like a swindle! He hasn't made any gold, that's merely a lie, like everything else.

DOCTOR. I don't know, but that's what's being said. But in our enlightened age anything whatever may be expected.

CAESAR. There's a professor at the high table, who's supposed to be an authority. But what subject is he professor of?

DOCTOR: I've no idea. It must be metallurgy and applied chemistry.

CAESAR. Can you see what order he's wearing?

DOCTOR. I don't know it. I expect it's some tenth rate foreign order.

CAESAR. Well, at a subscription dinner like this the company's always rather mixed.

DOCTOR. Hm!

CAESAR. You mean, that we . . . hm. . . . I admit we're not well dressed, but as far as intelligence goes. . . .

DOCTOR. Listen, Caesar, you're a lunatic in my charge, and you must avoid speaking about intelligence as much as you can.

CAESAR. That's the greatest impertinence I've heard for a long time. Don't you realise, idiot, that I've been engaged to look after you, since you lost your wits?

PROFESSOR (taping his goblet). Gentlemen!

CAESAR. Hear, hear!

PROFESSOR. Gentlemen! Our small society is today honoured by the presence of the great man, who is our guest of honour, and when the committee . . .

CAESAR (to the DOCTOR). That's the government, you know!

PROFESSOR. . . . and when the committee asked me to act as interpreter and to explain the motives that prompted them I was at first doubtful whether I could accept the honour. But when I compared my own incapacity with that of others, I discovered that neither lost in the comparison.

VOICES. Bravo!

PROFESSOR. Gentlemen! A century of discovery is ending with the greatest of all discoveries—foreseen by Pythagoras, prepared for by Albertus and Paracelsus and first carried out by our guest of honour. You will permit me to give this feeble expression of our admiration for the greatest man of a great century. A laurel crown from the society! (He places a laurel frown on the STRANGER'S head.) And from the committee: this! (He hangs a shining order round the STRANGER'S neck.) Gentlemen! Three cheers for the Great Man who has made gold!

ALL (with the exception of the STRANGER). Hurrah!

(The band plays chords from Mendelssohn's Dead March. During the last part of the foregoing speech servants have exchanged the golden goblets for dull tin ones, and they now begin to take away the pheasants, peacocks, etc. The music plays softly. General conversation.)

CAESAR. Oughtn't we to taste these things before they take them away?

DOCTOR. It all seems humbug, except that about making gold.

STRANGER (knocking on the table). Gentlemen! I've always been proud of the fact that I'm not easy to deceive . . .

CAESAR. Hear, hear!

STRANGER. . . . that I'm not easily carried away, but I am touched at the sincerity so obvious in the great tribute you've just paid me; and when I say touched, I mean it.

CAESAR. Bravo!

STRANGER. There are always sceptics; and moments in the life of every man, when doubts creep into the hearts of even the strongest. I'll confess that I myself have doubted; but after finding myself the object this sincere and hearty demonstration, and after taking part in this royal feast, for it is royal; and seeing that, finally, the government itself . . .

VOICE. The committee!

STRANGER. . . . the committee, if you like, has so signally recognised my modest merits, I doubt no longer, but believe! (The Civil Uniform creeps out.) Yes, gentlemen, this is the greatest and most satisfying moment of my life, because it has given me back the greatest thing any man can possess, the belief in himself.

CAESAR. Splendid! Bravo!

STRANGER. I thank you. Your health!

(The PROFESSOR gets up. Everyone rises and the company begins to mix. Most of the musicians go out, but two remain.)

GUEST (to the STRANGER). A delightful evening!

175

STRANGER. Wonderful.

(All the Frock Coats creep away.)

FATHER (an elderly, overdressed man with an eye-glass and military bearing crosses to the doctor). What? Are you here?

DOCTOR. Yes, Father-in-law. I'm here. I go everywhere he goes.

FATHER. It's too late in the day to call me father-in-law. Besides, I'm *his* father-in-law now.

DOCTOR. Does he know you?

FATHER. No. He's not had that honour; and I must ask you to preserve my incognito. Is it true he's made gold?

DOCTOR. So it's said. But it's certain he left his wife while she was in childbed.

FATHER. Does that mean I can expect a third son-in-law soon? I don't like the idea! The uncertainty of my position makes me hate being a father-in-law at all. Of course, I've nothing to say against it, since. . . .

(The tables have now been cleared; the cloths and the candelabra have been removed, so that the tables themselves, which are merely boards supported on trestles, are all that remain. A big stoneware jug has been brought in and small jugs of simple form have been put on the high table. The people in rags sit down next to the STRANGER at the high table; and the FATHER sits astride a chair and stares at him.)

CAESAR (knocking on the table). Gentlemen! This feast has been called royal, not on account of the excellence of the service which, on the contrary, has been wretched; but because the man, whom we have

176

honoured, is a king, a king in the realm of the Intellect. Only I am able to judge of that. (One of the people in rags laughs.) Quiet. Wretch! But he's more than a king, he's a man of the people, of the humblest. A friend of the oppressed, the guardian of fools, the bringer of happiness to idiots. I don't know whether he's succeeded in making gold. I don't worry about that, and I hardly believe it . . . (There is a murmur. Two policemen come in and sit by the door; the musicians come down and take seats at the tables.) . . . but supposing he has, he has answered all the questions that the daily press has been trying to solve for the last fifty years. . . . It's only an assumption—

STRANGER. Gentlemen!

RAGGED PERSON. No. Don't interrupt him.

CAESAR. A mere assumption without real foundation, and the analysis may be wrong!

ANOTHER RAGGED PERSON. Don't talk nonsense!

STRANGER. Speaking in my capacity as guest of honour at this gathering I should say that it would be of interest to those taking part to hear the grounds on which I've based my proof. . . .

CAESAR. We don't want to hear that. No, no.

FATHER. Wait! I think justice demands that the accused should be allowed to explain himself. Couldn't our guest of honour tell the company his secret in a few words?

STRANGER. As the discoverer I can't give away my secret. But that's not necessary, because I've submitted my results to an authority under oath.

CAESAR. Then the whole thing's nonsense, the whole thing! We don't believe authorities—we're free-thinkers. Did you ever hear anything so impudent? That we should honour a mystery man, an arch-swindler, a charlatan, in good faith.

FATHER. Wait a little, my good people!

(During this scene a wall screen, charmingly decorated with palm trees and birds of paradise, has been taken away, disclosing a wretched serving-counter and stand for beer mugs, behind which a waitress is seen dispensing tots of spirits. Scavengers and dirty-looking women go over to the counter and start drinking.)

STRANGER. Was I asked here to be insulted?

FATHER. Not at all. My friend's rather loquacious, but he's not said anything insulting yet.

STRANGER. Isn't it insulting to be called a charlatan?

FATHER. He didn't mean it seriously.

STRANGER. Even as a joke I think the word arch-swindler slanderous.

FATHER. He didn't use *that* word.

STRANGER. What? I appeal to the company: wasn't the word he used arch-swindler?

ALL. No. He never said that!

STRANGER. Then I don't know where I am—or what company I've got into.

RAGGED PERSON. Is there anything wrong with it?

(The people murmur.)

BEGGAR (comes forward, supporting himself on crutches; he strikes the table so hard with his crutch, that some mugs are broken.) Mr. Chairman! May I speak? (He breaks some more crockery.) Gentlemen, in this life I've not allowed thyself to be easily deceived, but this time I have been. My friend in the chair there has convinced me that I've been completely deceived on the question of his power of judgment and sound understanding, and I feel touched. There are limits to pity and limits also to cruelty. I don't like to see real merit being dragged into the dust, and this man's worth a better fate than his folly's leading him to.

STRANGER. What does this mean?

(The FATHER and the DOCTOR have gone out during this scene without attracting attention. Only beggars remain at the high table. Those who are drinking gather into groups and stare at the STRANGER.)

BEGGAR. You take yourself to be the man of the century, and accept the invitation of the Drunkards' Society, in order to have yourself fêted as a man of science. . . .

STRANGER (rising). But the government. . . .

BEGGAR. Oh yes, the Committee of the Drunkards' Society have given you their highest distinction—that order you've had to pay for yourself. . . .

STRANGER. What about the professor?

BEGGAR. He only calls himself that; he's no professor really, though he does give lessons. And the uniform that must have impressed you most was that of a lackey in a chancellery.

STRANGER (tearing of the wreath and the ribbon of the order). Very well! But who was the elderly man with the eyeglass?

BEGGAR. Your father-in-law!

STRANGER. Who got up this hoax?

BEGGAR. It's no hoax, it's quite serious. The professor came on behalf of the Society, for so they call themselves, and asked you whether you'd accept the fête. You accepted it; so it became serious!

(Two dirty-looking women carry in a dust-bin suspended from a stick and set it down on the high table.)

FIRST WOMAN. If you're the man who makes gold, you might buy two brandies for us.

STRANGER. What's this mean?

BEGGAR. It's the last part of the reception; and it's supposed to mean that gold's mere rubbish.

STRANGER. If only that were true, rubbish could be exchanged for gold.

BEGGAR. Well, it's only the philosophy of the Society of Drunkards. And you've got to take your philosophy where you find it.

SECOND WOMAN (sitting down next to the STRANGER). Do you recognise me?

STRANGER. No.

SECOND WOMAN. Oh, you needn't be embarrassed so late in the evening as this!

STRANGER. You believe you're one of my victims? That I was amongst the first hundred who seduced you?

SECOND WOMAN. No. It's not what you think. But I once came across a printed paper, when I was about to be confirmed, which said that it was a duty to oneself to give way to all desires of the flesh. Well, I grew free and blossomed; and this is the fruit of my highly developed self!

STRANGER (rising). Perhaps I may go now?

WAITRESS (coming over with a bill). Yes. But the bill must be paid first.

STRANGER. What? By me? I haven't ordered anything.

WAITRESS. I know nothing of that; but you're the last of the company to have had anything.

STRANGER (to the BEGGAR). Is this all a part of the reception?

BEGGAR. Yes, certainly. And, as you know, everything costs money, even honour. . . .

STRANGER (taking a visiting card and handing it to the waitress). There's my card. You'll be paid tomorrow.

WAITRESS (putting the card in the dust-bin). Hm! I don't know the name; and I've put a lot of such cards into the dust-bin. I want the money.

BEGGAR. Listen, madam, I'll guarantee this man will pay.

WAITRESS. So you'd like to play tricks on me too! Officer! One moment, please.

POLICEMAN. What's all this about? Payment, I suppose. Come to the station; we'll arrange things there. (He writes something in his note-book.)

STRANGER. I'd rather do that than stay here and quarrel. . . . (To the BEGGAR.) I don't mind a joke, but I never expected such cruel reality as this.

BEGGAR. Anything's to be expected, once you challenge persons as powerful as you have! Let me tell you this in confidence. You'd better be prepared for worse, for the very worst!

STRANGER. To think I've been so duped . . . so . . .

BEGGAR. Feasts of Belshazzar always end in one way a hand's stretched out—and writes a bill. And another hand's laid on the guest's shoulder and leads him to the police station! But it must be done royally!

POLICEMAN (laying his hand on the STRANGER). Have you talked enough?

THE WOMEN and RAGGED ONES. The alchemist can't pay. Hurrah! He's going to gaol. He's going to gaol!

SECOND WOMAN. Yes, but it's a shame.

STRANGER. You're sorry for me? I thank you for that, even if I don't quite deserve it! *You* felt pity for me!

SECOND WOMAN. Yes. That's also something I learnt from you.

(The scene is changed without lowering the curtain. The stage is darkened, and a medley of scenes, representing landscapes, palaces, rooms, is lowered and brought forward; so that characters and furniture are no longer seen, but the STRANGER alone remains visible and seems to be standing stiffly as though unconscious. At last even he disappears, and from the confusion a prison cell emerges.)

SCENE II
PRISON CELL

[On the right a door; and above it a barred opening, through which a ray of sunlight is shining, throwing a patch of light on the left-hand wall, where a large crucifix hangs.]

[The STRANGER, dressed in a brown cloak and wearing a hat, is sitting at the table looking at the patch of sunlight. The door is opened and the BEGGAR is let in.]

BEGGAR. What are you brooding over?

STRANGER. I'm asking myself why I'm here; and then: where I was yesterday?

BEGGAR. Where do you think?

STRANGER. It seems in hell; unless I dreamed everything.

BEGGAR. Then wake up now, for this is going to be reality.

STRANGER. Let it come. I'm only afraid of ghosts.

BEGGAR (taking out a newspaper). Firstly, the great authority has withdrawn the certificate he gave you for making gold. He says, in this paper, that you deceived him. The result is that the paper calls you a charlatan!

STRANGER. O God! What is it I'm fighting?

BEGGAR. Difficulties, like other men.

STRANGER. No, this is something else. . . .

BEGGAR. Your own credulity, then.

STRANGER. No, I'm not credulous, and I know I'm right.

BEGGAR. What's the good of that, if no one else does,

STRANGER. Shall I ever get out of this prison? If I do, I'll settle everything.

BEGGAR. The matter's arranged; everything's paid for.

STRANGER. Oh? Who paid, then?

BEGGAR. The Society, I suppose; or the Drunkard's Government.

STRANGER. Then I can go?

BEGGAR. Yes. But there's one thing. . . .

STRANGER. Well, what is it?

BEGGAR. Remember, an enlightened man of the world mustn't let himself be taken by surprise.

STRANGER. I begin to divine. . . .

BEGGAR. The announcement's on the front page.

STRANGER. That means: she's already married again, and my children have a stepfather. Who is he?

BEGGAR. Whoever he is, don't murder him; for he's not to blame for taking in a forsaken woman.

STRANGER. My children! O God, my children!

BEGGAR. I notice you didn't foresee what's happened; but why not look ahead, if you're so old and such an enlightened man of the world.

STRANGER (beside himself). O God! My children!

BEGGAR. Enlightened men of the world don't weep! Stop it, my son. When such disasters happen men of the world . . . either . . . well, tell me. . . .

STRANGER. Shoot themselves!

BEGGAR. Or?

STRANGER. No, not that!

BEGGAR. Yes, my son, precisely that! He's throwing out a sheet-anchor as an experiment.

STRANGER. This is irrevocable. Irrevocable!

BEGGAR. Yes, it is. Quite irrevocable. And you can live another lifetime, in order to contemplate your own rascality in peace.

STRANGER. You should be ashamed to talk like that.

BEGGAR. And you?

STRANGER. Have you ever seen a human destiny like mine?

BEGGAR. Well, look at mine!

STRANGER. I know nothing of yours.

BEGGAR. It's never occurred to you, in all our long acquaintance, to ask about my affairs. You once scorned the friendship I offered you, and fell straightway into the arms of boon companions. I hope it'll do you good. And so farewell, till the next time.

STRANGER. Don't go.

BEGGAR. Perhaps you'd like company when you get out of prison?

STRANGER. Why not?

BEGGAR. It hasn't occurred to you I mightn't want to show myself in *your* company?

STRANGER. It certainly hasn't.

BEGGAR. But it's true. Do you think I want to be suspected of having been at that immortal banquet in the alchemist's honour, of which there's an account in the morning paper?

STRANGER. He doesn't want to be seen with me!

BEGGAR. Even a beggar has his pride and fears ridicule.

STRANGER. He doesn't want to be seen with me. Am I then sunk to such misery?

BEGGAR. You must ask yourself that, and answer it, too.

(A mournful cradle song is heard in the distance.)

STRANGER. What's that?

BEGGAR. A song sung by a mother at her baby's cradle.

STRANGER. Why must I be reminded of it just now?

BEGGAR. Probably so that you can feel really keenly what you've left for a chimera.

STRANGER. Is it possible I could have been wrong? If so it's the devil's work, and I'll lay down my arms.

BEGGAR. You'd better do that as soon as you can. . . .

STRANGER. Not yet! (A rosary can be heard being repeated in the distance.) What's that? (A sustained note of a horn is heard.) That's the unknown huntsman! (The chord from the Dead March is heard.) Where am I? (He remains where he is as if hypnotised.)

BEGGAR. Bow yourself or break!

STRANGER. I cannot bow!

BEGGAR. Then break.

(The STRANGER falls to the ground. The same confused medley of scenes as before.)

Curtain.

SCENE III
THE 'ROSE' ROOM

[The same scene as Act I. The kneeling Sisters of Mercy are now reading their prayer books, ' . . . exules filii Evae; Ad to suspiramus et flentes In hac lacrymarum aalle.' The MOTHER is by the door at the back; the FATHER by the door on the right.]

MOTHER (going towards him). So you've come back again?

FATHER (humbly). Yes.

MOTHER. Your lady-love's left you?

RATHER. Don't be more cruel than you need!

MOTHER. You say that to me, you who gave my wedding presents to your mistress. You, who were so dishonourable as to expect me, your wife, to choose presents for her. You, who wanted my advice about colour and cut, in order to educate her taste in dress! What do you want here?

FATHER. I heard that my daughter . . .

MOTHER. Your daughter's lying there, between life and death; and you know that her feelings for you have grown hostile. That's why I ask you to go; before she suspects your presence.

FATHER. You're right, and I can't answer you. But let me sit in the kitchen, for I'm tired. Very tired.

MOTHER. Where were you last night?

FATHER. At the club. But I wanted to ask you if the husband weren't here?

MOTHER. Am I to lay bare all this misery? Don't you know your daughter's tragic fate?

FATHER. Yes . . . I do. And what a husband!

MOTHER. What men! Go downstairs now and sleep off your liquor.

FATHER. The sins of the fathers. . . .

MOTHER. You're talking nonsense.

FATHER. Of course I don't mean my sins . . . but those of our parents. And now they say the lake up there's to be drained, so that the river will rise. . . .

MOTHER (pushing him out of the door). Silence. Misfortune will overtake us soon enough, without you calling it up.

MAID (from the bedroom at the back). The lady's asking for the master.

MOTHER. She means her husband.

MAID. Yes. The master of the house, her husband.

MOTHER. He went out a little while ago.

(The STRANGER comes in.)

STRANGER. Has the child been born?

MOTHER. No. Not yet.

STRANGER (putting his hand to his forehead). What? Can it take so long?

MOTHER. Long? What do you mean?

STRANGER (looking about him). I don't know what I mean. How is it with the mother?

MOTHER. She's just the same.

STRANGER. The same?

MOTHER. Don't you want to get back to your gold making?

STRANGER. I can't make head or tail of it! But there's still hope my worst dream was nothing but a dream.

MOTHER. You really look as if you were walking in your sleep.

STRANGER. Do I? Oh, I wish I were! The one thing I fear I'd fear no longer.

MOTHER. He who guides your destiny seems to know your weakest spots.

STRANGER. And when there was only one left, he found that too; happily for me only in a dream! Blind Powers! Powerless Ones!

MAID (coming in again). The lady asks you to do her a service.

STRANGER. There she lies like an electric eel, giving shocks from a distance. What kind of service is it to be now?

MAID. There's a letter in the pocket of her green coat.

STRANGER. No good will come of that! (He takes the letter out of the green coat, which is hanging near the dress by fireplace.) I must be dead. I dreamed this, and now it's happening. My children have a stepfather!

MOTHER. Who are you going to blame?

STRANGER. Myself! I'd rather blame no one. I've lost my children.

MOTHER. You'll get a new one here.

STRANGER. He might be cruel to them. . . .

MOTHER. Then their sufferings will burden your conscience, if you have one.

STRANGER. Supposing he were to beat them?

MOTHER. Do you know what I'd do in your place?

STRANGER. Yes, I know what you'd do; but I don't know what I'll do.

MOTHER (to the Sisters of Mercy). Pray for this man!

STRANGER. No, no. Not that! It'll do no good, and I don't believe in prayer.

MOTHER. But you believe in your gold?

STRANGER. Not even in that. It's over. All over!

(The MIDWIFE comes out of the bedroom.)

MIDWIFE. A child's born. Praise the Lord!

MOTHER. Let the Lord be praised!

SISTERS. Let the Lord be praised!

MIDWIFE (to the STRANGER). Your wife's given you daughter.

191

MOTHER (to the STRANGER). Don't you want to see your child?

STRANGER. No. I no longer want to tie myself anything on earth. I'm afraid I'd get to love her, and then you'd tear the heart from my body. Let me get out of this atmosphere, which is too pure for me. Don' t let that innocent child come near me, for I'm a man already damned, already sentenced, and for me there's no joy, no peace, and no . . . forgiveness!

MOTHER. My son, now you're speaking words of wisdom! Truthfully and without malice: I welcome your decision. There's no place for you here, and amongst us women you'd be plagued to death. So go in peace.

STRANGER. There'll be no more peace, but I'll go. Farewell!

MOTHER. Exules filii Evae; on earth you shall be a fugitive and a vagabond.

STRANGER. Because I have slain my brother.

Curtain.

ACT IV

SCENE I
BANQUETING HALL

[The room in which the banquet took place in Act III. It is dirty, and furnished with unpainted wooden tables. Beggars, scavengers and loose women. Cripples are seated here and there drinking by the light of tallow dips.]

[The STRANGER and the SECOND WOMAN are sitting together drinking brandy, which stands on the table in front of them in a carafe. The STRANGER is drinking heavily.]

WOMAN. Don't drink so much!

STRANGER. You see. You've scruples, too!

WOMAN. No. But I don't like to see a man I respect lowering himself so.

STRANGER. But I came here specially to do so; to take a mud-bath that would harden my skin against the pricks of life. To find immoral support about me. And I chose your company, because you're the most despicable, though you've still retained a spark of humanity. You were sorry for me, when no one else was. Not even myself! Why?

WOMAN. Really, I don't know.

STRANGER. But you must know that there are moments when you look almost beautiful.

WOMAN. Oh, listen to him!

STRANGER. Yes. And then you resemble a woman who was dear to me.

WOMAN. Thank you!

WAITRESS. Don't talk so loud, there's a sick man here.

STRANGER. Tell me, have you ever been in love?

WOMAN. We don't use that word, but I know what you mean. Yes. I had a lover once and we had a child.

STRANGER. That was foolish!

WOMAN. I thought so, too, but he said the days liberation were at hand, when all chains would he struck off, all barriers thrown down, and . . .

STRANGER (tortured). And then . . . ?

WOMAN. Then he left me.

STRANGER. He was a scoundrel. (He drinks.)

WOMAN (looking at him.) You think so?

STRANGER. Yes. He must have been.

WOMAN. Now you're so intolerant.

STRANGER (drinking). Am I?

194

WOMAN. Don't drink so much; I want to see you far above me, otherwise you can't raise me up.

STRANGER. What illusions you must have! Childish! I lift you up! I who am down below. Yet I'm not; it's not I who sit here, for I'm dead. I know that my soul's far away, far, far away. . . . (He stares in front of him with an absent-minded air) . . . where a great lake lies in the sunshine like molten gold; where roses blossom on the wall amongst the vines; where a white cot stands under the acacias. But the child's asleep and the mother's sitting beside the cot doing crochet work. There's a long, long strip coming from her mouth and on the strip is written . . . wait . . . 'Blessed are the sorrowful, for they shall be comforted.' But that's not so, really. I shall never be comforted. Tell me, isn't there thunder in the air, it's so close, so hot?

WOMAN (looking out of the window). No. I can see no clouds out there. . . .

STRANGER. Strange . . . that's lightning.

WOMAN. No. You're wrong.

STRANGER. One, two, three, four, five . . . now the thunder must come! But it doesn't. I've never been frightened of a thunderstorm until today—I mean, until tonight. But is it day or night?

WOMAN. My dear, it's night.

STRANGER. Yes. It *is* night.

(The DOCTOR has come in during this scene and has sat down behind the STRANGER, without having been seen by him.)

WAITRESS. Don't speak so loud, there's a sick person in here.

STRANGER (to the WOMAN). Give me your hand.

WOMAN (wiping it on her apron). Oh, why?

STRANGER. You've a lovely white hand. But . . . look at mine. It's black. Can't you see it's black?

WOMAN. Yes. So it is!

STRANGER. Blackened already, perhaps even rotten? I must see if my heart's stopped. (He puts his hand to his heart.) Yes. It has! So I'm dead, and I know when I died. Strange, to be dead, and yet to be going about. But where am I? Are all these people dead, too? They look as if they'd risen from the sewers of the town, or as if they'd come from prison, poorhouse or lock hospital. They're workers of the night, suffering, groaning, cursing, quarrelling, torturing one another, dishonouring one another, envying one another, as if they possessed anything worthy of envy! The fire of sleep courses through their veins, their tongues cleave to their palates, grown dry through cursing; and then they put out the blaze with water, with fire-water, that engenders fresh thirst. With fire-water, that itself burns with a blue flame and consumes the soul like a prairie fire, that leaves nothing behind it but red sand. (He drinks.) Set fire to it. Put it out again. Set fire to it. Put it out again! But what you can't burn up—unluckily—is the memory of what's past. How can that memory be burned to ashes?

WAITRESS. Please don't speak so loud, there's a sick man in here. So ill, that he's already asked to be given the sacrament.

STRANGER. May he soon go to hell!

(Those present murmur at this, resenting it.)

196

WAITRESS. Take care! Take care!

WOMAN (to the STRANGER). Do you know that man who's been sitting behind you, staring at you all the time?

STRANGER (turning. He and the DOCTOR stare at one another for a moment, without speaking). Yes. I used to know him once.

WOMAN. He looks as if he'd like to bite you in the back.

(The DOCTOR sits down opposite the STRANGER and stares at him.)

STRANGER. What are you looking at?

DOCTOR. Your grey hairs.

STRANGER (to the WOMAN). Is my hair grey?

WOMAN. Yes. Indeed it is!

DOCTOR. And now I'm looking at your fair companion. Sometimes you have good taste. Sometimes not.

STRANGER. And sometimes you have the misfortune to have the same taste as I.

DOCTOR. That wasn't a kind remark! But you've killed me twice in your lifetime; so go on.

STRANGER (to the WOMAN). Let's get away from here.

DOCTOR. You know when I'm near you. You feel my presence from afar. And I shall reach you, as the thunder will, whether you hide in the depths of the earth or of the sea. . . . Try to escape me, if you can!

197

STRANGER (to the WOMAN). Come with me. Lead me . . . I can't see. . . .

WOMAN. No, I don't want to go yet. I don't want to be bored.

DOCTOR. You're right there, daughter of joy! Life's hard enough without taking on yourself the sorrows others have brought on themselves. That man won't bear his own sorrows, but makes his wife shoulder the burden for him.

STRANGER. What's that? Wait! She bore false witness of a breach of the peace and attempted murder!

DOCTOR. Now he's putting the blame on her!

STRANGER (resting his head in his hands and letting it sink on to the table. In the far distance a violin and guitar are heard playing the following melody):

DOCTOR (to the WOMAN). Is he ill?

WOMAN. He must be mad; he says he's dead.

(In the distance drums beat the reveille and bugles are blown, but very softly.)

STRANGER. Is it morning? Night's passing, the sun's rising and ghosts lie down to sleep again in graves. Now I can go. Come!

WOMAN (going nearer to the DOCTOR). No. I said no.

STRANGER. Even you, the last of all my friends! Am I such a wretched being, that not even a prostitute will bear me company for money?

DOCTOR. You must be.

STRANGER. I don't believe it yet; although everyone tells me so. I don't believe anything at all, for every time I have, I've been deceived. But tell me this hasn't the sun yet risen? A little while ago I heard a cock crow and a dog bark; and now they're ringing the Angelus. . . . Have they put out the lights, that it's so dark?

DOCTOR (to the WOMAN). He must be blind.

WOMAN. Yes. I think he is.

STRANGER. No. I can see you; but I can't see the lights.

DOCTOR. For you it's growing dark. . . . You've played with the lightning, and looked too long at the sun. That is forbidden to men.

STRANGER. We're born with the desire to do it; but may not. That's Envy. . . .

DOCTOR. What do you possess that's worthy of envy?

STRANGER. Something you'll never understand, and that only I can value.

DOCTOR. You mean, the child?

MANGER. You know I didn't mean it. If I had I'd have said that I possessed something you could never let.

DOCTOR. So you're back at that! Then I'll express myself as clearly: you took what I'd done with.

WOMAN. Oh! I shan't stay in the company of such swine! (She gets up and moves to another seat.)

STRANGER. I know we've sunk very low; yet I believe the deeper I sink the nearer I'll come to my goal: the end!

WAITRESS. Don't speak so loud, there's a dying man in there!

STRANGER. Yes, I believe you. The whole time there's been a smell of corpses here.

DOCTOR. Perhaps that's us?

STRANGER. Can one be dead, without suspecting it?

DOCTOR. The dead maintain that they don't know the difference.

STRANGER. You terrify me. Is it possible? And all these shadowy figures, whose faces I think I recognise as memories of my youth at school in the swimming bath, the gymnasium. . . . (He clutches his heart.) Oh! Now he's coming: the Terrible One, who tears the heart out of the breast. The Terrible One, who's been following me for years. He's here!

(He is beside himself. The doors are thrown open; a choir boy comes in carrying a lantern made of blue glass that throws a blue light on the guests; he rings the silver bell. All present begin to howl like wild beasts. The DOMINICAN then enters with the sacrament. The WAITRESS and the WOMAN throw themselves on their knees, the others howl. The DOMINICAN raises the monstrance; all fall on their knees. The choir boy and the DOMINICAN go into the room on the left.)

BEGGAR (entering and going towards the STRANGER). Come away from here. You're ill. And the bailiffs have a summons for you.

STRANGER. Summons? From whom?

BEGGAR. Your wife.

DOCTOR. The electric eel strikes at a great distance. She once wanted to bring a charge of slander against me, because she couldn't stay out at night.

STRANGER. Couldn't stay out at night?

DOCTOR. Yes. Didn't you know who you were married to?

STRANGER. I heard she'd been engaged before she . . . married you.

DOCTOR. Yes. That's what it was called, but in reality she'd been the mistress of a married man, whom she denounced for rape, after she'd forced herself into his studio and posed to him naked, as a model.

STRANGER. And that was the woman you married?

DOCTOR. Yes. After she'd seduced me, she denounced me for breach of promise, so I had to marry her. She'd engaged two detectives to see I didn't get away. And that was the woman you married!

STRANGER. I did it because I soon saw it was no good choosing when all were alike.

BEGGAR. Come away from here. You'll be sorry if you don't.

STRANGER (to the DOCTOR). Was she always religious?

DOCTOR. Always.

STRANGER. And tender, good-hearted, self-sacrificing?

DOCTOR. Certainly!

STRANGER. Can one understand her?

DOCTOR. No. But you can go mad thinking about her. That's why one had to accept her as she was. Charming, intoxicating!

STRANGER. Yes, I know. But one's powerless against pity. That's why I don't want to fight this case. I can't defend myself without attacking her; and I don't want to do that.

DOCTOR. You were married before. How was that?

STRANGER. Just the same.

DOCTOR. This love acts like henbane: you see suns, where there are none, and stars where no stars are! But it's pleasant, while it lasts!

STRANGER. And the morning after? Oh, the morning after!

BEGGAR. Come, unhappy man! He's poisoning you, and you don't know it. Come!

STRANGER (getting up). Poisoning me, you say? Do you think he's lying?

BEGGAR. Every word he's said's a lie.

STRANGER. I don't believe it.

BEGGAR. No. You only believe lies. But that serves you right.

STRANGER. Has he been lying? Has he?

BEGGAR. How can you believe your enemies?

STRANGER. But he's my friend, because he's told me the bitter truth.

BEGGAR. Eternal Powers, save his reason! For he believes everything evil's true, and everything good evil. Come, or you'll be lost!

DOCTOR. He's lost already! And now he'll be whipped into froth, broken up into atoms, and used as an ingredient in the great pan-cake. Away with you hell! (To those present.) Howl like victims of the pit. (The guests all howl.) And no more womanly pity. Howl, woman! (The WOMAN refuses with a gesture of her hand.)

STRANGER (to the BEGGAR). That man's not lying.

Curtain.

SCENE II
IN A RAVINE

[A ravine with a stream in the middle, which is crossed by a foot-bridge. In the foreground a smithy and a mill, both of which are in ruins. Fallen trees choke the stream. In the background a starry sky above the pine wood. The constellation of Orion is clearly visible.]

[The STRANGER and the BEGGAR enter. In the foreground there is snow; in the background the green of summer.]

STRANGER. I feel afraid! Tonight the stars seem to hang so low, that I fear they'll fall on me like drops of molten silver. Where are we?

BEGGAR. In the ravine, by the stream. You must know the place.

STRANGER. Know it? As if I could ever forget it! It reminds me of my honeymoon journey. But where are the smithy and the mill?

BEGGAR. All in ruins! The lake of tears was drained a week ago. The stream rose, then the river, till everything was laid waste—meadows, fields and gardens.

STRANGER. And the quiet house?

BEGGAR. The old sin was washed away, but the walls in left.

STRANGER. And those who lived there?

BEGGAR. They've gone to the colonies; so that the story's now at an end.

STRANGER. Then my story's at an end too. So thoroughly at an end, that no happy memories remain. The last was fouled by the poisoner. . . .

BEGGAR. Whose poison you prepared! You should declare your bankruptcy.

STRANGER. Yes. Now I'll have to give in.

BEGGAR. Then the day of reckoning will draw near.

STRANGER. I think we might call it quits; because, if I've sinned, I've been punished.

BEGGAR. But others certainly won't think so.

STRANGER. I've stopped taking account of others, since I saw that the Powers that guide the destinies of mankind brook no accomplices. The crime I committed in this life was that I wanted to set men free. . . .

BEGGAR. Set men free from their duties, and criminals from their feeling of guilt, so that they could really become unscrupulous! You're not the first, and not the 1ast to dabble in the Devil's work. Lucifer a non lucendo! But when Reynard grows old, he turns monk—so wisely is it ordained—and then he's forced to split himself in n two and drive out Beelzebub with his own penance.

STRANGER. Shall I be driven to that?

BEGGAR. Yes. Though you don't want it! You'll be forced to preach against yourself from the housetops. To unpick your fabric thread by thread. To flay yourself alive at every street corner, and show what you really are. But that needs courage. All the same, a man who's played with the thunder will not tremble! Yet, sometimes, when night falls and the Invisible Ones, who can only be seen in darkness, ride on his chest, then he will fear—even the stars, and most of all the Mill of Sins, that grinds the past, and grinds it . . . and grinds it! One of the seven-and-seventeen Wise Men said that the greatest victory he ever won was over himself; but foolish men don't believe it, and that's why they're deceived; because they only credit what nine-and-ninety fools have said a thousand times.

STRANGER. Enough! Tell me; isn't this snow here on the ground?

BEGGAR. Yes. It's winter here.

STRANGER. But over there it's green.

BEGGAR. It's summer there.

STRANGER. And growing light! (A clear beam of light falls on the foot-bridge.)

BEGGAR. Yes. It's light there, and dark here.

STRANGER. And who are they? (Three children, dressed is summer clothing, two girls and a boy, come on to the bridge from the right.) Ho! My children! (The children stop to listen, and then look at the STRANGER without seeming to recognise him. The STRANGER calls.) Gerda! Erik! Thyra! It's your father! (The children appear to recognise him; they turn away to the left.) They don't know me. They don't want to know me.

(A man and a woman enter from the right. The children dance of to the left and disappear. The STRANGER falls on his face on the ground.)

BEGGAR. Something like that was to be expected. Such things happen. Get up again!

STRANGER (raising himself up). Where am I? Where have I been? Is it spring, winter or summer? In what century am I living, in what hemisphere? Am I a child or an old man, male or female, a god or a devil? And who are you? Are you, you; or are you me? Are those my own entrails that I see about me? Are those stars or bundles of nerves in my eye; is that water, or is it tears? Wait! Now I'm moving forward in time for a thousand years, and beginning to shrink, to grow heavier and to crystallise! Soon I'll be re-created, and from the dark waters of Chaos the Lotus flower will stretch up her head towards the sun and say: it is I! I must have been sleeping for a few thousand years; and have dreamed I'd exploded and become ether, and could no longer feel, no longer suffer, no longer be joyful; but had entered into peace and equilibrium. But now! Now! I suffer as much as if I were all mankind. I suffer and have no right to complain. . . .

BEGGAR. Then suffer, and the more you suffer the earlier pain will leave you.

STRANGER. No. Mine are eternal sufferings. . . .

BEGGAR. And only a minute's passed.

STRANGER. I can't bear it.

BEGGAR. Then you must look for help.

STRANGER. What's coming now? Isn't it the end yet?

(It grows light above the bridge. CAESAR comes in and throws himself from the parapet; then the DOCTOR appears on the right, with bare head and a wild look. He behaves as if he would throw himself into the stream too.)

STRANGER. He's revenged himself so thoroughly, that he awakes no qualms of conscience! (The DOCTOR goes out, left. The SISTER enters, right, as if searching for someone.) Who's that?

BEGGAR. His unmarried sister, who's unprovided for, and has now no home to go to. She's grown desperate since her brother was driven out of his wits by sorrow and went to pieces.

STRANGER. That's a harder fate. Poor creature, what can one do? Even if I felt her sufferings, would that help her?

BEGGAR. No. It wouldn't.

STRANGER. Why do qualms of conscience come after, and not beforehand? Can you help me over that?

BEGGAR. No. No one can. Let us go on.

STRANGER. Where to?

BEGGAR. Come with me.

Curtain.

SCENE III
THE 'ROSE' ROOM

[The LADY, dressed in white, is sitting by the cradle doing crochet work. The green dress is hanging up by the door on the right. The STRANGER comes an, and looks round in astonishment.]

LADY (simply, mildly, without a trace of surprise). Tread softly and come here, if you'd see something lovely.

STRANGER. Where am I?

LADY. Quiet! Look at the little stranger who came when you were away.

STRANGER. They told me the river had risen and swept everything off.

LADY. Why do you believe everything you're told? The river did rise, but this little creature has someone who protects both her and hers. Wouldn't you like to see your daughter? (The STRANGER goes towards the cradle. The LADY lifts the curtain.) She's lovely! Isn't she? (The STRANGER gazes darkly in front of him.) Won't you look?

STRANGER. Everything's poisoned. Everything!

LADY. Well, perhaps!

STRANGER. Do you know that he has lost his wits and is wandering in the neighbourhood, followed by his sister, who's searching for him? He's penniless, and drinking. . . .

LADY. Oh, my God!

STRANGER. Why don't you reproach me?

LADY. You'll reproach yourself enough: I'd rather give you good advice. Go to the Convent of St. Saviour's, there you'll find a man who can free you from the evil you fear.

STRANGER. What, in the convent, where they curse and bind?

LADY. And deliver also!

STRANGER. Frankly, I think you're trying to deceive me; I don't trust you any more.

LADY. Nor I, you! So look on this as your farewell visit.

STRANGER. That was my intention; but first I wanted to find out if we're of the same mind. . . .

LADY. You see, we can build no happiness on the sorrows of others; so we must part. That's the only way to lessen his sufferings. I have my child, who'll fill my life for me; and you have the great goal of your ambition. . . .

STRANGER. Will you still mock me?

LADY. No, why? You've solved the great problem.

STRANGER. Be quiet! No more of that, even if you believe it.

LADY. But if all the rest believe it too. . . .

STRANGER. No one believes it now.

LADY. It says in the paper today that gold's been made in England. That it's been proved possible.

STRANGER. You've been deceived.

LADY. No! Oh, heaven, he won't believe his own good fortune.

STRANGER. I no longer believe anything.

LADY. Get the newspaper from the pocket of my dress over there.

STRANGER. The green witch's dress, that laid a spell on me one Sunday afternoon, between the inn and the church door! That'll bring no good.

LADY (fetching the paper herself and also a large parcel that is in the pocket of the dress). See for yourself.

STRANGER (tearing up the paper). No need for me to look!

LADY. He won't believe it. He won't. Yet the chemists want to give a banquet in your honour next Saturday.

STRANGER. Is that in the paper too? About the banquet?

LADY (handing him the packet). And here's the diploma of honour. Read it!

STRANGER (tearing up the packet). Perhaps there's a Government Order too!

LADY. Those whom the gods would destroy they first make blind! You made your discovery with no good intentions, and therefore you weren't permitted to be the only one to succeed.

STRANGER. Now I shall go. For I won't stay here and lay bare my shame! I've become a laughing-stock, so I'll go and hide myself—bury myself alive, because I don't dare to die.

LADY. Then go! We start for the colonies in a few days.

STRANGER. That's frank at least! Perhaps we're nearing a solution.

LADY. Of the riddle: why we had to meet?

STRANGER. Why did we have to?

LADY. To torture one another.

STRANGER. Is that all?

LADY. You thought you could save me from a werewolf, who really was no such thing, and so you become one yourself. And then I was to save you from evil by taking all the evil in you on myself, and I did so; but the result was that you only became more evil. My poor deliverer! Now you're bound hand and foot and no magician can set you free.

STRANGER. Farewell, and thank you for all you've done.

LADY. Farewell, and thank you . . . for this! (She points to the cradle.)

STRANGER (going towards the back). First perhaps I ought to take my leave in there.

LADY. Yes, my dear. Do!

(The STRANGER goes out through the door at the back. The LADY crosses to the door on the right and lets in the DOMINICAN—who is also the BEGGAR.)

CONFESSOR. Is he ready now?

LADY. Nothing remains for this unhappy man but to leave the world and bury himself in a monastery.

CONFESSOR. So he doesn't believe he's the great inventor he undoubtedly is?

LADY. No. He can believe good of no one, not even of himself.

CONFESSOR. That is the punishment Heaven sent him: to believe lies, because he wouldn't listen to the truth.

LADY. Lighten his guilty burden for him, if you can.

CONFESSOR. No. If I did he'd only grow insolent and accuse God of malice and injustice. This man is a demon, who must be kept confined. He belongs to the dangerous race of rebels; he'd misuse his gifts, if he could, to do evil. And men's power for evil is immeasurable.

LADY. For the sake of the . . . attachment you've shown me, can't you ease his burden a little; where it presses on him most and where he's least to blame?

CONFESSOR. You must do that, not I; so that he can leave you in the belief that you've a good side, and that you're not what your first husband told him you were. If he believes you, I'll deliver him later, just as I once bound him when he confessed to me, during his illness, in the convent of St. Saviour's.

LADY (going to the back and opening the door). As you wish!

STRANGER (re-entering). So there's the Terrible One! How did he come here? But isn't he the beggar, after all?

CONFESSOR. Yes, I am your terrible friend, and I've come for you.

212

STRANGER. What? Have I . . . ?

CONFESSOR. Yes. Once already you promised me your soul, on oath, when you lay ill and felt near madness. It was then you offered to serve the powers of good; but when you got well again you broke your oath, and therefore were plagued with unrest, and wandered abroad unable to find peace—tortured by your own conscience.

STRANGER. Who are you really? Who dares lay a hand on my destiny?

CONFESSOR. You must ask her that.

LADY. This is the man to whom I was first engaged, and who dedicated his life to the service of God, when I left him.

STRANGER. Even if he were!

LADY. So you needn't think so ill of yourself because it was you who punished my faithlessness and another's lack of conscience.

STRANGER. His sin cannot justify mine. Of course it's untrue, like everything else; and you only say it to console me.

CONFESSOR. What an unhappy soul he is. . . .

STRANGER. A damned one too!

CONFESSOR. No! (To the LADY.) Say something good of him.

LADY. He won't believe it, if I do; he only believes evil!

CONFESSOR. Then I shall have to say it. A beggar once came and asked him for a drink of water; but he gave me wine instead and let me sit at his table. You remember that?

213

STRANGER. No. I don't load my memory with such trifles.

CONFESSOR. Pride! Pride!

STRANGER. Call it pride, if you like. It's the last vestige of our god-like origin. Let's go, before it grows dark.

CONFESSOR. 'For the whole world shined with clear light and none were hindered in their labour. Over these only was spread a heavy night, an image of darkness which should afterward receive them; but yet were they unto themselves more grievous than the darkness.'

LADY. Don't hurt him!

STRANGER (with passion). How beautifully she can speak, though she is evil. Look at her eyes; they cannot weep tears, but they can flatter, sting, or lie! And yet she says: Don't hurt him! See, now she fears I'll wake her child, the little monster that robbed me of her! Come, priest, before I change my mind.

Curtain.

PART III.

CHARACTERS

THE STRANGER
THE LADY
THE CONFESSOR
THE MAGISTRATE
THE PRIOR
THE TEMPTER
THE DAUGHTER

less important figures
HOSTESS
FIRST VOICE
SECOND VOICE
WORSHIPPERS OF VENUS
MAIA
PILGRIM
FATHER
WOMAN
EVE
PRIOR
PATER ISIDOR (the Doctor of Part I)
PATER CLEMENS
PATER MELCHER

SCENES

ACT I

ON THE RIVER BANK

[The foreground represents the bank of a large river. On the right a projecting tongue of land covered with old willow trees. Farther up stage the river can be seen flowing quietly past. The background represents the farther bank, a steep mountain slope covered with woodland. Above the tops of the forest trees the Monastery can be seen; it is an enormous four-cornered building completely white, with two rows of small windows. The façade is broken by the Church belonging to the Monastery, which is flanked by two towers in the style favoured by the Jesuits. The Church door is open, and at a certain moment the monstrance on the altar is visible in the light of the sun. On the near bank in the foreground, which is low and sandy, purple and yellow loose-strife are growing. A shallow boat is moored nearby. On the left the ferryman's hut. It is an evening in early summer and the sun is low; foreground, river and the lower part of the background lie in shadow; and the trees on the far bank sway gently in the breeze. Only the Monastery is lit by the sun.]

[The STRANGER and the CONFESSOR enter from the right. The STRANGER is wearing alpine clothing: a brown cloak with a cape and hood; he has a staff and wallet. He is limping slightly. The CONFESSOR is to the black and white habit of the Dominicans. They stop at a place where a willow tree prevents any view of the Monastery.]

217

STRANGER. Why do you lead me along this winding, hilly path, that never comes to an end?

CONFESSOR. Such is the way, my friend. But now we'll soon be there. (He leads the STRANGER farther up stage. The STRANGER sees the Monastery, and is enchanted by it; he takes off his hat, and puts down his wallet and staff.) Well?

STRANGER. I've never seen anything so white on this polluted earth. At most, only in my dreams! Yes, that's my youthful dream of a house in which peace and purity should dwell. A blessing on you, white house! Now I've come home!

CONFESSOR. Good! But first we must await the pilgrims on this bank. It's called the bank of farewell, because it's the custom to say farewell here, before the ferryman ferries one across.

STRANGER. Haven't I said enough farewells already? Wasn't my whole life one thorny path of farewells? At post offices, steamer-quays, railway stations—with the waving of handkerchiefs damp with tears?

CONFESSOR. Yet your voice trembles with the pain what you've lost.

STRANGER. I don't feel I've lost anything. I don't want anything back.

CONFESSOR. Not even your youth?

STRANGER. That least of all. What should I do with it, and its capacity for suffering?

CONFESSOR. And for enjoyment?

STRANGER. I never enjoyed anything, for I was born with a thorn in my flesh; every time I stretched out my hand to grasp a pleasure, I pricked my finger and Satan struck me in the face.

CONFESSOR. Because your pleasures have been base ones.

STRANGER. Not so base. I had my own home, a wife, children, duties, obligations to others! No, I was born in disfavour, a step-child of life; and I was pursued, hunted, in a word, cursed!

CONFESSOR. Because you didn't obey God's commandment.

STRANGER. But no one can, as St. Paul says himself! Why should I be able to do what no one else can do? I of all men? Because I'm supposed to be a scoundrel. Because more's demanded of me than of others. . . . (Crying out.) Because I was treated with injustice.

CONFESSOR. Have you got back to that, rebellious one?

STRANGER. Yes. I've always been there. Now let's cross the river.

CONFESSOR. Do you think one can climb up to that white house without preparation?

STRANGER. I'm ready: you can examine me.

CONFESSOR. Good! The first monastic vow is: humility.

STRANGER. And the second: obedience! Neither of them was ever a special virtue of mine; it's for that very reason that I want to make the great attempt.

CONFESSOR. And show your pride through your humility.

STRANGER. Whatever it is, it's all the same to me.

CONFESSOR. What, everything? The world and its best gifts; the joy of innocent children, the pleasant warmth of home, the approbation of your fellow-men, the satisfaction brought by the fulfilment of duty—are you indifferent to them all?

STRANGER. Yes! Because I was born without the power of enjoyment. There have been moments when I've been an object of envy; but I've never understood what it was I was envied for: my sufferings in misfortune, my lack of peace in success, or the fact I hadn't long to live.

CONFESSOR. It's true that life has given you everything you wished; even a little gold at the last. Why, I even seem to remember that a sculptor was commissioned to make a portrait bust of you.

STRANGER. Oh yes! A bust was made of me.

CONFESSOR. Are you, of all men, impressed by such things?

STRANGER. Of course not! But they do at least mark well founded appreciation, that neither envy nor lack of understanding can shake.

CONFESSOR. You think so? It seems to me that human greatness resides in the good opinion of others; and that, if this opinion changes, the greatest can quickly dwindle into nothing.

STRANGER. The opinions of others have never meant much to me.

CONFESSOR. Haven't they? Really?

STRANGER. No one's been so strict with himself as I! And no one's been so humble! All have demanded my respect; whilst they spurned me and spat on me. And when at last I found I'd duties towards the immortal soul given into my keeping, I began to demand respect for this immortal soul. Then I was branded as the proudest of the proud! And by whom? By the proudest of all amongst the humble and lowly.

CONFESSOR. I think you're entangling yourself in contradictions.

STRANGER. I think so, too! For the whole of life consists of nothing but contradictions. The rich are the poor in spirit; the many little men hold the power, and the great only serve the little men. I've never met such proud people as the humble; I've never met an uneducated man who didn't believe himself in a position to criticise learning and to do without it. I've found the unpleasantest of deadly sins amongst the Saints: I mean self-complacency. In my youth I was a saint myself; but I've never been so worthless as I was then. The better I thought myself, the worse I became.

CONFESSOR. Then what do you seek here?

STRANGER. What I've told you already; but I'll add this: I'm seeking death without the need to die!

CONFESSOR. The mortification of your flesh, of your old self! Good! Now keep still: the pilgrims are coming on their wooden rafts to celebrate the festival of Corpus Christi.

STRANGER (looking to the right in surprise). Who are they?

CONFESSOR. People who believe in something.

STRANGER. Then help my unbelief! (Sunlight now falls on the monstrance in the church above, so that it shines like a window pane at sunset.) Has the sun entered the church, or. . . .

CONFESSOR. Yes. The sun has entered. . . .

(The first raft comes in from the right. Children clothed in white, with garlands on their heads and with lighted lanterns in their hands, are seen standing round an altar decked with flowers, on which a white flag with a golden lily has been planted. They sing, whilst the raft glides slowly by.)

Blessèd be he, who fears the Lord,
Beati omnes, qui timent Dominum,
And walks in his ways,
Qui ambulant in viis ejus.
Thou shalt feed thyself with the work of thy hands,
Labores manuum tuarum quia manducabis;
Blessèd be thou and peace be with thee,
Beatus es et bene tibi erit.

(A second raft appears with boys on one side and girls on the other. It has a flag with a rose on it.)

Thy wife shall be like a fruitful vine,
Uxor tua sicut vitis abundans,
Within thy house,
In lateribus domus tuae.

(The third raft carries men and women. There is a flag with fruit upon it: figs, grapes, pomegranates, melons, ears of wheat, etc.)

Filii tui sicut novellae olivarum,
Thy children shall be like olive branches about thy table,
In circuitu mensae tuae.

(The fourth raft is filled with older men and women. The flag has a representation of a fir-tree under snow.)

222

See, how blessèd is the man,
Ecce sic benedicetur homo,
Who feareth the Lord,
Qui timet Dominum!

(The raft glides by.)

STRANGER. What were they singing?

CONFESSOR. A pilgrim's song.

STRANGER. Who wrote it?

CONFESSOR. A royal person.

STRANGER. Here? What was his name? Has he written anything else?

CONFESSOR. About fifty songs; he was called David, the son of Isaiah! But he didn't always write psalms. When he was young, he did other things. Yes. Such things will happen!

STRANGER. Can we go on now?

CONFESSOR. In a moment. I've something to say to you first.

STRANGER. Speak.

CONFESSOR. Good. But don't be either sad or angry.

STRANGER. Certainly not.

CONFESSOR. Here, you see, on this bank, you're a well-known—let's say famous—person; but over there, on the other, you'll be quite unknown to the brothers. Nothing more, in fact, than an ordinary simple man.

STRANGER. Oh! Don't they read in the monastery?

CONFESSOR. Nothing light; only serious books.

STRANGER. They take in papers, I suppose?

CONFESSOR. Not the kind that write about you!

STRANGER. Then on the other side of this river my life-work doesn't exist?

CONFESSOR. What work?

STRANGER. I see. Very well. Can't we cross now?

CONFESSOR. In a minute. Is there no one you'd like to take leave of?

STRANGER (after a pause.) Yes. But it's beyond the bounds of possibility.

CONFESSOR. Have you ever seen anything impossible?

STRANGER. Not really, since I've seen my own destiny.

CONFESSOR. Well, who is it you'd like to meet?

STRANGER. I had a daughter once; I called her Sylvia, because she sang all day long like a wren. It's some years since I saw her; she must be a girl of sixteen now. But I'm afraid if I were to meet her, life would regain its value for me.

CONFESSOR. You fear nothing else?

STRANGER. What do you mean?

CONFESSOR. That she may have changed!

STRANGER. She could only have changed for the better.

CONFESSOR. Are you sure?

STRANGER. Yes.

CONFESSOR. She'll come to you. (He goes down to the bank and beckons to the right.)

STRANGER. Wait! I'm wondering whether it's wise!

CONFESSOR. It can do no harm.

(He beckons once more. A boat appears on the river, rowed by a young girl. She is wearing summer clothing, her head is bare and her fair hair is hanging loose. She gets out of the boat behind the willow tree. The CONFESSOR draws back until he is near the ferryman's hut, but remains in sight of the audience. The STRANGER has waved to the girl and she has answered him. She now comes on to the stage, runs into the STRANGER'S arms, and kisses him.)

DAUGHTER. Father. My dear father!

STRANGER. Sylvia! My child!

DAUGHTER. How in the world do you come to be up here in the mountains?

STRANGER. And how have *you* got here? I thought I'd managed to hide so well.

DAUGHTER. Why did you want to hide?

STRANGER. Ask me as little as possible! You've grown into a big girl. And I've gone grey.

DAUGHTER. No. You're not grey. You're just as young as you were when we parted.

STRANGER. When we . . . parted!

DAUGHTER. When you left us. . . . (The STRANGER does not reply.) Aren't you glad we're meeting again?

STRANGER (faintly). Yes!

DAUGHTER. Then show it.

STRANGER. How can I be glad, when we're parting today for life?

DAUGHTER. Why, where do you want to go?

STRANGER (pointing to the monastery). Up there!

DAUGHTER (with a sophisticated air). Into the monastery? Yes, now I come to think of it, perhaps it's best.

STRANGER. You think so?

DAUGHTER (with pity, but good-will.) I mean, if you've a ruined life behind you. . . . (Coaxingly.) Now you look sad. Tell me one thing.

STRANGER. Tell *me* one thing, my child, that's been worrying me more than anything else. You've a stepfather?

DAUGHTER. Yes.

STRANGER. Well?

226

DAUGHTER. He's very good and kind.

STRANGER. With every virtue that I lack. . . .

DAUGHTER. Aren't you glad we've got into better hands?

STRANGER. Good, better, best! Why do you come here bare-headed?

DAUGHTER. Because George is carrying my hat.

STRANGER. Who's George? And where is he?

DAUGHTER. George is a friend of mine; and he's waiting for me on the bank down below.

STRANGER. Are you engaged to him?

DAUGHTER. No. Certainly not!

STRANGER. Do you want to marry?

DAUGHTER. Never!

STRANGER. I can see it by your mottled cheeks, like those of a child that has got up too early; I can hear it by your voice, that's no longer that of a warbler, but a jay; I can feel it in your kisses, that burn cold like the sun in May; and by your steady icy look that tells me you're nursing a secret of which you're ashamed, but of which you'd like to boast. And your brothers and sisters?

DAUGHTER. They're quite well, thank you.

STRANGER. Have we anything else to say to one another?

DAUGHTER (coldly). Perhaps not.

STRANGER. Now you look so like your mother.

DAUGHTER. How do you know, when you've never been able to see her as she was!

STRANGER. So you understood that, though you were so young?

DAUGHTER. I learnt to understand it from you. If only you'd understand yourself.

STRANGER. Have you anything else to teach me?

DAUGHTER. Perhaps! But in your day that wasn't considered seemly.

STRANGER. My day's over and exists no longer; just as Sylvia exists no longer, but is merely a name, a memory. (He takes a guide-book out of his pocket.) Look at this guide-book! Can you see small marks made here by tiny fingers, and others by little damp lips? You made them when you were five years old; you were sitting on my knee in the train, and we saw the Alps for the first time. You thought what you saw was Heaven; and when I explained that the mountain was the Jungfrau, you asked if you could kiss the name in the book.

DAUGHTER. I don't remember that!

STRANGER. Delightful memories pass, but hateful ones remain! Don't you remember anything about me?

DAUGHTER. Oh yes.

STRANGER. Quiet! I know what you mean. One night . . . one dreadful, horrible night . . . Sylvia, my child, when I shut my eyes I see a pale little angel, who slept in my arms when she was ill; and who thanked me when I gave her a present. Where is she whom I long for so and who exists no more, although she isn't dead? You, as you are, seem a stranger, whom I've never known and certainly don't long to see again. If Sylvia at least were dead and lay in her grave, there'd be a churchyard where I could take my flowers. . . . How strange it is! She's neither among the living, nor the dead. Perhaps she never existed, and was only a dream like everything else.

DAUGHTER (wheedling).Father, dear!

STRANGER. It's she! No, only her voice. (Pause.) So you think my life's been ruined?

DAUGHTER. Yes. But why speak of it now?

STRANGER. Because remember I once saved *your* life. You had brain fever for a whole month and suffered a great deal. Your mother wanted the doctor to deliver you from your unhappy existence by some powerful drug. But I prevented it, and so saved you from death and your mother from prison.

DAUGHTER. I don't believe it!

STRANGER. But a fact may be true, even if you don't believe it.

DAUGHTER. You dreamed it.

STRANGER. Who knows if I haven't dreamed everything, and am not even dreaming now. How I wish it were so!

DAUGHTER. I must be going, father.

STRANGER. Then good-bye!

DAUGHTER. May I write to you?

STRANGER. What? One of the dead write to another? Letters won't reach me in future. And I mayn't receive visitors. But I'm glad we've met, for now there's nothing else on earth I cling to. (Going to the left.) Good-bye, girl or woman, whatever I should call you. There's no need to weep!

DAUGHTER. I wasn't thinking of weeping, though I dare say good breeding would demand I should. Well, good-bye! (She goes out right.)

STRANGER (to the CONFESSOR). I think I came out of that well! It's a mercy to part with content on both sides. Mankind, after all, makes rapid progress, and self-control increases as the flow of the tear-ducts lessens. I've seen so many tears shed in my lifetime, that I'm almost taken aback at this dryness. She was a strong child, just the kind I once wished to be. The most beautiful thing that life can offer! She lay, like an angel, wrapped in the white veils of her cradle, with a blue coverlet when she slept. Blue and arched like the sky. That was the best: what will the worst look like?

CONFESSOR. Don't excite yourself, but be of good cheer. First throw away that foolish guide-book, for this is your last journey.

STRANGER. You mean this? Very well. (He opens the book, kisses one of the pages and then throws it into the river.) Anything else?

CONFESSOR. If you've any gold or silver, you must give it to the poor.

STRANGER. I've a silver watch. I never got as far as a gold one.

CONFESSOR. Give that to the ferryman; and then you'll get a glass of wine.

STRANGER. The last! It's like an execution! Perhaps I'll have to have my hair cut, too?

CONFESSOR. Yes. Later. (He takes the watch and goes to the door of the ferryman's hut, speaking a few whispered words to someone within. He receives a bottle of wine and a glass in exchange, which he puts on the table.)

STRANGER (filling his glass, but not drinking it.) Shall I never get wine up there?

CONFESSOR. No wine; and you'll see no women. You may hear singing; but not the kind of songs that go with women and wine.

STRANGER. I've had enough of women; they can't tempt me any more.

CONFESSOR. Are you sure?

STRANGER. Quite sure. . . . But tell me this: what do you think of women, who mayn't even set their feet within your consecrated walls?

CONFESSOR. So you're still asking questions?

STRANGER. And why may an abbess never hear confession, never read mass, and never preach?

CONFESSOR. I can't answer that.

STRANGER. Because the answer would accord with my thoughts on that theme.

CONFESSOR. It wouldn't be a disaster if we were to agree for once.

STRANGER. Not at all!

CONFESSOR. Now drink up your wine.

STRANGER. No. I only want to look at it for the last time. It's beautiful. . . .

CONFESSOR. Don't lose yourself in meditation; memories lie at the bottom of the cup.

STRANGER. And oblivion, and songs, and power—imaginary power, but for that reason all the greater.

CONFESSOR. Wait here a moment; I'll go and order the ferry.

STRANGER. 'Sh! I can hear singing, and I can see. . . . I can see. . . . For a moment I saw a flag unfurling in a puff of wind, only to fall back on the flagstaff and hang there limply as if it were nothing but a dishcloth. I've witnessed my whole life flashing past in a second, with its joys and sorrows, its beauty and its misery! But now I can see nothing.

CONFESSOR (going to the left). Wait here a moment, I'll go and order the ferry.

(The STRANGER goes so far up stage that the rays of the setting sun, which are streaming from the right through the trees, throw his shadow across the bank and the river. The LADY enters from the right, in deep mourning. Her shadow slowly approaches that of the STRANGER.)

STRANGER (who, to begin with, looks only at his own shadow). Ah! The sun! It makes me a bloodless shape, a giant, who can walk on the water of the river, climb the mountain, stride over the roof of the monastery church, and rise, as he does now, up into the firmament—up to the stars.

Ah, now I'm up here with the stars. . . . (He notices the shadow thrown by the LADY.) But who's following me? Who's interrupting my ascension? Trying to climb on my shoulders? (Turning.) You!

LADY. Yes. I!

STRANGER. So black! So black and so evil.

LADY. No longer evil. I'm in mourning. . . .

STRANGER. For whom?

LADY. For our Mizzi.

STRANGER. My daughter! (The LADY opens her arms, in order to throw herself on to his breast, but he avoids her.) I congratulate the dead child. I'm sorry for you. I myself feel outside everything.

LADY. Comfort me, too.

STRANGER. A fine idea! I'm to comfort my fury, weep with my hangman, amuse my tormentor.

LADY. Have you no feelings?

STRANGER. None! I wasted the feelings I used to have on you and others.

LADY. You're right. You can reproach me.

STRANGER. I've neither the time nor the wish to do that. Where are you going?

LADY. I want to cross with the ferry.

233

STRANGER. Then I've no luck, for I wanted to do the same. (The LADY weeps into her handkerchief. The STRANGER takes it from her and dries her eyes.) Dry your eyes, child, and be yourself! As hard, and lacking in feeling, as you really are! (The LADY tries to put her arm round his neck. The STRANGER taps her gently on the fingers.) You mustn't touch me. When your words and glances weren't enough, you always wanted to touch me. You'll excuse a rather trivial question: are you hungry?

LADY. No. Thank you.

STRANGER. But you're tired. Sit down. (The LADY sits down at the table. The STRANGER throws the bottle and glass into the river.) Well, what are you going to live for now?

LADY (sadly). I don't know.

STRANGER. Where will you go?

LADY (sobbing). I don't know.

STRANGER. So you're in despair? You see no reason for living and no end to your misery! How like me you are! What a pity there's no monastery for both sexes, so that we could pair off together. Is the werewolf still alive?

LADY. You mean . . . ?

STRANGER. Your first husband.

LADY. He never seems to die.

STRANGER. Like a certain worm! (Pause.) And now that we're so far from the world and its pettiness, tell me this: why did you leave him in those days, and come to me?

234

LADY. Because I loved you.

STRANGER. And how long did that last?

LADY. Until I read your book, and the child was born.

STRANGER. And then?

LADY. I hated you! That is, I wanted to be rid of all the evil you'd given me, but I couldn't.

STRANGER. So that's how it was! But we'll never really know the truth.

LADY. Have you noticed how impossible it is to find things out? You can live with a person and their relations for twenty years, and yet not know anything about them.

STRANGER. So you've discovered that? As you see so much, tell me this: how was it you came to love me?

LADY. I don't know; but I'll try to remember. (Pause.) Well, you had the masculine courage to be rude to a lady. In me you sought the companionship of a human being and not merely of a woman. That honoured me; and, I thought, you too.

STRANGER. Tell me also whether you held me to be a misogynist?

LADY. A woman-hater? Every healthy man is one, in the secret places of his heart; and all perverted men are admirers of women.

STRANGER. You're not trying to flatter me, are you?

LADY. A woman who'd try to flatter a man's not normal.

STRANGER. I see you've thought a great deal!

LADY. Thinking's the least I've done; for when I've thought least I've understood most. Besides, what I said just how is perhaps only improvised, as you call it, and not true in the least.

STRANGER. But if it agrees with many of my observations it becomes most probable. (The LADY weeps into her handkerchief.) You're weeping again?

LADY. I was thinking of Mizzi. The loveliest thing we ever had is gone.

STRANGER. No. You were the loveliest thing, when you sat all night watching over your child, who was lying in your bed, because her cradle was too cold! (Three loud knocks are heard on the ferryman's door.) 'Sh!

LADY. What's that?

STRANGER. My companion, who's waiting for me.

LADY (continuing the conversation). I never thought life would give me anything so sweet as a child.

STRANGER. And at the same time anything so bitter.

LADY. Why bitter?

STRANGER. You've been a child yourself, and you must remember how we, when we'd just married, came to your mother in rags, dirty and without money. I seem to remember she didn't find us very sweet.

LADY. That's true.

STRANGER. And I . . . well, just now I met Sylvia. And I expected that all that was beautiful and good in the child would have blossomed in the girl. . . .

LADY. Well?

STRANGER. I found a faded rose, that seemed to have blown too soon. Her breasts were sunken, her hair untidy like that of a neglected child, and her teeth decayed.

LADY. Oh!

STRANGER. You mustn't grieve. Not for the child! You might perhaps have had to grieve for her later, as I did.

LADY. So that's what life is?

STRANGER. Yes. That's what life is. And that's why I'm going to bury myself alive.

LADY. Where?

STRANGER (pointing to the monastery). Up there!

LADY. In the monastery? No, don't leave me. Bear me company. I'm so alone in the world and so poor, so poor! When the child died, my mother turned me out, and ever since I've been living in an attic with a dressmaker. At first she was kind and pleasant, but then the lonely evenings got too long for her, and she went out in search of company— so we parted. Now I'm on the road, and I've nothing but the clothes I'm wearing; nothing but my grief. I eat it and drink it; it nourishes me and sends me to sleep. I'd rather lose anything in the world than that! (The STRANGER weeps.) You're weeping. You! Let me kiss your eyelids.

STRANGER. You've suffered all that for my sake!

LADY. Not for your sake! You never did me an ill turn; but I plagued you till you left your fireside and your child!

STRANGER. I'd forgotten that; but if you say so. . . . So you still love me?

LADY. Probably. I don't know.

STRANGER. And you'd like to begin all over again?

LADY. All over again? The quarrels? No, we won't do that.

STRANGER. You're right. The quarrels would only begin all over again. And yet it's difficult to part.

LADY. To part. The word alone's terrible enough.

STRANGER. Then what are we to do?

LADY. I don't know.

STRANGER. No, one knows nothing, hardly even that one knows nothing; and that's why, you see, I've got as far as to *believe*.

LADY. How do you know you can believe, if belief's a gift?

STRANGER. You can receive a gift, if you ask for it.

LADY. Oh yes, if you ask; but I've never been able to beg.

STRANGER. I've had to learn to. Why can't you?

LADY. Because one has to demean oneself first.

238

STRANGER. Life does that for one very well.

LADY. Mizzi, Mizzi, Mizzi! . . . (She has taken a shawl she was carrying over her arm, rolled it up and put it on her knee like a baby in long clothes.) Sleep! Sleep! Sleep! Think of it! I can see her here! She's smiling at me; but she's dressed in black; she seems to be in mourning too! How stupid I am! Her mother's in mourning! She's got two teeth down below, and they're white—milk teeth; she should never have cut any others. Oh, can't you see her, when I can? It's no vision. It *is* her!

CONFESSOR (in the door of the ferryman's hut; sternly to the STRANGER). Come. Everything's ready!

STRANGER. No. Not yet. I must first set my house in order; and look after this woman, who was once my wife.

CONFESSOR. Oh, so you want to stay!

STRANGER. No. I don't want to stay; but I can't leave duties behind me unfulfilled. This woman's on the road, deserted, without a home, without money!

CONFESSOR. What has that to do with us? Let the dead bury their dead!

STRANGER. Is that your teaching?

CONFESSOR. No, yours. . . . Mine, on the other hand, commands me to send a Sister of Mercy here, to look after this unhappy one, who . . . who . . . The Sister will soon be here!

STRANGER. I shall count on it.

CONFESSOR (taking the STRANGER by the hand and drawing him away.) Then come!

STRANGER (in despair). Oh, God in heaven! Help us every one!

CONFESSOR. Amen!

(The LADY, who has not been looking at the CONFESSOR and the STRANGER, now raises her eyes and glances at the STRANGER as if she wanted to spring up and hold him back; but she is prevented by the imaginary child she has put to her breast.)

Curtain.

ACT II

CROSS-ROADS IN THE MOUNTAINS

[A cross-roads high up in the mountains. On the right, huts. On the left a small pool, round which invalids are sitting. Their clothes are blue and their hands cinnabar-red. From the pond blue vapour and small blue flames rise now and then. Whenever this happens the invalids put them hands to their mouths and cough. The background is formed by a mountain covered with pine-wood, which is obscured above by a stationary bank of mist.]

[The STRANGER is sitting at a table outside one of the huts. The CONFESSOR comes forward from the right.]

STRANGER. At last!

CONFESSOR. What do you mean: at last?

STRANGER. You left me here a week ago and told me to wait till you came back.

CONFESSOR. Hadn't I prepared you for the fact that the way to the white house up there would be long and difficult.

STRANGER. I don't deny it. How far have we come?

CONFESSOR. Five hundred yards. We've still got fifteen hundred.

STRANGER. But where's the sun?

CONFESSOR. Up there, above the clouds. . . .

STRANGER. Then we shall have to go through them?

CONFESSOR. Yes. Of course.

STRANGER. What are those patients doing there? What a company! And why are their hands so red?

CONFESSOR. For both our sakes I want to avoid using impure words, so I'll speak in pleasant riddles, which you, as a writer, will understand.

STRANGER. Yes. Speak beautifully. There's so much that's ugly here.

CONFESSOR. You may have noticed that the signs given to the planets correspond with those of certain metals? Good! Then you'll have seen that Venus is represented by a mirror. This mirror was originally made of copper, so that copper was called Venus and bore her stamp. But now the reverse of Venus' mirror is covered with quicksilver or mercury!

STRANGER. The reverse of Venus . . . is Mercury. Oh!

CONFESSOR. Quicksilver is therefore the reverse side of Venus. Quicksilver is itself as bright as a calm sea, as a lake at the height of summer; but when mercury meets firestone and burns, it blushes and turns red like newly-shed blood, like the cloth on the scaffold, like the cinnabar lips of the whore! Do you understand now, or not?

STRANGER. Wait a moment! Cinnabar is quicksilver and sulphur.

CONFESSOR. Yes. Mercury must be burnt, if it comes too near to Venus! Have we said enough now?

242

STRANGER. So these are sulphur springs?

CONFESSOR. Yes. And the sulphur flames purify or burn everything rotten! So when the source of life's grown tainted, one is sent to the sulphur springs. . . .

STRANGER. How does the source of life grow tainted?

CONFESSOR. When Aphrodite, born of the pure seafoam, wallows in the mire. . . . When Aphrodite Urania, the heaven-born, degrades herself to Pandemos, the Venus of the streets.

STRANGER. Why is desire born?

CONFESSOR. Pure desire, to be satisfied; impure, to be stifled.

STRANGER. What is pure, and what impure?

CONFESSOR. Have you got back to that?

STRANGER. Ask these men here. . . .

CONFESSOR. Take care! (He looks at the STRANGER, who is unable to support his gaze.)

STRANGER. You're choking me. . . . My chest. . . .

CONFESSOR. Yes, I'll steal the air you use to form rebellious words, and ask outrageous questions. Sit down there, I'll come back—when you've learnt patience and undergone your probation. But don't forget that I can hear and see you, and am aware of you, wherever I may be!

STRANGER. So I'm to be tested! I'm glad to know it!

CONFESSOR. But you mustn't speak to the worshippers of Venus.

(MAIA, an old woman, appears in the background.)

STRANGER (rising in horror). Who am I meeting here after all this time? Who is it?

CONFESSOR. Who are you speaking of?

STRANGER. That old woman there?

CONFESSOR. Who's she?

STRANGER (calling). Maia! Listen! (Old Maia has disappeared. The STRANGER hurries after her.) Maia, my friend, listen! She's gone!

CONFESSOR. Who was it?

STRANGER (sitting down). O God! Now, when I find her again at last, she goes. . . . I've looked for her for seven long years, written letters, advertised. . . .

CONFESSOR. Why?

STRANGER. I'll tell you how her fate was linked to mine! (Pause.) Maia was the nurse in my first family . . . during those hard years . . . when I was fighting the Invisible Ones, who wouldn't bless my work! I wrote till my brain and nerves dissolved like fat in alcohol . . . but it wasn't enough! I was one of those who never could earn enough. And the day came when I couldn't pay the maids their wages—it was terrible—and I became the servant of my servant, and she became my mistress. At last . . . in order, at least, to save my soul, I fled from what was too powerful for me. I fled into the wilderness, where I collected my spirit in solitude and recovered my strength! My first thought then was—my debts! For seven years I

244

looked for Maia, but in vain! For seven years I saw her shadow, out of the windows of trains, from the decks of steamers, in strange towns, in distant lands, but without ever being able to find her. I dreamed of her for seven years; and whenever I drank a glass of wine I blushed at the thought of old Maia, who perhaps was drinking water in a poorhouse! I tried to give the sum I owed her to the poor; but it was no use. And now—she's found and lost in the same moment! (He gets up and goes towards the back as if searching for her.) Explain this, if you can! I want to pay my debt; I can pay it now, but I'm not allowed to.

CONFESSOR. Foolishness' Bow to what seems inexplicable; you'll see that the explanation will come later. Farewell!

STRANGER. Later. Everything comes later.

CONFESSOR. Yes. If it doesn't come at once! (He goes out. The LADY enters pensively and sits down at the table, opposite the STRANGER.)

STRANGER. What? You back again? The same and not the same? How beautiful you've grown; as beautiful as you were the first time I ever saw you; when I asked if I might be your friend, your dog.

LADY. That you can see beauty I don't possess shows that once more you have a mirror of beauty in your eye. The werewolf never thought me beautiful, for he'd nothing beautiful with which to see me.

STRANGER. Why did you kiss me that day? What made you do it?

LADY. You've often asked me that, and I've never been able to find the answer, because I don't know. But just now, when I was away from you, here in the mountains, where the air's purer and the sun nearer. . . . Hush! Now I can see that Sunday afternoon, when you sat on that seat like a lost and helpless child, with a broken look in your eyes, and stared at your own destiny. . . . A maternal feeling I'd never known before welled up in me then, and I was overcome with pity, pity for a human soul—so that I forgot myself.

STRANGER. I'm ashamed. Now I believe it was so.

LADY. But you took it another way. You thought . . .

STRANGER. Don't tell me. I'm ashamed.

LADY. Why did you think so badly of me? Didn't you notice that I drew down my veil; so that it was between us, like the knight's sword in the bridal bed. . . .

STRANGER. I'm ashamed. I attributed my evil thoughts to you. Ingeborg, you were made of better stuff than I. I'm ashamed!

LADY. Now you look handsome. How handsome!

STRANGER. Oh no. Not I. You!

LADY (ecstatically). No, you! Yes, now I've seen through the mask and the false beard. Now I can see the man you hid from me, the man I thought I'd found in you . . . the man I was always searching for. I've often thought you a hypocrite; but we're no hypocrites. No, no, we can't pretend.

STRANGER. Ingeborg, now we're on the other side of the river, and have life beneath us, behind us . . . how different everything seems. Now, now, I can see your soul; the ideal, the angel, who was imprisoned in the flesh because of sin. So there is an Above, and an Earlier Age. When we began it wasn't the beginning, and it won't be the end when we are ended. Life is a fragment, without beginning or end! That's why it's so difficult to make head or tail of it.

246

LADY (kindly). So difficult. So difficult. Tell me, for instance—now we're beyond guilt or innocence—how was it you came to hate women?

STRANGER. Let me think! To hate women? Hate them? I never hated them. On the contrary! Ever since I was eight years old I've always had some love affair, preferably an innocent one. And I've loved like a volcano three times! But wait—I've always felt that women hated me . . . and they've always tortured me.

LADY. How strange!

STRANGER. Let me think about it a little. . . . Perhaps I've been jealous of my own personality; and been afraid of being influenced too much. My first love made herself into a sort of governess and nurse to me. But, of course, there *are* men who detest children; who detest women too, if they're superior to them, that is!

LADY (amiably). But you've called women the enemies of mankind. Did you mean it?

STRANGER. Of course I meant it, if I wrote it! For I wrote out of experience, not theory. . . . In woman I sought an angel, who could lend me wings, and I fell into the arms of an earth-spirit, who suffocated me under mattresses stuffed with the feathers of wings! I sought an Ariel and I found a Caliban; when I wanted to rise she dragged me down; and continually reminded me of the fall. . . .

LADY (kindly). Solomon knew much of women; do you know what he said? 'I find more bitter than death a woman, whose heart is snares and nets and her hands as bands; whoso pleaseth God shall escape from her; but the sinner shall be taken by her.'

STRANGER. I was never acceptable in God's sight. Was that a punishment? Perhaps. But I was never acceptable to anyone, and I've never had a good word addressed to me! Have I never done a good action? Is it possible for a man never to have done anything good? (Pause.) It's terrible never to hear any good words about oneself!

LADY. You've heard them. But when people have spoken well of you, you've refused to listen, as if it hurt you.

STRANGER. That's true, now you remind me. But can you explain it?

LADY. Explain it? You're always asking for explanations of the inexplicable. 'When I applied my heart to know wisdom . . . I beheld all the work of God, that a man cannot find out that is done under the sun. Because, though a man labour to seek it out, yet he shall not find it; yea, further, though a wise man think to know it, yet shall he not be able to find it!'

STRANGER. Who says that?

LADY. The Prophet Ecclesiastes. (She takes a doll out of her pocket.) This is Mizzi's doll. You see she longs for her little mistress! How pale she's grown . . . and she seems to know where Mizzi is, for she's always gazing up to heaven, whichever way I hold her. Look! Her eyes follow the stars as the compass the pole. She is my compass and always shows me where heaven is. She should, of course, be dressed in black, because she's in mourning; but we're so poor. . . . Do you know why we never had money? Because God was angry with us for our sins. 'The righteous suffer no dearth.'

STRANGER. Where did you learn that?

LADY. In a book in which everything's written. Everything! (She wraps the doll up in her cloak.) See, she's beginning to get cold—that's because of the cloud up there. . . .

STRANGER. How can you dare to wander up here in the mountains?

LADY. God is with me; so what have I to fear from human beings?

STRANGER. Aren't you tormented by those people at the pool?

LADY (turning towards them). I can't see them. I can't see anything horrible now.

STRANGER. Ingeborg! I have made you evil, yet you're on the way to make me good! It was my dream, you know, to seek redemption through a woman. You don't believe it! But it's true. In the old days nothing was of value to me if I couldn't lay it at a woman's feet. Not as a tribute to an overbearing mistress, . . . but as a sacrifice to the beautiful and good. It was my pleasure to give; but she wanted to take and not receive: that's why she hated me! When I was helpless and thought the end was near, a desire grew in me to fall asleep on a mother's knee, on a tremendous breast where I could bury my tired head and drink in the tenderness I'd been deprived of.

LADY. You had no mother?

STRANGER. Hardly! And I've never felt any bond between myself and my father or my brothers and sisters. . . . Ingeborg, I was the son of a servant of whom it is written. 'Drive forth the handmaid with her son, for this son shall not inherit with the son of peace.'

LADY. Do you know why Ishmael was driven out? It says just before—that he was a scoffer. And then it goes on: 'He will be a wild man, his hand will be against every man, and every man's hand against him; and against all his brothers.'

STRANGER. Is that also written?

LADY. Oh yes, my child; it's all there!

STRANGER. All?

LADY. All. There you'll find answers to all your questions even the most inquisitive!

STRANGER. Call me your child, and then I'll love you. . . . And if I love anyone, I long to serve them, to obey them, to let myself be ill-treated, to suffer and to bear it.

LADY. You shouldn't love me, but your Creator.

STRANGER. He's unfriendly—like my father!

LADY. He is Love itself; and you are Hate.

STRANGER. You're his daughter; but I'm his cast-out son.

LADY (coaxingly). Quiet! Be still!

STRANGER. If you only knew what I've suffered this last week. I don't know where I am.

LADY. Where do you think?

STRANGER. There's a woman in that but who looks at me as if I'd come to rob her of her last mite. She says nothing—that's the trouble. But I think it's prayers she mutters, when she sees me.

LADY. What sort of prayers?

STRANGER. The sort one whispers behind the backs of those who have the evil eye or bring misfortune.

LADY. How strange! Don't you realise that one's sight can be blinded?

STRANGER. Yes, of course. But who can do it?

HOSTESS (coming across to their table). Well, look at that! I suppose she's your sister?

STRANGER. Yes. We can say so now.

HOSTESS (to the LADY). Fancy meeting someone I can speak to at last! This gentleman's so silent, you see, that one feels at once one must respect him; particularly as he seems to have had trouble. But I can say this to his sister, and he shall hear it: that from the moment he entered the house I felt that I was blessed. I'd been dogged by misfortune; I'd no lodger, my only cow had died, my husband was in a home for drunkards and my children had nothing to eat. I prayed God to send me help from heaven, because I expected nothing more on earth. Then this gentleman came. And apart from giving me double what I asked, he brought me good luck—and my house was blessed. God bless you, good sir!

STRANGER (getting up excitedly). Silence, woman. That's blasphemy!

LADY. He won't believe. O God! He won't believe. Look at me!

STRANGER. When I look at you, I do believe. She's giving me her blessing! And I, who'm damned, have brought a blessing on her! How can I believe it? I, of all men! (He falls down by the table and weeps in his hands.)

LADY. He's weeping! Tears, rain from heaven, that can soften rocks, are falling on his stony heart. . . . He's weeping!

HOSTESS. He? Who has a heart of gold! Who's been so open handed and so good to my children!

LADY. You hear what she says!

HOSTESS. There's only one thing about him I don't understand; but I don't want to say anything unpleasant. . . .

LADY. What is it?

HOSTESS. Only a trifle; and yet . . .

LADY. Well?

HOSTESS. He didn't like my dogs.

LADY. I can't blame him for not caring for an impure beast. I hate everything animal, in myself and others. I don't hate animals on that account, for I hate nothing that's created. . . .

STRANGER. Thank you, Ingeborg!

LADY. You see! I've an eye for your merits, even though you don't believe it. . . . Here comes the Confessor.

(The CONFESSOR enters.)

HOSTESS. Then I'll go; for the Confessor has no love for me.

LADY. The Confessor loves all mankind.

CONFESSOR (coming forward and speaking to the LADY). You best of all, my child; for you're goodness itself. Whether you're beautiful to look at, I can't see; but I know you must be, because you're good. Yes, you were the bride of my youth, and my spiritual mate; and you'll always be so, for you gave me what you were never able to give to others. I've lived your life in my spirit, suffered your pains, enjoyed your pleasures—pleasure rather, for you'd no others than what your child gave you. I alone have seen the beauty of your soul—my friend here has divined it; that's why he felt attracted to you—but the evil in him was too strong; you had to draw it out of him into yourself to free him. Then, being evil, you had to suffer the worst pains of hell for his sake, to bring atonement. Your work's ended. You can go in peace!

LADY. Where?

CONFESSOR. Up there. Where the sun's always shining.

LADY (rising). Is there a home for me there, too?

CONFESSOR. There's a home for everyone! I'll show you the way. (He goes with her into the background. The STRANGER makes a movement.) You're impatient? You mustn't be! (He goes out. The STRANGER remains sitting alone. The WORSHIPPERS OF VENUS get up, go towards him and form a circle round him.)

STRANGER. What do you want with me?

WORSHIPPERS. Hail! Father.

STRANGER (much upset). Why call me that?

FIRST VOICE. Because we're your children. Your dear ones!

STRANGER (tries to escape, but is surrounded and cannot). Let me go. Let me go!

SECOND VOICE (that of a pale youth). Don't you recognise me, Father?

TEMPTER (appearing in the background at the left-hand fork of the path). Ha!

STRANGER (to the Second Voice). Who are you? I seem to know your face.

SECOND VOICE. I'm Erik—your son!

STRANGER. Erik! You here?

SECOND VOICE. Yes. I'm here.

STRANGER. God have mercy! And you, my boy, forgive me!

SECOND VOICE. Never! You showed us the way to the sulphur springs! Is it far to the lake?

(The STRANGER falls to the ground.)

TEMPTER. Ha! Jubilate, temptatores!

VENUS WORSHIPPERS. Sulphur! Sulphur! Sulphur! Mercury!

TEMPTER (coming forward and touching the STRANGER with his foot). The worm! You can make him believe whatever you like. That comes from his unbelievable pride. Does he think he's the mainspring of the universe, the originator of all evil? This foolish man believes he taught youth to go in search of Venus; as if youth hadn't done that long before he was born! His pride's insupportable, and he's been rash enough to try to botch my work for me. Give him another greeting, lying Erik! (The SECOND VOICE—that is the youth—bends over the STRANGER and whispers in his ear.) There were seven deadly sins; but now there are eight. The eighth I discovered! It's called despair. For to despair of what is good, and not to hope for forgiveness, is to call . . . (He hesitates before pronouncing the word God, as if it burnt his lips.) God wicked. That is calumny, denial, blasphemy. . . . Look how he winces!

STRANGER (rising quickly, and looking the TEMPTER to the eyes). Who are you?

TEMPTER. Your brother. Don't we resemble one another? Some of your features seem to remind me of my portrait.

STRANGER. Where have I seen it?

TEMPTER. Almost everywhere! I'm often to be found in churches, though not amongst the saints.

STRANGER. I can't remember. . . .

TEMPTER. Is it so long since you've been to church? I'm usually represented with St. George. (The STRANGER totters and would like to fly, but cannot.) Michael and I are sometimes to be seen in a group, in which, to be sure, I don't appear in the most favourable light; but that can be altered. All can be altered; and one day the last shall be first. It's just the same in your case. For the moment, things are going badly with you, but that can be altered too . . . if you've enough intelligence to change your company. You've had too much to do with skirts, my son. Skirts raise dust, and dust lies on eyes and breast. . . . Come and sit down. We'll have a chat. . . . (He takes the STRANGER jocularly by the ear and leads him round the table.) Sit down and tremble, young man! (They both sit

255

down.) Well? What shall we do? Call for wine—and a woman? No! That's too old a trick, as old as Doctor Faust! Bon! We modern are in search of mental dissipation. . . . So you're on your way to those holy men up there, who think that they who sleep can't sin; to the cowardly ones, who've given up the battle of life, because they were defeated once or twice; to those that bind souls rather than free them. . . . And talking of that! Has any saintly man ever freed you from the burden of sin? No! Do you know why sin has been oppressing you for so long? Through renunciation and abstinence, you've grown so weak that anyone can seize your soul and take possession of it. Why, they can even do it from a distance! You've so destroyed your personality that you see with strange eyes, hear with strange ears and think strange thoughts. In a word you've murdered your own soul. Just now, didn't you speak well of the enemies of mankind; of Woman, who made a hell of paradise? You needn't answer me; I can read your answer in your eyes and hear it on your lips. You talk of pure love for a woman! That's lust, young man, lust after a woman, which we have to pay for so dearly. You say you don't desire her. Then why do you want to be near her? You'd like to have a friend? Take a male friend, many of them! You've let them convince you you're no woman hater. But the woman gave you the right answer; every healthy man's a woman hater, but can't live without linking himself to his enemy, and so must fight her! All perverse and unmanly men are admirers of women! How's it with you now? So you saw those invalids and thought yourself responsible for their misery? They're tough fellows, you can believe me; they'll be able to leave here in a few days and go back to their occupations. Oh yes, lying Erik's a wag! But things have gone so far with you, that you can't distinguish between your own and other people's children. Wouldn't it be a great thing to escape from all this? What do you say? Oh, I could free you . . . but I'm no saint. Now we'll call old Maia. (He whistles between his fingers: MAIA appears.) Ah, there you are! Well, what are you doing here? Have you any business with this fellow?

MAIA. No. He's good and always was; but he'd a terrible wife.

TEMPTER (to the STRANGER). Listen! You've not heard that yet, have you? Rather the opposite. She was the good angel, whom you ruined . . . we've all been told that! Now, old Maia, what kind of story is it he prattles of? He says he was plagued with remorse for seven years because he owed you money.

MAIA. He owed me a small sum once; but I got it back from him—and with good interest—much better than the savings bank would have given me. It was very good of him—very kind.

STRANGER (starting up). What's that you said? Is it possible I've forgotten?

TEMPTER. Have you the receipt, Maia? If so, give it me.

MAIA. The gentleman must have the receipt; but I've got the savings bank book here. He paid the money into it in my name. (She produces a savings bank book, and hands it to the STRANGER, who looks at it.)

STRANGER. Yes, that's quite right. Now I remember. Then why this seven-year torment, shame and disgrace? Those reproaches during sleepless nights? Why? Why? Why?

TEMPTER. Old Maia, you can go now. But first say something nice about this self-tormentor. Can't you remember any human quality in this wild beast, whom human beings have baited for years?

STRANGER (to MAIA). Quiet, don't answer him! (He stops his ears with his fingers.)

TEMPTER. Well, Maia?

257

MAIA. I know well enough what they say about him, but that refers to what he writes—and I've not read it for I can't read. Still, no one need read it, if they don't want to. Anyhow the gentleman's been very kind. Now he's stopping his ears. I don't know how to flatter; but I can say this in a whisper. . . . (She whispers some thing to the TEMPTER.)

TEMPTER. Yes. All human beings who are easily moved are baited like wild beasts! It's the rule. Good bye, old Maia!

MAIA. Good-bye, kind gentlemen. (She goes out.)

STRANGER. Why did I suffer innocently for seven years?

TEMPTER (pointing upwards with one finger). Ask up there!

STRANGER. Where I never get an answer!

TEMPTER. Well, that may be. (Pause.) Do you think *I* look good?

STRANGER. I can't say I do.

TEMPTER. You look extremely wicked, too! Do you know why we look like that?

STRANGER. No.

TEMPTER. The hate and malice of our fellow human beings have fastened themselves on us. Up there, you know, there are real saints, who've never done anything wicked themselves, but who suffer for others, for relations, who've committed unexpiated sins. Those angels, who've taken the depravity of others on themselves, really resemble bandits. What do you say to that?

258

STRANGER. I don't know who you are; but you're the first to answer questions that might reconcile me to life. You are. . . .

TEMPTER. Well, say it!

STRANGER. The deliverer!

TEMPTER. And therefore. . . . ?

STRANGER. Therefore you've been given a vulture. . . . But listen, have you ever thought that there's as good a reason for this as for everything else? Granted the earth's a prison, on which dangerous prisoners are confined—is it a good thing to set them free? Is it right?

TEMPTER. What a question! I've never really thought about it. Hm!

STRANGER. And have you ever thought of this: we may be born in guilt?

TEMPTER. That's nothing to do with me: I concern myself with the present.

STRANGER. Good! Don't you think we're sometimes punished wrongly, so that we fail to see the logical connection, though it exists?

TEMPTER. Logic's not missing; but all life's a tissue of offences, mistakes, errors, that are comparatively blameless owing to human weakness, but that are punished by the most consistent revenge. Everything's revenged, even our injudicious actions. Who forgives? A magnanimous man-sometimes; heavenly justice, never! (A PILGRIM appears in the background.) See! A penitent! I'd like to know what wrong he's done. We'll ask him. Welcome to our quiet meadows, peaceful wanderer! Take your place at the simple table of the ascetic, at which there are no more temptations.

PILGRIM. Thank you, fellow traveller in the vale of woe.

TEMPTER. What kind of woe is yours?

PILGRIM. None in particular; on the contrary, the hour of liberation's struck, and I'm going up there to receive absolution.

STRANGER. Listen, haven't we two met before?

PILGRIM. I think so, certainly.

STRANGER. Caesar! You're Caesar!

PILGRIM. I used to be; but I am no longer.

TEMPTER. Ha ha! Imperial acquaintance. Really! But tell us, tell us!

PILGRIM. You shall hear. Now I've a right to speak, for my penance is at an end. When we met at a certain doctor's house, I was shut up there as a madman and supposed to be suffering from the illusion that I was Caesar. Now the Stranger shall hear the truth of the matter: I never believed it, but I was forced by scruples of conscience to put a good face on it. . . . A friend of mine, a bad friend, had written proof that I was the victim of a misunderstanding; but he didn't speak when he should have, and I took his silence as a request not to speak either-and to suffer. Why did I? Well, in my youth I was once in great need. I was received as a guest in a house on an island far out to sea by a man who, in spite of unusual gifts, had been passed over for promotion—owing to his senseless pride. This man, by solitary brooding on his lot, had come to hold quite extraordinary views about himself. I noticed it, but I said nothing. One day this man's wife told me that he was sometimes mentally unbalanced; and then thought he was Julius Caesar. For many years I kept this secret conscientiously, for I'm not ungrateful by nature.

But life's tricky. It happened a few years later that this Caesar laid rough hands on my most intimate fate. In anger at this I betrayed the secret of his Caesar mania and made my erstwhile benefactor such a laughing stock, that his existence became unbearable to him. And now listen how Nemesis overtakes one! A year later I wrote a book-I am, you must know, an author who's not made his name. . . . And in this book I described incidents of family life: how I played with my daughter— she was called Julia, as Caesar's daughter was—and with my wife, whom we called Caesar's wife because no one spoke evil of her. . . . Well, this recreation, in which my mother-in-law joined too, cost me dear. When I was looking through the proofs of my book, I saw the danger and said to myself: you'll trip yourself up. I wanted to cut it out but, if you'll believe it, the pen refused, and an inner voice said to me: let it stand! It did stand! And I fell.

STRANGER. Why didn't you publish the letter from your friend that would have explained everything?

PILGRIM. When the disaster had happened I felt at once that it was the finger of God, and that I must suffer for my ingratitude.

STRANGER. And you did suffer?

PILGRIM. Not at all! I smiled to myself and wouldn't let myself be put out. And because I accepted my punishment with calmness and humility God lightened my burden; and I didn't feel myself ridiculous.

TEMPTER. That's a strange story; but such things happen. Shall we move on now? We'll go for an excursion, now we've weathered the storms. Pull yourself up by the roots, and then we'll climb the mountain.

STRANGER. The Confessor told me to wait for him.

TEMPTER. He'll find you, anyhow! And up here in the village the court's sitting today. A particularly interesting case is to be tried; and I dare say I'll be called as a witness. Come!

STRANGER. Well, whether I sit here, or up there, is all the same to me.

PILGRIM (to the STRANGER). Who's that?

STRANGER. I don't know. He looks like an anarchist.

PILGRIM. Interesting, anyhow!

STRANGER. He's a sceptical gentleman, who's seen life.

TEMPTER. Come, children; I'll tell you stories on the way. Come. Come!

(They go out towards the background.)

Curtain.

ACT III

SCENE I
TERRACE ON THE MOUNTAIN

[A Terrace on the mountain on which the Monastery stands. On the right a rocky cliff and a similar one on the left. In the far background a bird's-eye view of a river landscape with towns, villages, ploughed fields and woods; in the very far distance the sea can be seen. Down stage an apple tree laden with fruit. Under it a long table with a chair at the end and benches at the sides. Down stage, right, a corner of the village town hall. A cloud seems to be hanging immediately over the village.]

[The MAGISTRATE sits at the end of the table in the capacity of judge; the assessors on the benches. The ACCUSED MAN is standing on the right by the MAGISTRATE; the witnesses on the left, amongst them the TEMPTER. Members of the public, with the PILGRIM and the STRANGER, are standing here and there not far from the judge's seat.]

MAGISTRATE. Is the accused present?

ACCUSED MAN. Yes. Present.

MAGISTRATE. This is a very sad story, that's brought trouble and shame on our small community. Florian Reicher, twenty-three years old, is accused of shooting at Fritz Schlipitska's affianced wife, with the clear intention of killing her. It's a case of premeditated murder, and the provisions of the law are perfectly clear. Has the accused anything to say in his defence, or can he plead mitigating circumstances?

ACCUSED MAN. No.

TEMPTER. Ho, there!

MAGISTRATE. Who are you?

TEMPTER. Counsel for the accused.

MAGISTRATE. The accused man certainly has a right to the services of counsel, but in the present case I think the facts are so clear that the people have reached a certain conclusion; and the murderer will hardly be able to regain their sympathy. Isn't that so?

PEOPLE. He's condemned already!

TEMPTER. Who by?

PEOPLE. The Law and his own deed.

TEMPTER. Listen to me! As counsel for the accused I represent him and take the accusation on myself. I ask permission to address the court.

MAGISTRATE. I can't refuse it.

PEOPLE. Florian's been condemned already.

TEMPTER. The case must first be heard. (Pause.) I'd reached my eighteenth year—it's Florian speaking—and my thoughts, as I grew up under my mother's watchful eye, were pure; and my heart without deceit, for I'd never seen or heard anything wicked. Then I—Florian, that is— met a young girl who seemed to me the most beautiful creature I'd ever set eyes on in this wicked world, for she was goodness itself. I offered her my hand, my heart, and my future. She accepted everything and swore that she'd be true. I was to serve five years for my Rachel—and I did serve, collecting one straw after another for the little nest we were going to build. My whole life was centred on the love of this woman! As I was true to her myself, I never mistrusted her. By the fifth year I'd built the hut and collected our household goods . . . when I discovered she'd been playing with me and had deceived me with at least three men. . . .

MAGISTRATE. Have you witnesses?

BAILIFF. Three valid ones; I'm one of them.

MAGISTRATE. The bailiff alone will be sufficient.

TEMPTER. Then I shot her; not out of revenge, but in order to free myself from the unhealthy thoughts her faithlessness had forced on me; for when I tried to tear her picture out of my heart, images of her lovers always rose and crept into my blood, so that at last I seemed to be living in unlawful relationship with three men—with a woman as the link between us!

MAGISTRATE. Well, that was jealousy!

ACCUSED MAN. Yes, that was jealousy.

TEMPTER. Yes, jealousy, that feeling for cleanliness, that seeks to preserve thoughts from pollution by strangers. If I'd been content to do nothing, if I'd not been jealous, I'd have got into vicious company, and I didn't want to do that. That's why she had to die so that my thoughts might be cleansed of deadly sin, which alone is to be condemned. I've finished.

PEOPLE. The dead woman's guilty! Her blood's on her own head.

MAGISTRATE. She's guilty, for she was the cause of the crime.

(The FATHER of the dead woman steps forward.)

FATHER. Your Worship, judge of my dead child; and you, countrymen, let me speak!

MAGISTRATE. The dead girl's father may speak.

FATHER. You're accusing a dead girl; and I shall answer. Maria, my child, has undoubtedly been guilty of a crime and is to blame for the misdeeds of this man. There's no doubt of it!

PEOPLE. No doubt! It's she who's guilty!

FATHER. Permit her father to add a word of explanation, if not of defence. (Pause.) When she was fifteen, Maria fell into the hands of a man who seemed to have made it his business to entrap young girls, much as a bird-catcher traps small birds. He was no seducer, in the ordinary sense, for he contented himself with binding her senses and entangling her feelings only to thrust her away and watch how she suffered with torn wings and a broken heart—tortured by the agony of love, which is worse than any other agony. For three years Maria was cared for in an institution for the mentally deranged. And when she came out again, she was divided, broken into several pieces—it might be said that she was several persons. She was an angel and feared God with one side of her spirit; but with another she was a devil, and reviled all that was holy. I've seen her go straight from dancing and frenzy to her beloved Florian, and have heard her, in his presence, speak so differently and so alter her expression, that I could have sworn she was another being. But to me she seemed equally sincere in both her shapes. Is she to blame, or her seducer?

PEOPLE. She's not to blame! Where is her seducer?

FATHER. There!

TEMPTER. Yes. It was I.

PEOPLE. Stone him!

MAGISTRATE. The law must run its course. He must be heard.

TEMPTER. Bon! Then listen, Argives! It was like this. Your humble servant, born of poor but fairly honourable parents, was from the beginning one of those strange birds who, in their youth, go in search of their Creator—but without ever finding him, naturally! It's more usual for old cuckoos to look for him in their dotage—and for good reasons! The urge for this youthful quest was accompanied by a purity of heart and a modesty that even caused his nurses to smile—yes, we can laugh now when we hear that this boy would only change his underclothing in the dark! But even if we're corrupted by the crudities of life, we're still bound to find something beautiful in it; and if we're older something touching! And so we can afford today to laugh at his childish innocence. Scornful laughter, listeners, please.

MAGISTRATE (seriously). He mistakes his listeners.

TEMPTER. Then I ought to be ashamed of myself! (Pause.) He became a youth—your humble servant—and fell into a series of traps that were laid for his innocence. I'm an old sinner, but I blush at this moment. . . . (He takes of his hat.) Yes, look at me now—when I think of the insight this young man got into the world of Potiphar's wives that surrounded him! There wasn't a single woman. . . . Really, I'm ashamed in the name of mankind and the female sex—excuse me, please. . . . There were moments when I didn't believe my eyes, but thought a devil had blinded my sight. The holiest bands. . . . (He pinches his tongue.) No, quiet! Mankind will feel itself calumniated! Enough, until my twenty-fifth year I fought the good fight; and I fell because. . . . Well, I was called Joseph, and I *was* Joseph! I grew jealous of my virtue, and felt injured by the glances of a lewd woman. . . . And at last, cunningly seduced, I fell. Then I became a slave of my passions; often and often I sat by Omphalos and span, until I sank into the deepest degradation and suffered, suffered, suffered! But in reality it was only my body that was degraded; my soul lived her own life—her own pure life, I can say—on her own account. And I raved innocently for pure young virgins who, it seems, felt the bond that drew us together. Because, without boasting, I can say they were attracted to me. I didn't want to overstep the mark, but they did! And when I fled the danger, their hearts were broken, so they said. In a word, I've never seduced an innocent girl. I swear it! Am I therefore to blame for the emotional sorrows of this young woman, who went out of her mind? On the contrary, mayn't I count it a virtue that I shrank in horror from the step that brought about her fall? Who'll cast the first stone at me? No one! Then I mistake my listeners. Indeed, I thought I might be an object of scorn, if I were to plead here for my masculine innocence! Now, however, I feel young again; and there's something for which I'd like to ask mankind's forgiveness. If it weren't that I happened to see a cynical smile on the lips of the woman who seduced me when I was young. Come forward, woman, and look upon your work of destruction. Observe, how the seed has grown!

WOMAN (coming forward with dignity and modesty). It was I! Let me be heard, and let me tell the simple story of my seduction. (Pause.) Luckily my seducer is here, too. . . .

MAGISTRATE. Friends! I must break off the proceedings; otherwise we'll get back to Eve in Paradise.

268

TEMPTER. Who was Adam's seducer! That's just where we want to get back to. Eve! Come forward, Eve. Eve! (He waves his cloak in the air. The trunk of the tree becomes transparent and EVE appears, wrapped in her hair and with a girdle about her loins.) Now, Mother Eve, it was you who seduced our father. You are the accused: what have you to say in your defence?

EVE (simply and with dignity). The serpent tempted me!

TEMPTER. Well answered! Eve has proved her innocence. The serpent! Let the serpent come forward. (EVE disappears.) The serpent! (The serpent appears in the tree trunk.) Here you can see the seducer of us all. Now, serpent, who was it that beguiled you?

ALL (terrified). Silence! Blasphemer!

TEMPTER. Answer, serpent! (Lightning and a clap of thunder; all flee, except the TEMPTER, who has fallen to the ground, and the PILGRIM, the STRANGER and the LADY. The TEMPTER begins to recover; he then gets up and sits down in an attitude that recalls the classical statue 'The Polisher,' or 'The Slave.') Causa finalis, or the first cause—you can't discover that! For if the serpent's to blame, then we're comparatively innocent—but mankind mustn't be told that! The Accused, however, seems to have got out of this business! And the Court of justice has dissolved like smoke! Judge not. Judge not, O Judges!

LADY (to the STRANGER). Come with me.

STRANGER. But I'd like to listen to this man.

LADY. Why? He's like a small child, putting all those questions that can't be answered. You know how little children ask about everything. 'Papa, why does the sun rise in the east?' You know the answer?

STRANGER. Hm!

LADY. Or: 'Mama, who made God?' You think that profound? Well, come with me.

STRANGER (fighting his admiration for the TEMPTER). But that about Eve was new. . . .

LADY. Not at all. I learnt it in my Bible history, when I was eight. And that we inherit the debts of our fathers is part of the law of the land. Come, my son.

TEMPTER (rising, shaking his limbs and climbing up the rocky wall to the right with a limp). Come, I'll show you the world you think you know, but don't.

LADY (climbing up the rocky wall to the left). Come with me, my son, and I'll show you God's beautiful world, as I've come to see it, since the tears of sorrow washed the dust from my eyes. Come with me!

(The STRANGER stands irresolute between them.)

TEMPTER (to the LADY). And how have you seen the world through your tears? Like meadow banks reflected in troubled water! A chaos of curved lines in which the trees seemed to be standing on their heads. (To the STRANGER.) No, my son, with my field-glasses, dried in the fire of hate—with my telescope I can see everything as it is. Clear and sharp, precisely as it is.

LADY. What do you know of things, my son? You can never see the thing itself, only its picture; and the picture is illusion and not the thing. So you argue about pictures and illusions.

TEMPTER. Listen to her! A little philosopher in skirts. By Jupiter Chronos, such a disputation in this giant amphitheatre of the mountains demands a proper audience. Hullo!

LADY. I have mine here: my friend, my husband, my child! If he'll only listen to me, good; all will be well with me, and him. Come to me, my friend, for this is the way. This is the mountain Gerizim, where blessings are given. And that is Ebal, where they curse.

TEMPTER. Yes, this is Ebal, where they curse. 'Cursed be the earth, woman, for thy sake; in sorrow shalt thou bring forth children; and thy desire shall be to thy husband, and he shall rule over thee.' And then to the man this: 'Cursed is the ground for thy sake, thorns and thistle shall it bring forth to thee, and in the sweat of thy brow shalt thou labour!' So spoke the Lord, not I!

LADY. 'And God. blessed the first pair; and He blessed the seventh day, on which He had completed His work—and the work was good.' But you, and we, have made it something evil, and that is why. . . . But he who obeys the commandments of the Lord dwells on Gerizim, where blessings are given. Thus saith the Lord. 'Blessed shalt thou be in the city, and blessed shalt thou be in the field. Blessed shall be thy basket and thy store. Blessed shalt thou be when thou comest in, and blessed when thou goest out. And the Lord shall give rain unto thy land in his season to increase thy harvest, and thy children shall flourish. And the Lord shall make thee plenteous in goods, to lend to the peoples, and never to borrow. And the Lord will bless all the work of thy hand, if thou shalt keep the commandments of the Lord thy God!' (Pause.) So come, my friend, and lay your hand in mine. (She falls on her knees with clasped hands.) I beg you, by the love that once united us, by the memory of the child that drew us together; by the strength of a mother's love—a mother's—for so have I loved you, erring child, whom I've sought in the dark places of the wood and whom at last I've found, hungry and withered for want of love! Come back to me, prodigal one; and bury your tired head on my heart, where you rested before ever you saw the light of the sun. (A change comes over her during this speech; her clothing falls from her and she is seen to have changed into a white-robed woman with her hair let down and with a full maternal bosom.)

STRANGER. Mother!

LADY. Yes, my child, your mother! In life I could never caress you—the will of higher powers denied it me. Why that was I don't dare to ask.

STRANGER. But my mother's dead?

LADY. She was; but the dead aren't dead, and maternal love can conquer death. Didn't you know that? Come, my child, I'll repay where I have been to blame. I'll rock you to sleep on my knees. I'll wash you clean from the . . . (She omits the word she cannot bring herself to utter) of hate and sin. I'll comb your hair, matted with the sweat of fear; and air a pure white sheet for you at the fire of a home—a home you've never had, you who've known no peace, you homeless one, son of Hagar, the serving woman, born of a slave, against whom every man's hand was raised. The ploughmen ploughed your back and seared deep furrows there. Come, I'll heal your wounds, and suffer your sorrows. Come!

STRANGER (who has been weeping so violently that his whole body has been trembling, now goes to the cliff on the left where the MOTHER stands with open arms.) I'm coming!

TEMPTER. I can do nothing now. But one day we shall meet again! (He disappears behind the cliff.)

Curtain.

SCENE II
ROCKY LANDSCAPE ON THE MOUNTAIN

[Higher up the mountain; among the clouds a rocky landscape with a bog round it. The MOTHER on a rock, climbing until she disappears into the cloud. The STRANGER stops, bewildered.]

STRANGER. Oh, Mother, Mother! Why are you leaving me? At the very moment when my loveliest dream was on the point of fulfilment!

TEMPTER (coming forward). What have you been dreaming? Tell me!

STRANGER. My dearest hope, most secret desire and last prayer! Reconciliation with mankind, through a woman.

TEMPTER. Through a woman who taught you to hate.

STRANGER. Yes, because she bound me to earth—like the round shot a slave drags on his foot, so that he can't escape.

TEMPTER. You talk of woman. Always woman.

STRANGER. Yes. Woman. The beginning and the end—for us men anyhow. In relationship to one another they are nothing.

TEMPTER. So that's it; nothing in themselves; but everything for us, through us! Our honour and our shame; our greatest joy, our deepest pain; our redemption and our fall; our wages and our punishment; our strength and our weakness.

STRANGER. Our shame! You've said so. Explain this riddle to me, you who're wise. Whenever I appeared in public arm in arm with a woman, my wife, who was beautiful and whom I adored, I felt ashamed of my own weakness. Explain that riddle to me.

TEMPTER. You felt ashamed? I don't know why.

STRANGER. Can't you answer? You, of all men?

TEMPTER. No, I can't. But I too always suffered when I was with my wife in company, because I felt she was being soiled by men's glances, and I through her.

STRANGER. And when she did the shameful deed, you were dishonoured. Why?

TEMPTER. The Eve of the Greeks was called Pandora, and Zeus created her out of wickedness, in order to torture men and master them. As a wedding gift she received a box, containing all the unhappiness of the world. Perhaps the riddle of this sphinx can more easily be guessed, if it's seen from. Olympus, rather than from the pleasure garden of Paradise. Its full meaning will never be known to us. Though I'm as able as you. (Pause.) And, by the way, I can still enjoy the greatest pleasure creation ever offered! Go you and do likewise!

STRANGER. You mean Satan's greatest illusion! For the woman who seems most beautiful to me, can seem horrible to others! Even for me, when she's angry, she can be uglier than any other woman. Then what is beauty?

TEMPTER. A semblance, a reflection of your own goodness! (He puts his hand over his mouth.) Curses on it! I let it out that time. And now the devil's loose. . . .

STRANGER. Devil? Yes. But if she's a devil, how can a devil make me desire virtue and goodness? For that's what happened to me when I first saw her beauty; I was seized with a longing to be like her, and so to be worthy of her. To begin with I tried to be by taking exercise, having

274

baths, using cosmetics and wearing good clothes; but I only made myself ridiculous. Then I began from within; I accustomed myself to thinking good thoughts, speaking well of people and acting nobly! And one day, when my outward form had moulded itself on the soul within, I became her likeness, as she said. And it was she who first uttered those wonderful words: I love you! How can a devil ennoble us; how can a spirit of hell fill us with goodness; how . . . ? No, she was an angel! A fallen angel, of course, and her love a broken ray of that great light—that great eternal light—that warms and loves. . . . That loves. . . .

TEMPTER. What, old friend, must we stand here like two youths and spell out the riddles of love?

CONFESSOR (coming in). What's this chatterer saying? He's talked away his whole life; and never done anything.

TEMPTER. I wanted to be a priest, but had no vocation.

CONFESSOR. Whilst you're waiting for it, help me to find a drunkard who's drowned himself in the bog. It must be near here, because I've been following his tracks till now.

TEMPTER. Then it's the man lying beneath that brushwood there.

CONFESSOR (picking up some twigs, and disclosing a fully clothed corpse, with a white, young face.) Yes, it is! (He grows pensive as he looks at the dead man.)

TEMPTER. Who was he?

CONFESSOR. It's extraordinary!

TEMPTER. He must have been a good-looking man. And quite young.

275

CONFESSOR. Oh no. He was fifty-four. And when I saw him a week ago, he looked like sixty-four. His eyes were as yellow as the slime of a garden snail and bloodshot from drunkenness; but also because he'd shed tears of blood over his vices and misery. His face was brown and swollen like a piece of liver on a butcher's table, and he hid himself from men's eyes out of shame—up to the end he seems to have been ashamed of the broken mirror of his soul, for he covered his face with brushwood. I saw him fighting his vices; I saw him praying to God on his knees for deliverance, after he'd been dismissed from his post as a teacher. . . . But . . . Well, now he's been delivered. And look, now the evil's been taken from him, the good and beautiful that was in him has again become apparent; that's what he looked like when he was nineteen! (Pause.) This is sin—imposed as a punishment. Why? That we don't know. 'He who hateth the righteous, shall himself be guilty!' So it is written, as an indication. I knew him when he was young! And now I remember . . . he was always very angry with those who never drank. He criticised and condemned, and always set his cult of the grape on the altar of earthly joys! Now he's been set free. Free from sin, from shame, from ugliness. Yes, in death he looks beautiful. Death is the deliverer! (To the STRANGER.) Do you hear that, Deliverer, you who couldn't even free a drunkard from his evil passions!

TEMPTER. Crime as punishment? That's not so bad. Most penetrating!

CONFESSOR. So I think. You'll have new matter for argument.

TEMPTER. Now I'll leave you gentlemen for a while. But soon we'll meet again. (He goes out.)

CONFESSOR. I saw you just now with a woman! So there are still temptations?

STRANGER. Not the kind you mean.

CONFESSOR. Then what kind?

STRANGER. I could still imagine a reconciliation between mankind and woman—through woman herself! And indeed, through that woman who was my wife and has now become what I once held her to be having been purified and lifted up by sorrow and need. But . . .

CONFESSOR. But what?

STRANGER. Experience teaches; the nearer, the further off: the further from one another, the nearer one can be.

CONFESSOR. I've always known that—it was known by Dante, who all his life possessed the soul of Beatrice; and Beethoven, who was united from afar with Therese von Brunswick, knew it, though she was the wife of another!

STRANGER. And yet! Happiness is only to be found in her company.

CONFESSOR. Then stay with her.

STRANGER. You're forgetting one thing: we're divorced.

CONFESSOR. Good! Then you can begin a new marriage. And it'll promise all the more, because both of you are new people.

STRANGER. Do you think anyone would marry us?

CONFESSOR. I, for instance? That's asking too much.

STRANGER. Yes. I'd forgotten! But I daresay someone could be found. It's another thing to get a home together. . . .

CONFESSOR. You're sometimes lucky, even if you won't see it. There's a small house down there by the river; it's quite new and the owner's never even seen it. He was an Englishman who wanted to marry; but at the last moment *she* broke off the engagement. It was built by his secretary, and neither of the engaged couple ever set eyes on it. It's quite intact, you see!

STRANGER. IS it to let?

CONFESSOR. Yes.

STRANGER. Then I'll risk it. And I'll try to begin life all over again.

CONFESSOR. Then you'll go down?

STRANGER. Out of the clouds. Below the sun's shining, and up here the air's a little thin.

CONFESSOR. Good! Then we must part—for a time.

STRANGER. Where are you going?

CONFESSOR. Up.

STRANGER. And I down; to the earth, the mother with the soft bosom and warm lap. . . .

CONFESSOR. Until you long once more for what's hard as stone, as cold and as white . . . Farewell! Greetings to those below!

(Each of them goes of in the direction he has chosen.)

Curtain.

SCENE III
A SMALL HOUSE ON THE MOUNTAIN

[A pleasant, panelled dining-room, with a tiled stove of majolica. On the dining-table, which is in the middle of the room, stand vases filled with flowers; also two candelabra with many lighted candles. A large carved sideboard on the left. On the right, two windows. At the back, two doors; that on the left is open and gives a view of the drawing-room, belonging to the lady of the house, which is furnished in light green and mahogany, and has a standard lamp of brass with a large, lemon-coloured lampshade, which is lit. The door on the right is closed. On the left behind the sideboard the entrance from the hall.]

[From the left the STRANGER enters, dressed as a bridegroom; and the LADY, dressed as a bride; both radiant with youth and beauty.]

STRANGER. Welcome to my house, belovèd; to your home and mine, my bride; to your dwelling-place, my wife!

LADY. I'm grateful, dear friend! It's like a fairy tale!

STRANGER. Yes, it is. A whole book of fairy tales, my dear, written by me.

(They sit down on either side of the table.)

LADY. Is this real? It seems too lovely to me.

STRANGER. I've never seen you look so young, so beautiful.

LADY. It's your own eyes. . . .

STRANGER. Yes, my own eyes that have learnt to see. And your goodness taught them. . . .

LADY. Which itself was taught by sorrow.

STRANGER. Ingeborg!

LADY. It's the first time you've called me by that name.

STRANGER. The first? I've never met Ingeborg; I've never known you, as you are, sitting here in our home! Home! An enchanting word. An enchanting thing I've never yet possessed. A home and a wife! You are my first, my only one; for what once happened exists no longer—no more than the hour that's past!

LADY. Orpheus! Your song has made these dead stones live. Make life sing in me!

STRANGER. Eurydice, whom I rescued from the underworld! I'll love you to life again; revivify you with my imagination. Now happiness will come to us, for we know the dangers to avoid.

LADY. The dangers, yes! It's lovely in this house. It seems as if these rooms were full of invisible guests, who've come to welcome us. Kind spirits, who'll bless us and our home.

STRANGER. The candle flames are still, as if in prayer. The flowers are pensive. . . . And yet!

LADY. Hush! The summer night's outside, warm and dark. And stars hang in the sky; large and tearful in the fir trees, like Christmas candles. This is happiness. Hold it fast!

STRANGER (still thinking). And yet!

LADY. Hush!

280

STRANGER (getting up). A poem's coming: I can hear it. It's for you.

LADY. Don't tell it me. I can see it—in your eyes.

STRANGER. For I read it in yours! Well, I couldn't repeat it, because it has no words. Only scent, and colour. If I were to, I should destroy it. What's unborn is always most beautiful. What's unwon, most dear!

LADY. Quiet. Or, our guests will leave us.

(They do not speak.)

STRANGER. This *is* happiness—but I can't grasp it.

LADY. See it and breath it; for it can't be grasped.

(They do not speak.)

STRANGER. You're looking at your little room.

LADY. It's as bright green as a summer meadow. There's someone in there. Several people!

STRANGER. Only my thoughts.

LADY. Your good, your beautiful thoughts. . . .

STRANGER. Given me by you.

LADY. Had I anything to give you?

STRANGER. You? Everything! But up to now my hands have not been free to take it. Not clean enough to stroke your little heart. . . .

LADY. Beloved! The time for reconciliation's coming.

STRANGER. With mankind, and woman—through a woman? Yes, that time has come; and blessed may you be amongst women.

(The candles and lamps go out; it grows dark in the dining-room; but a weak ray of light can be seen, coming from the brass standard lamp in the LADY's room.)

LADY. Why's it grown dark? Oh!

STRANGER. Where are you, beloved? Give me your hand. I'm afraid!

LADY. Here, dearest.

STRANGER. The little hand, held out to me in the darkness, that's led me over stones and thorns. That little, soft, dear hand! Lead me into the light, into your bright, warm room; fresh green like hope.

LADY (leading him towards the pale-green room). Are you afraid?

STRANGER. You're a white dove, with whom the startled eagle finds sanctuary, when heaven's thunder clouds grow black, for the dove has no fear. She has not provoked the thunders of heaven!

(They have reached the doorway leading to the other room, when the curtain falls.)

* * * * *

[The same room; but the table has been cleared. The LADY is sitting at it, doing nothing. She seems bored. On the right, down stage, a window is open. It is still. The STRANGER comes in, with a piece of paper in his hand.]

STRANGER. Now you shall hear it.

282

LADY (acquiescing absent-mindedly). Finished already?

STRANGER. Already? Do you mean that seriously? I've taken seven days to write this little poem. (Silence.) Perhaps it'll bore you to hear it?

LADY (drily). No. Certainly not. (The STRANGER sits down at the table and looks at the LADY.) Why are you looking at me?

STRANGER. I'd like to see your thoughts.

LADY. But you've heard them.

STRANGER. That's nothing; I want to see them! (Pause.) What one says is mostly worthless. (Pause.) May I read them? No, I see I mayn't. You want nothing more from me. (The LADY makes a gesture as if she were going to speak.) Your face tells me enough. Now you've sucked me dry, eaten me hollow, killed my ego, my personality. To that I answer: how, my beloved? Have *I* killed your ego, when I wanted to give you the whole of mine; when I let you skim the cream off my bowl, that I'd filled with all the experience of along life, with incursions into the deserts and groves of knowledge and art?

LADY. I don't deny it, but my ego wasn't my own.

STRANGER. Not yours? Then what is? Something that belongs to others?

LADY. Is yours something that belongs to others too?

STRANGER. No. What I've experienced is my own, mine and no other's. What I've read becomes mine, because I've broken it in two like glass, melted it down, and from this substance blown new glass in novel forms.

LADY. But I can never be yours.

STRANGER. I've become yours.

LADY. What have you got from me?

STRANGER. How can you ask me that?

LADY. All the same—I'm not sure that you think it, though I feel you feel it—you wish me far away.

STRANGER. I must be a certain distance from you, if I'm to see you. Now you're within the focus, and your image is unclear.

LADY. The nearer, the farther off!

STRANGER. Yes. When we part, we long for one another; and when we meet again, we long to part.

LADY. Do you really think we love each other?

STRANGER. Yes. Not like ordinary people, but unusual ones. We resemble two drops of water, that fear to get close together, in case they should cease to be two and become one.

LADY. This time we knew the dangers and wanted to avoid them. But it seems that they can't be avoided.

STRANGER. Perhaps they weren't dangers, but rude necessities; laws inscribed in the councils of the immortals. (Silence.) Your love always seemed to have the effect of hate. When you made me happy, you envied the happiness you'd given me. And when you saw I was unhappy, you loved me.

LADY. Do you want me to leave you?

STRANGER. If you do, I shall die.

LADY. And, if I stay, it's I who'll die.

STRANGER. Then let's die together and live out our love in a higher life; our love, that doesn't seem to be of this world. Let's live it out in another planet, where there's no nearness and no distance, where two are one; where number, time and space are no longer what they are in this.

LADY. I'd like to die, yet I don't want to. I think I must be dead already.

STRANGER. The air up here's too strong.

LADY. You can't love me if you speak like that.

STRANGER. To be frank, there are moments when you don't exist for me. But in others I feel your hatred like suffocating smoke.

LADY. And I feel my heart creeping from my breast, when you are angry with me.

STRANGER. Then we must hate one other.

LADY. And love one another too.

STRANGER. And hate because we love. We hate each other, because we're bound together. We hate the bond, we hate our love; we hate what is most loveable, what is the bitterest, the best this life can offer. We've come to an end!

LADY. Yes.

STRANGER. What a joke life is, if you take it seriously. And how serious, if you take it as a joke! You wanted to lead me by the hand towards the light; your easier fate was to make mine easier too. I wanted to raise you above the bogs and quicksands; but you longed for the lower regions, and wanted to convince me they were the upper ones. I ask myself if it's possible that you took what was wicked from me, when I was freed from it; and that what was good in you entered into me? If I've made you wicked I ask your pardon, and I kiss your little hand, that caressed and scratched me . . . the little hand that led me into the darkness . . . and on the long journey to Damascus. . . .

LADY. To a parting? (Silence.) Yes, a parting!

(The LADY goes on her way. The STRANGER falls on to a chair by the table. The TEMPTER puts his head in at the window, and rests himself on his elbows whilst he smokes a cigarette.)

TEMPTER. Ah, yes! C'est l'amour! The most mysterious of all mysteries, the most inexplicable of all that can't be explained, the most precarious of all that's insecure.

STRANGER. So you're here?

TEMPTER. I'm always everywhere, where it smells of quarrels. And in love affairs there are always quarrels.

STRANGER. Always?

TEMPTER. Always! I was invited to a silver wedding yesterday. Twenty-five years are no trifle—and for twenty-five years they'd been quarrelling. The whole love affair had been one long shindy, with many little ones in between! And yet they loved one another, and were grateful for all the good that had come to them; the evil was forgotten, wiped out—for a

286

moment's happiness is worth ten days of blows and pinpricks. Oh yes! Those who won't accept evil never get anything good. The rind's very bitter, though the kernel's sweet.

STRANGER. But very small.

TEMPTER. It may be small, but it's good! (Pause.) Tell me, why did your madonna go her way? No answer; because he doesn't know! Now we'll have to let the hotel again. Here's a board. I'll hang it out at once. 'To Let.' One comes, another goes! C'est la vie, quoi? Rooms for Travellers!

STRANGER. Have you ever been married?

TEMPTER. Oh yes. Of course.

STRANGER. Then why did you part?

TEMPTER. Chiefly—perhaps it's a peculiarity of mine—chiefly because—well, you know, a man marries to get a home, to get into a home; and a woman to get out of one. She wanted to get out, and I wanted to get in! I was so made that I couldn't take her into company, because I felt as if she were soiled by men's glances. And in company, my splendid, wonderful wife turned into a little grimacing monkey I couldn't bear the sight of. So I stayed at home; and then, she stayed away. And when I met her again, she'd changed into someone else. She, my pure white notepaper, was scribbled all over; her clear and lovely features changed in imitation of the satyr-like looks of strange men. I could see miniature photographs of bull-fighters and guardsmen in her eyes, and hear the strange accents of strange men in her voice. On our grand piano, on which only the harmonies of the great masters used to be heard, she now played the cabaret songs of strange men; and on our table there lay nothing but the favourite reading of strange men. In a word, my whole existence was on the way to becoming an intellectual concubinage with strange men—and that was contrary to my nature, which has always longed for women! And—I need hardly say this— the tastes of these strange men were always the reverse of mine. She developed a real genius for discovering things I detested! That's what she called 'saving her personality.' Can you understand that?

STRANGER. I can; but I won't attempt to explain it.

TEMPTER. Yet this woman maintained she loved me, and that I didn't love her. But I loved her so much I didn't want to speak to any other human being; because I feared to be untrue to her if I found pleasure in the company of others, even if they were men. I'd married for feminine society; and in order to enjoy it I'd left my friends. I'd married in order to find company, but what I got was complete solitude! And I was supporting house and home, in order to provide strange men with feminine companionship. *C'est l'amour*, my friend!

STRANGER. You should never talk about your wife.

TEMPTER. No! For if you speak well of her, people will laugh; and if you speak ill, all their sympathy will go out to her; and if, in the first instance, you ask why they laugh, you get no answer.

STRANGER. No. You can never find out who you've married. Never get hold of her—it seems she's no one. Tell me—what is woman?

TEMPTER. I don't know! Perhaps a larva or a chrysalis, out of whose trance-like life a man one day will be created. She seems a child, but isn't one; she is a sort of child, and yet not like one. Drags downward, when the man pulls up. Drags upward, when the man pulls down.

STRANGER. She always wants to disagree with her husband; always has a lot of sympathy for what he dislikes; is crudest beneath the greatest superficial refinement; the wickedest amongst the best. And yet, whenever I've been in love, I've always grown more sensitive to the refinements of civilisation.

TEMPTER. You, I dare say. What about her?

STRANGER. Oh, whilst our love was growing *she* was always developing backwards. And getting cruder and more wicked.

TEMPTER. Can you explain that?

STRANGER. No. But once, when I was trying to find the solution to the riddle by disagreeing with myself, I took it that she absorbed my evil and I her good.

TEMPTER. Do you think woman's particularly false?

STRANGER. Yes and no. She seeks to hide her weakness but that only means that she's ambitious and has a sense of shame. Only whores are honest, and therefore cynical.

TEMPTER. Tell me some more about her that's good.

STRANGER. I once had a woman friend. She soon noticed that when I drank I looked uglier than usual; so she begged me not to. I remember one night we'd been talking in a café for many hours. When it was nearly ten o'clock, she begged me to go home and not to drink any more. We parted, after we'd said goodnight. A few days later I heard she'd left me only to go to a large party, where she drank till morning. Well, I said, as in those days I looked for all that was good in women, she meant well by me, but had to pollute herself for business reasons.

TEMPTER. That's well thought out; and, as a view, can be defended. She wanted to make you better than herself, higher and purer, so that she could look up to you! But you can find an equally good explanation for that. A wife's always angry and out of humour with her husband; and the husband's always kind and grateful to his wife. He does all he can to make things easy for her, and she does all she can to torture him.

STRANGER. That's not true. Of course it may sometimes appear to be so. I once had a woman friend who shifted all the defects that she had on to me. For instance, she was very much in love with herself, and therefore called me the most egoistical of men. She drank, and called me a drunkard; she rarely changed her linen and said I was dirty; she was jealous, even of my men friends, and called me Othello. She was masterful and called me Nero. Niggardly and called me Harpagon.

TEMPTER. Why didn't you answer her?

STRANGER. You know why very well! If I'd made clear to her what she really was, I'd have lost her favour that moment—and it was precisely her favour I wanted to keep.

TEMPTER. *A tout prix*! Yes, that's the source of degradation! You grow accustomed to holding your tongue, and at last find yourself caught in a tissue of falsehoods.

STRANGER. Wait! Don't you agree that married people so mix their personalities that they can no longer distinguish between meum and tuum, no longer remain separate from one another, or cannot tell their own weaknesses from those of the other. My jealous friend, who called me Othello, took me for herself, identified me with herself.

TEMPTER. That sounds conceivable.

STRANGER. You see! You can often explain most if you don't ask who's to blame. For when married people begin to differ, it's like a realm divided against itself, and that's the worst kind of disharmony.

TEMPTER. There are moments when I think a woman cannot love a man.

STRANGER. Perhaps not. To love is an active verb and woman's a passive noun. He loves and she is loved; he asks questions and she merely answers.

TEMPTER. Then what is woman's love?

STRANGER. The man's.

TEMPTER. Well said. And therefore when the man ceases to love her, she severs herself from him!

STRANGER. And then?

TEMPTER. 'Sh! Someone's coming. Perhaps to take the house!

STRANGER. A woman or a man?

TEMPTER. A woman! And a man. But he's waiting outside. Now he's turned and is going into the wood. Interesting!

STRANGER. Who is it?

TEMPTER. You can see for yourself.

STRANGER (looking out of the window). It's she! My first wife! My first love!

TEMPTER. It seems she's left her second husband recently . . . and arrived here with number three; who, if one can judge by certain movements of his back and calves, is escaping from a stormy scene. Oh, well! But she didn't notice his spiteful intentions. Very interesting! I'll go out and listen.

(He disappears. The WOMAN knocks.)

STRANGER. Come in!

(The WOMAN comes in. There is a silence.)

WOMAN (excitedly). I only came here because the house was to let.

STRANGER. Oh!

WOMAN (slowly). Had I known who wanted to let it, I shouldn't have come.

STRANGER. What does it matter?

WOMAN. May I sit down a moment? I'm tired.

STRANGER. Please do. (They sit down at the table opposite one another, in the seats occupied by the STRANGER and the LADY in the first scene.) It's a long time since we've sat facing one another like this.

WOMAN. With flowers and lights on the table. One night . . .

STRANGER. When I was dressed as a bridegroom and you as a bride . . .

WOMAN. And the candle flames were still as in prayer and the flowers pensive. . . .

STRANGER. Is your husband outside?

WOMAN. No.

STRANGER. You're still seeking . . . what doesn't exist?

WOMAN. Doesn't it?

STRANGER. No. I always told you so, but you wouldn't believe me; you wanted to find out for yourself. Have you found out now?

WOMAN. Not yet.

STRANGER. Why did you leave your husband? (The WOMAN doesn't reply.) Did he beat you?

WOMAN. Yes.

STRANGER. How did he come to forget himself so far?

WOMAN. He was angry.

STRANGER. What about?

WOMAN. Nothing.

STRANGER. Why was he angry about nothing?

WOMAN (rising). No, thank you! I won't sit here and be picked to pieces. Where's your wife?

STRANGER. She left me just now.

WOMAN. Why?

STRANGER. Why did you leave me?

WOMAN. I felt you wanted to leave me; so, not to be deserted, I went myself.

STRANGER. I dare say that's true. But how could you read my thoughts?

WOMAN (sitting down again). What? We didn't need to speak in order to know one another's thoughts.

STRANGER. We made a mistake when we were living together, because we accused each other of wicked thoughts before they'd become actions; and lived in mental reservations instead of realities. For instance, I once noticed how you enjoyed the defiling gaze of a strange man, and I accused you of unfaithfulness.

WOMAN. You were wrong to do so, and right. Because my thoughts were sinful.

STRANGER. Don't you think my habit of 'anticipating you' prevented your bad designs from being put in practice?

WOMAN. Let me think! Yes, perhaps it did. But I was annoyed to find a spy always at my side, watching my inmost self, that was my own.

STRANGER. But it wasn't your own: it was ours!

WOMAN. Yes, but I held it to be mine, and believed you'd no right to force your way in. When you did so I hated you; I said you were abnormally suspicious out of self-defence. Now I can admit that your suspicions were never wrong; that they were, in fact, the purest wisdom.

STRANGER. Oh! Do you know that, at night, when we'd said good-night as friends and gone to sleep, I used to wake and feel your hatred poisoning me; and think of getting out of bed so as not to be suffocated. One night I woke and felt a pressure on the top of my head. I saw you were awake and had put your hand close to my mouth. I thought you were making me inhale poison from a phial; and, to make sure, I seized your hand.

WOMAN. I remember.

STRANGER. What did you do then?

WOMAN. Nothing. Only hated you.

STRANGER. Why?

WOMAN. Because you were my husband. Because I ate your bread.

STRANGER. Do you think it's always the same?

WOMAN. I don't know. I suspect it is.

STRANGER. But sometimes you've even despised me?

WOMAN. Yes, when you were ridiculous. A man in love is always ridiculous. Do you know what a cox-comb is? That's what a lover's like.

STRANGER. But if any man who loves you is ridiculous, how can you respond to his love?

WOMAN. We don't! We submit to it, and search for another man who doesn't love us.

STRANGER. But if he, in turn, begins to love you, do you look for a third?

WOMAN. Perhaps it's like that.

STRANGER. Very strange. (There is a silence.) I remember you were always dreaming of someone you called your Toreador, which I translated by 'horse butcher.' You eventually got him, but he gave you no children, and no bread; only beatings! A toreador's always fighting. (Silence.) Once I let myself be tempted into trying to compete with the toreador. I started to bicycle and fence and do other things of the kind. But you only began to detest me for it. That means that the husband mayn't do what the lover may. Later you had a passion for page boys. One of them used to sit on the Brussels carpet and read you bad verses. . . . My good ones were of no use to you. Did you get your page boy?

WOMAN. Yes. But his verses weren't bad, really.

STRANGER. Oh yes, they were, my dear. I know him! He stole my rhythms and set them for the barrel organ.

WOMAN (rising and going to the door.) You should be ashamed of yourself.

(The TEMPTER conies in, holding a letter in his hand.)

TEMPTER. Here's a letter. It's for you. (The WOMAN takes it, reads it and falls into a chair.) A farewell note! Oh, well! All beginnings are hard—in love affairs. And those who lack the patience to surmount initial difficulties—lose the golden fruit. Pages are always impatient. Unknown youth, have you had enough?

STRANGER (rising and picking up his hat). My poor Anna!

WOMAN. Don't leave me.

STRANGER. I must.

WOMAN. Don't go. You were the best of them all.

TEMPTER. Do you want to begin again from the beginning? That would be a sure way to make an end of this. For if lovers only find one another, they lose one another! What is love? Say something witty, each one of you, before we part.

WOMAN. I don't know what it is. The highest and the loveliest of things, that has to sink to the lowest and the ugliest.

STRANGER. A caricature of godly love.

TEMPTER. An annual plant, that blossoms during the engagement, goes to seed in marriage and then sinks to the earth to wither and die.

WOMAN. The loveliest flowers have no seed. The rose is the flower of love.

STRANGER. And the lily that of innocence. That can form seeds, but only opens her white cup to kisses.

TEMPTER. And propagates her kind with buds, out of which fresh lilies spring, like chaste Minerva who sprang fully armed from the head of Zeus, and not from his royal loins. Oh yes, children, I've understood much, but never this: what the beloved of my soul has to do with. . . . (He hesitates.)

STRANGER. Well, go on!

TEMPTER. What all-powerful love, that is the marriage of souls, has to do with the propagation of the species!

STRANGER and WOMAN. Now he's come to the point!

TEMPTER. I've never been able to understand how a kiss, that's an unborn word, a soundless speech, a quiet language of the soul, can be exchanged, by means of a hallowed procedure, for a surgical operation, that always ends in tears and the chattering of teeth. I've never understood how that holy night, the first in which two souls embrace each other in love, can end in the shedding of blood, in quarrelling, hate, mutual contempt—and lint! (He holds his mouth shut.)

STRANGER. Suppose the story of the fall were true? In pain shalt thou bring forth children.

TEMPTER. In that case one could understand.

WOMAN. Who is the man who says these things?

TEMPTER. Only a wanderer on the quicksands of this life. (The WOMAN rises.) So you're ready to go. Who will go first?

STRANGER. I shall.

TEMPTER. Where?

STRANGER. Upwards. And you?

TEMPTER. I shall stay down here, in between. . . .

Curtain.

ACT IV

SCENE I
CHAPTER HOUSE OF THE MONASTERY

[A Gothic chapter house. In the background arcades lead to the cloisters and the courtyard of the monastery. In the middle of the courtyard there is a well with a statue of the Virgin Mary, surrounded by long-stemmed white roses. The walls of the chapter house are filled with built-in choir stalls of oak. The PRIOR'S own stall is in the middle to the right and rather higher than the rest. In the middle of the chapter house an enormous crucifix. The sun is shining on the statue of the Virgin in the courtyard. The STRANGER enters from the back. He is wearing a coarse monkish cowl, with a rope round his waist and sandals on his feet. He halts in the doorway and looks at the chapter house, then goes over to the crucifix and stops in front of it. The last strophe of the choral service can be heard from across the courtyard. The CONFESSOR enters from the back; he is dressed in black and white; he has long hair and along beard and a very small tonsure that can hardly be seen.]

CONFESSOR. Peace be with you!

STRANGER. And with you.

CONFESSOR. How do you like this white house?

STRANGER. I can only see blackness.

CONFESSOR. You still are black; but you'll grow white, quite white! Did you sleep well last night?

STRANGER. Dreamlessly, like a tired child. But tell me: why do I find so many locked doors?

CONFESSOR. You'll gradually learn to open them.

STRANGER. Is this a large building?

CONFESSOR. Endless! It dates from the time of Charlemagne and has continually grown through pious benefactions. Untouched by the spiritual upheavals and changes of different epochs, it stands on its rocky height as a monument of Western culture. That is to say: Christian faith wedded to the knowledge of Hellas and Rome.

STRANGER. So it's not merely a religious foundation?

CONFESSOR. No. It embraces all the arts and sciences as well. There's a library, museum, observatory and laboratory—as you'll see later. Agriculture and horticulture are also studied here; and a hospital for laymen, with its own sulphur springs, is attached to the monastery.

STRANGER. One word more, before the chapter assembles. What kind of man is the Prior?

CONFESSOR (smiling). He is the Prior! Aloof, without peer, dwelling on the summits of human knowledge, and . . . well, you'll see him soon.

STRANGER. Is it true that he's so old?

CONFESSOR. He's reached an unusual age. He was born at the beginning of the century that's now nearing its end.

STRANGER. Has he always been in the monastery?

CONFESSOR. No. He's not always been a monk, though always a priest. Once he was a minister, but that was seventy years ago. Twice curator of the university. Archbishop. . . . 'Sh! Mass is over.

STRANGER. I presume he's not the kind of unprejudiced priest who pretends to have vices when he has none?

CONFESSOR. Not at all. But he's seen life and mankind, and he's more human than priestly.

STRANGER. And the fathers?

CONFESSOR. Wise men, with strange histories, and none of them alike.

STRANGER. Who can never have known life as it's lived. . . .

CONFESSOR. All have lived their lives, more than once; have suffered shipwreck, started again, gone to pieces and risen once more. You must wait.

STRANGER. The Prior's sure to ask me questions. I don't think I can agree to everything.

CONFESSOR. On the contrary, you must show yourself as you are; and defend your opinions to the last.

STRANGER. Will contradiction be permitted here?

CONFESSOR. Here? You're a child, who's lived in a childish world, where you've played with thoughts and words. You've lived in the erroneous belief that language, a material thing, can be a vehicle for anything so subtle as thoughts and feelings. We've discovered that error, and therefore speak as little as possible; for we are aware of, and can divine, the innermost thoughts of our neighbour. We've so developed our perceptive faculties by spiritual exercises that we are linked in a single chain; and can detect a feeling of pleasure and harmony, when there's complete accord. The Prior, who has trained himself most rigorously, can feel if anyone's thoughts have strayed into wrong paths. In some respects he's like—merely like, I say—a telephone engineer's galvanometer, that shows when and where a current has been interrupted. Therefore we can have no secrets from one another, and so do not need the confessional. Think of all this when you confront the searching eye of the Prior!

STRANGER. Is there any intention of examining me?

CONFESSOR. Oh no. There are merely a few questions to answer without any deep meaning, before the practical examinations. Quiet! Here they are.

(He goes to one side. The PRIOR enters from the back. He is dressed entirely in white and he has pulled up his hood. He is a tall man with long white hair and along white beard-his head is like that of Jupiter. His face is pale, but full and without wrinkles. His eyes are large, surrounded by shadows and his eyebrows strongly marked. A quiet, majestic calm reigns over his whole personality. The PRIOR is followed by twelve Fathers, dressed in black and white, with black hoods, also pulled up. All bow to the crucifix and then go to their places.)

PRIOR (after looking at the STRANGER for a moment.) What do you seek here? (The STRANGER is confused and tries to find an answer, but cannot. The PRIOR goes on, calmly, firmly, but indulgently.) Peace? Isn't that so? (The STRANGER makes a sign of assent with head and mouth.) But if the whole of life is a struggle, how can you find peace amongst the living? (The STRANGER is not able to answer.) Do you want to turn your back on life because you feel you've been injured, cheated?

STRANGER (in a weak voice). Yes.

PRIOR. So you've been defrauded, unjustly dealt with? And this injustice began so early that you, an innocent child, couldn't imagine you'd committed any crime that was worthy of punishment. Well, once you were unjustly accused of stealing fruit; tormented into taking the offence on yourself; tortured into telling lies about yourself and forced to beg forgiveness for a fault you'd not committed. Wasn't it so?

STRANGER (with certainty). Yes. It was.

PRIOR. It was; and you've never been able to forget it. Never. Now listen, you've a good memory; can you remember *The Swiss Family Robinson*?

STRANGER (shrinking). *The Swiss Family Robinson*?

PRIOR. Yes. Those events that caused you such mental torture happened in 1857, but at Christmas 1856, that is the year before, you tore a copy of that book and out of fear of punishment hid it under a chest in the kitchen. (The STRANGER is taken aback.) The wardrobe was painted in oak graining, and clothes hung in its upper part, whilst shoes stood below. This wardrobe seemed enormously big to you, for you were a small child, and you couldn't imagine it could ever be moved; but during spring cleaning at Easter what was hidden was brought to light. Fear drove you to put the blame on a schoolfellow. And now he had to endure torture, because appearances were against him, for you were thought to be trustworthy. After this the history of your sorrows comes as a logical sequence. You accept this logic?

STRANGER. Yes. Punish me!

PRIOR. No. I don't punish; when I was a child I did—similar things. But will you now promise to forget this history of your own sufferings for all time and never to recount it again?

STRANGER. I promise! If only he whom I took advantage of could forgive me.

PRIOR. He has already. Isn't that so, Pater Isidor?

ISIDOR (who was the DOCTOR in the first part of 'The Road to Damascus,' rising). With my whole heart!

STRANGER. It's you!

ISIDOR. Yes. I.

PRIOR (to FATHER ISIDOR). Pater Isidor, say a word, just one.

ISIDOR. It was in the year 1856 that I had to endure my torture. But even in 1854 one of my brothers suffered in the same way, owing to a false accusation on my part. (To the STRANGER.) So we're all guilty and not one of us is without blemish; and I believe my victim had no clear conscience either. (He sits down.)

PRIOR. If we could only stop accusing one another and particularly Eternal Justice! But we're born in guilt and all resemble Adam! (To the STRANGER.) There was something you wanted to know, was there not?

STRANGER. I wanted to know life's inmost meaning.

PRIOR. The very innermost! So you wanted to learn what no man's permitted to know. Pater Uriel! (PATER URIEL, who is blind, rises. The PRIOR speaks to the STRANGER.) Look at this blind father! We call him Uriel in remembrance of Uriel Acosta, whom perhaps you've heard of? (The STRANGER makes a sign that he has not.) You haven't? All young people should have heard of him. Uriel Acosta was a Portuguese of Jewish descent, who, however, was brought up in the Christian faith. When he was still fairly young he began to inquire—you understand—to inquire if Christ were really God; with the result that he went over to the Jewish faith. And then he began research into the Mosaic writings and the immortality of the soul, with the result that the Rabbis handed him over to the Christian priesthood for punishment. A long time after he returned to the Jewish faith. But his thirst for knowledge knew no bounds, and he continued his researches till he found he'd reached absolute nullity; and in despair that he couldn't learn the final secret he took his own life with a pistol shot. (Pause.) Now look at our good father Uriel here. He, too, was once very young and anxious to know; he always wanted to be in the forefront of every modern movement, and he discovered new philosophies. I may add, by the way, that he's a friend of my boyhood and almost as old as I. Now about 1820 he came upon the so-called rational philosophy, that had already lain in its grave for twenty years. With this system of thought, which was supposed to be a master key, all locks were to be picked, all questions answered and all opponents confuted—everything was clear and simple. In those days Uriel was a strong opponent of all religions and in particular followed the Mesmerists, as the hypnotisers of that age were called. In 1830 our friend became a Hegelian, though, to be sure, rather late in the day. Then he re-discovered God, a God who was immanent in nature and in man, and found he was a little god himself. Now, as ill-luck would have it, there were two Hegels, just as there were two Voltaires; and the later, or more conservative Hegel, had developed his All-godhead till it had become a compromise with the Christian view. And so Father Uriel, who never wanted to be behind the times, became a rationalistic Christian, who was given the thankless task of combating Rationalism and himself. (Pause.) I'll shorten the whole sad history for Father Uriel's sake. In 1850 he again became a materialist and an enemy of Christianity. In 1870 he became a hypnotist, in 1880 a theosophist, and 1890 he wanted to shoot himself! I met him just at that time. He was sitting on a bench in Unter den Linden in Berlin, and he was blind. This Uriel was blind—and Uriel means 'God is my Light'—who for a century had marched with the torch of liberalism at the head of *every* modern movement! (To the STRANGER.) You see, he wanted to know, but he failed! And therefore he now believes. Is there anything else you'd like to know?

STRANGER. One thing only.

PRIOR. Speak.

STRANGER. If Father Uriel had held to his first faith in 1810, men would have called him conservative or old-fashioned; but now, as he's followed the developments of his time and has therefore discarded his youthful faith, men will call him a renegade—that's to say: whatever he does mankind will blame him.

PRIOR. Do you heed what men say? Father Clemens, may I tell him how you heeded what men said? (PATER CLEMENS rises and makes a gesture of assent.) Father Clemens is our greatest figure painter. In the world outside he's known by another name, a very famous one. Father Clemens was a young man in 1830. He felt he had a talent for painting and gave himself up to it with his whole soul. When he was twenty he was exhibiting. The public, the critics, his teachers, and his parents were all of the opinion that he'd made a mistake in the choice of his profession. Young Clemens heeded what men were saying, so he laid down his brush and turned bookseller. When he was fifty years of age, and had his life behind him, the paintings of his early years were discovered by some stranger; and were then recognised as masterpieces by the public, the critics, his teachers and relations! But it was too late.

And when Father Clemens complained of the wickedness of the world, the world answered with a heartless grin: 'Why did you let yourself be taken in?' Father Clemens grieved so much at this, that he came to us. But he doesn't grieve any longer now. Or do you, Father Clemens?

CLEMENS. No! But that isn't the end of the story. The paintings I'd done in 1830 were admired and hung in a museum till 1880. Taste then changed very quickly, and one day an important newspaper announced that their presence there was an outrage. So they were banished to the attic.

PRIOR (to the STRANGER). That's a good story!

CLEMENS. But it's still not finished. By 1890 taste had so changed again that a professor of the History of Art wrote that it was a national scandal that my works should be hanging in an attic. So the pictures were brought down again, and, for the time being, are classical. But for how long? From that you can see, young man, in what worldly fame consists? Vanitas vanitatum vanitas!

STRANGER. Then is life worth living?

PRIOR. Ask Pater Melcher, who is experienced not only in the world of deception and error, but also in that of lies and contradictions. Follow him: he'll show you the picture gallery and tell you stories.

STRANGER. I'll gladly follow anyone who can teach me something.

(PATER MELCHER takes the STRANGER by the hand and leads him out of the Chapter House.)

Curtain.

SCENE II
PICTURE GALLERY OF THE MONASTERY

[Picture Gallery of the Monastery. There are mostly portraits of people with two heads.]

MELCHER. Well, first we have here a small landscape, by an unknown master, called 'The Two Towers.' Perhaps you've been in Switzerland and know the originals.

STRANGER. I've been in Switzerland!

MELCHER. Exactly. Then near the station of Amsteg on the Gotthard railway you've seen a tower, called Zwing-Uri, sung of by Schiller in his *Wilhelm Tell*. It stands there as a monument to the cruel oppression which the inhabitants of Uri suffered at the hands of the German Emperors. Good! On the Italian side of the Gotthard lies Bellinzona, as you know. There are many towers to be seen there, but the most curious is called Castel d'Uri. That's the monument recalling the cruel oppression which the Italian cantons suffered at the hands of the inhabitants of Uri! Now do you understand?

STRANGER. So freedom means: freedom to oppress others. That's new to me.

MELCHER. Then let's go on without further comment to the portrait collection. Number one in the catalogue. Boccaccio, with two heads—all our portraits have at least two heads. His story's well known. The great man began his career by writing dissolute and godless tales, which he dedicated to Queen Johanna of Naples, who'd seduced the son of St. Brigitta. Boccaccio ended up as a saint in a monastery where he lectured on Dante's Hell and the devils that, in his youth, he had thought to drive out in a most original way. You'll notice now, how the two faces are meeting each other's gaze!

STRANGER. Yes. But all trace of humour's lacking; and humour's to be expected in a man who knew himself as well as our friend Boccaccio did.

MELCHER. Number two in the catalogue. Ah, yes; that's two-headed Doctor Luther. The youthful champion of tolerance and the aged upholder of intolerance. Have I said enough?

STRANGER. Quite enough.

MELCHER. Number three in the catalogue. The great Gustavus Adolphus accepting Catholic funds from Cardinal Richelieu in order to fight for Protestantism, whilst remaining neutral in the face of the Catholic League.

STRANGER. How do Protestants explain this threefold contradiction?

MELCHER. They say it's not true. Number four in the catalogue. Schiller, the author of The Robbers, who was offered the freedom of the City of Paris by the leaders of the French Revolution in 1792; but who had been made a State Councillor of Meiningen as early as 1790 and a royal Danish Stipendiary in 1791. The scene depicts the State Councillor—and friend of his Excellency Goethe—receiving the Diploma of Honour from the leaders of the French Revolution as late as 1798. Think of it, the diploma of the Reign of Terror in the year 1798, when the Revolution was over and the country under the Directory! I'd have liked to have seen the Councillor and his friend, His Excellency! But it didn't matter, for two years later he repaid his nomination by writing the *Song of the Bell*, in which he expressed his thanks and begged the revolutionaries to keep quiet! Well, that's life. We're intelligent people and love *The Robbers* as much as *The Song of the Bell*; Schiller as much as Goethe!

STRANGER. The work remains, the master perishes.

MELCHER. Goethe, yes! Number five in the catalogue. He began with Strassburg cathedral and *Götz von Berlichingen,* two hurrahs for gothic Germanic art against that of Greece and Rome. Later he fought against Germanism and for Classicism. Goethe against Goethe! There you see the traditional Olympic calm, harmony, etc., in the greatest disharmony with itself. But depression at this turns into uneasiness when the young Romantic school appears and combats the Goethe of *Iphigenia* with theories drawn from Goethe's *Goetz.* That the 'great heathen' ends up by converting Faust in the Second Part, and allowing him to be saved by the Virgin Mary and the angels, is usually passed over in silence by his admirers. Also the fact that a man of such clear vision should, towards the end of his life, have found everything so 'strange,' and 'curious,' even the simplest facts that he'd previously seen through. His last wish was for 'more light'! Yes; but it doesn't matter. We're intelligent people and love our Goethe just the same.

STRANGER. And rightly.

MELCHER. Number six in the catalogue. Voltaire! He has more than two heads. The Godless One, who spent his whole life defending God. The Mocker, who was mocked, because 'he believed in God like a child.' The author of the cynical 'Candide,' who wrote:

In my youth I sought the pleasures
Of the senses, but I learned
That their sweetness was illusion
Soon to bitterness it turned.
In old age I've come to see
Life is nought but vanity.

Dr. Knowall, who thought he could grasp everything between Heaven and Earth by means of reason and science, sings like this, when he comes to the end of his life:

I had thought to find in knowledge
Light to guide me on my way;
Yet I still must walk in darkness
All that's known must soon decay.
Ignorance, I turn to thee!
Knowledge is but vanity.

But that's no matter! Voltaire can be put to many uses. The Jews use him against the Christians, and the Christians use him against the Jews, because he was an anti-Semite, like Luther. Chateaubriand used him to defend Catholicism, and Protestants use him even today to attack Catholicism. He was a fine fellow!

STRANGER. Then what's your view?

MELCHER. We have no views here; we've faith, as I've told you already. And that's why we've only one head—placed exactly above the heart. (Pause.) In the meantime let's look at number seven in the catalogue. Ah, Napoleon! The creation of the Revolution itself! The Emperor of the People, the Nero of Freedom, the suppressor of Equality and the 'big brother' of Fraternity. He's the most cunning of all the two-headed, for he could laugh at himself, raise himself above his own contradictions, change his skin and his soul, and yet be quite explicable to himself in every transformation—convinced, self-authorised. There's only one other man who can be compared with him in this; Kierkegaard the Dane. From the beginning he was aware of this parthenogenesis of the soul, whose capacity to multiply by taking cuttings was equivalent to bringing forth young in this life without conception. And for that reason, and so as not to become life's fool, he wrote under a number of pseudonyms, of which each one constituted a 'stage on his life's way.' But did you realise this? The Lord of life, in spite of all these precautions, made a fool of him after all. Kierkegaard, who fought all his life against the priesthood and the professional preachers of the State Church, was eventually forced of necessity to become a professional preacher himself! Oh yes! Such things do happen.

STRANGER. The Powers That Be play tricks. . . .

MELCHER. The Powers play tricks on tricksters, and delude the arrogant, particularly those who alone believe they possess truth and knowledge! Number eight in the catalogue. Victor Hugo. He split himself into countless parts. He was a peer of France, a Grandee of Spain, a friend of Kings, and the socialist author of *Les Misérables*. The peers naturally called him a renegade, and the socialists a reformer. Number nine. Count Friedrich Leopold von Stollberg. He wrote a fanatical book for the Protestants, and then suddenly became a Catholic! Inexplicable in a sensible man. A miracle, eh? A little journey to Damascus, perhaps? Number ten. Lafayette. The heroic upholder of freedom, the revolutionary, who was forced to leave France as a suspected reactionary, because he wanted to help Louis XVI; and then was captured by the Austrians and carried off to Olmütz as a revolutionary! What was he in reality?

STRANGER. Both!

MELCHER. Yes, both. He had the two halves that made a whole—a whole man. Number eleven. Bismarck. A paradox. The honest diplomat, who maintained he'd discovered that to tell the truth was the greatest of ruses. And so was compelled—by the Powers, I suppose?—to spend the last six years of his life unmasking himself as a conscious liar. You're tired. Then we'll stop now.

STRANGER. Yes, if one clings to the same ideas all one's life, and holds the same opinions, one grows old according to nature's laws, and gets called conservative, old-fashioned, out of date. But if one goes on developing, keeping pace with one's own age, renewing oneself with the perennially youthful impulses of contemporary thought, one's called a waverer and a renegade.

MELCHER. That's as old as the world! But does an intelligent, man heed what he's called? One is, what one's becoming.

STRANGER. But who revises the periodically changing views of contemporary opinion?

MELCHER. You ought to answer that yourself, and indeed in this way. It is the Powers themselves who promulgate contemporary opinion, as they develop in *apparent* circles. Hegel, the philosopher of the present, himself dimorphous, for both a 'left'-minded and a 'right'-minded Hegel can always be quoted, has best explained the contradictions of life, of history and of the spirit, with his own magic formula. Thesis: affirmation; Antithesis: negation; Synthesis: comprehension! Young man, or rather, comparatively young man! You began life by accepting everything, then went on to denying everything on principle. Now end your life by comprehending everything. Be exclusive no longer. Do not say: either—or, but: not only—but also! In a word, or two words rather, Humanity and Resignation!

Curtain.

SCENE III
CHAPEL OF THE MONASTERY

[Choir of the Monastery Chapel. An open coffin with a bier cloth and two burning candles. The CONFESSOR leads in the STRANGER by the hand. The STRANGER is dressed in the white shirt of the novice.]

CONFESSOR. Have you carefully considered the step you wish to take?

STRANGER. Very carefully.

CONFESSOR. Have you no more questions?

STRANGER. Questions? No.

CONFESSOR. Then stay here, whilst I fetch the Chapter and the Fathers and Brothers, so that the solemn act may begin.

STRANGER. Yes. Let it come to pass.

(The CONFESSOR goes out. The STRANGER, left alone, is sunk in thought.)

TEMPTER (coming forward). Are you ready?

STRANGER. So ready, that I've no answer left for you.

TEMPTER. On the brink of the grave, I understand! You'll have to lie in your coffin and appear to die; the old Adam will be covered with three shovelfuls of earth, and a De Profundis will be sung. Then you'll rise again from the dead, having laid aside your old name, and be baptized once more like a new-born child! What will you be called? (The STRANGER does not reply.) It is written: Johannes, brother Johannes, because he preached in the wilderness and . . .

STRANGER. Do not trouble me.

TEMPTER. Speak to me a little, before you depart into the long silence. For you'll not be allowed to speak for a whole year.

STRANGER. All the better. Speaking at last becomes a vice, like drinking. And why speak, if words do not cloak thoughts?

TEMPTER. *You* at the graveside. . . . Was life so bitter?

STRANGER. Yes. My life was.

TEMPTER. Did you never know one pleasure?

STRANGER. Yes, many pleasures; but they were very brief and seemed only to exist in order to make the pain of their loss the sharper.

TEMPTER. Can't it be put the other way round: that pain exists in order to make joy more keen?

STRANGER. It can be put in any way.

(A woman enters with a child to be baptized.)

TEMPTER. Look! A little mortal, who's to be consecrated to suffering.

STRANGER. Poor child!

TEMPTER. A human history, that's about to begin. (A bridal couple cross the stage.) And there—what's loveliest, and most bitter. Adam and Eve in Paradise, that in a week will be a Hell, and in a fortnight Paradise again.

STRANGER. What is loveliest, brightest! The first, the only, the last that ever gave life meaning! I, too, once sat in the sunlight on a verandah, in the spring beneath the first tree to show new green, and a small crown crowned a head, and a white veil lay like thin morning mist over a face . . . that was not that of a human being. Then came darkness!

TEMPTER. Whence?

STRANGER. From the light itself. I know no more.

TEMPTER. It could only have been a shadow, for light is needed to throw shadows; but for darkness no light is needed.

STRANGER. Stop! Or we'll never come to an end.

(The CONFESSOR and the CHAPTER appear in procession.)

TEMPTER (disappearing). Farewell!

CONFESSOR (advancing with a large black bier-cloth). Lord! Grant him eternal peace!

CHOIR. May he be illumined with perpetual light!

CONFESSOR (wrapping the STRANGER to the bier-cloth). May he rest in peace!

CHOIR. Amen!

Curtain.

Milton Keynes UK
Ingram Content Group UK Ltd.
UKHW021939281223
435034UK00004B/28